IMPRISONED BY
HOPE

Imprisoned by
Hope

Dolores Rimblas Attias

iUniverse, Inc.
Bloomington

Imprisoned by Hope

iUniverse books may be ordered through booksellers or by contacting:

iUniverse
1663 Liberty Drive
Bloomington, IN 47403
www.iuniverse.com
1-800-Authors (1-800-288-4677)

ISBN: 978-1-4620-2507-7 (sc)
ISBN: 978-1-4620-2508-4 (ebk)

Printed in the United States of America

iUniverse rev. date: 03/30/2012

CONTENTS

ACKNOWLEDGMENTS

Deepest thanks to Helen Montgomery, leader of Southwest Writers Group, for editing my book *Imprisoned by Hope*. Thanks also to the members of the group for their insightful critique. Without them I could not have done it.

Special thanks to Patricia Gurk for the many hours she spent helping me with my project. I'll never forget it.

DEDICATION

With an aching heart for her recent passing, I dedicate this book, as I did all the previous ones, to my dearest mentor and friend Maria Elena Ramirez Cabañas, Principal and owner of Queen Elizabeth School in Mexico City; to her lovely daughter Maruca, and her dear husband Raul Miranda.

CHAPTER I

Elena Alcantara

Elena Alcantara stepped from the subway at the Riverside Drive Station in New York City. As she trudged through the snow on the two long blocks toward home, her mind flashed to thoughts of her native Cuba: The grinding poverty, the machismo, and the subservient attitude of women. She had worked hard, and, in spite of everything, she had beaten the insurmountable odds facing her as an immigrant. How different things were here in the United States!

Snow had accumulated and the freezing weather made the ground slippery. Young Elena marveled at the white snow and the way it sparkled with reflected light from streetlamps and passing cars. In the small town where she was born, dust from unpaved roads would have shrouded the lights of passing cars. She couldn't feel her toes and was sure her nose would break off if she didn't go indoors soon. This glorious city amazed her with its tall buildings that seemed to kiss the sky, and long trains that shot out of the earth with a deafening racket.

Elena Alcantara of Santiago de Cuba, island of year-round sun, walked on a snow-filled street in Manhattan—the major commercial, financial, and cultural center of the United States . . . well, of the world. She smiled internally, sure that the smile wouldn't reach her lips. Her face was completely numb.

Finally, she arrived at the tall brick building where she shared a studio apartment with Vilma, a good friend and co-worker. She climbed several steps to the front door, opened it and stepped into an anteroom. She welcomed the blast of heat that immediately enfolded her; then brought her hands to her lips and warmed her numb fingers with her breath. After a few seconds, the now familiar sensation of ants crawled up her extremities, as blood returned to her frozen limbs.

Elena reached for the key under the floor mat, unlocked the second door and placed the key back under the mat, oblivious to danger. She took the stairs to the third floor while humming a cheerful melody. She was still giddy with excitement, rehashing her earlier conversation with Gina Martinez, her fellow Cuban friend and boss at the hair salon.

Gina was getting married and Elena was thrilled. Still better, Gina had offered to sell to Elena her beauty salon. Just like that, in a few months she had gone from a Cuban *guajira* to a New York City business owner. What a dream! Could this be true? Would she wake up and find herself back in her country, still fighting her father's assaults or her ex-husband's emotional abuse?

"Anybody home? Vilma?"

Everything was silent and dark. Elena flipped on the light and turned on the radio. An improvised accordion wall gave privacy to Elena's bedroom. She undressed, looked in the mirror and was pleased at the reflection of the woman who stared back. Finally she was putting on some weight. Back in Cuba they called her *la reina de natacion, nada por delante y nada por detrás.* Nothing in front and nothing behind. *Nada!* Nothing! Well, if they could see her now! She actually had a curvaceous figure and men seemed to like her.

She mused at the difference between men in the United States and Cuba. Here they stole glances at her surreptitiously, but very few said anything. In Cuba they seemed to have contests to see who could come up with the most sensuous and inventive *piropo*. She liked it better here. She felt safer.

Elena put on her robe and slippers, grabbed her toiletry kit and headed for the communal bathroom out in the hall. She always felt uneasy when she thought about how many people on her floor had used the same toilet and shower she was about to use. She disinfected the toilet seat and the shower's floor before using them, and then proceeded to brush her long brown hair one hundred times, as she was used to doing three times a week with good results: bouncing, lustrous and robust hair. Then she returned to her apartment, hung and folded her clothes and sat in an armchair. She put her feet up and mulled over her situation with Gina.

Not only was she selling Elena her business, but Gina was also madly in love again. Given Gina's exotic looks and provocative figure, it was no wonder she had found someone to replace Roberto so soon—exactly as Elena had hoped. Oh, Elena's handsome Roberto was all hers—they were free to resume their love.

Elena remembered every word of her conversation with Gina, as they were straightening up the beauty salon earlier that evening.

"Yes Elena, everything happened so fast," Gina had said.

"I wish you the best, Gina. I'm dying to see you in your wedding gown." Elena paused for a second. "I . . . I wonder . . ."

"What do you want to ask, Elena?"

"I want to know if you are worried about leaving your business and your friends to move to another state with a man you don't know well."

"No problem, dear friend, he can be trusted." Gina leaned on the front counter of the salon, her dreamy eyes lost in space. "I just want to be with my *gringo*, no matter where."

"Did you ever love Roberto as much as you love him?"

Gina was pensive for a moment. "You know?" she said weighing her words, "with Roberto it was passion, caprice, lust—I loved myself more than I did him. With my Bryan it's different; he brings out the best in me. I care for his well-being more than mine. I never put Roberto first like I do Bryan." Gina stroked her chignon gently and asked, "Do you understand what I'm saying? I am in love when I thought I couldn't love again!" She shook her head and smiled. "It bothers me to remember how insane I was when I thought I was losing Roberto to another woman. I felt like I could kill them both. With Bryan I'd rather die than lose him."

Elena was brought back from her recollections by a creaking sound out in the hallway. She heard footsteps that seemed to stop at her door.

It's probably Vilma, she thought. *But why doesn't she come in? Maybe she's rummaging in her purse for the key.*

Elena started to get up to open the door for Vilma but stopped. Could Vilma be with a date? She certainly didn't want to interrupt anything. But something didn't feel right, and Elena froze when she saw the doorknob turning slowly.

"SINNER REPENT OR BURN IN HELL!" A loud male voice surged from within the apartment.

Elena jumped out of her skin. "*¿Que pasa?*" she shouted, looking around the tiny apartment in terror. The diatribe continued and Elena soon realized it was coming from the radio. She shut it off and looked at the door again, heart pounding; the door was ajar now. She heard fast, retreating footsteps. Elena approached cautiously and peaked out into the hallway. She saw her dark-skinned neighbor standing outside, eyes full of terror; nervously scrunching the bright African patterned skirt with one hand.

"What happen?" she asked, approaching the woman.

"You have white, clear aura child," the old woman said.

"Excuse me?"

"Big black man by your door. He listen. He wait. Gray aura surround him. Something scare him. He run away."

Elena was speechless.

"You have many angels watching you. Looking out for you. But you are stupid child, and one day the angels can't protect you."

Elena stared in disbelief as the woman peered back at her and pointed a shaking finger, saying, ". . . and no leave big key under mat. I see you do this. You will make us all dead. You must help angels."

The woman turned and slammed the door behind her. After a moment of paralysis, Elena was able to get back to her apartment and lock the door. Did the intruder still have the outside security key? Could the ranting of the man in the radio have scared him off?

Chapter II

Roberto Carvajal

Roberto Carvajal walked through the aisle of the Iberia Airliner that was to take him from Barcelona to New York and his beloved Elena. He picked up a newspaper on the way to his window seat and sat staring at the spinning propeller, his mind filled with the image of Elena.

The young man glanced at the headlines in the paper: "North Korea invades the South." He frowned and folded the paper, annoyed with the news. He didn't feel like reading or talking to the person seated next to him, so he closed his eyes and let his thoughts run free.

As if in a movie, he saw his last encounter with Elena, her body entwined with his. He had arranged a party for two in his apartment. It was a farewell for them after Elena had decided they should be apart for a year. She had refused to see him until his relationship with Gina was completely over.

Roberto fell in love with Elena the first time he saw her, at the time she was living with Gina. He had always dated sophisticated, worldly women, but Elena was so different! She was strikingly beautiful, yes, but also unassuming and candid. She showed compassion and genuine caring-values that were difficult to find in the circle in which he moved.

He had found the woman he wanted to marry, and he would do anything to keep her.

Although he didn't want to be away from her that long, he had finally capitulated, seeing the wisdom of a fresh start. He decided to go to Barcelona to be close to his mother Aisha and sister Ruth, and to strengthen some business connections.

Roberto came back to the present, startled by the voice of a stewardess. The plane had already taken off and was climbing into the clouds.

"Anything to drink, sir?" she asked again, leaning slightly toward him.

He cleared his throat. "A Virgin Bloody Mary, please."

His eyes followed the good-looking woman appreciatively, as she walked away and stopped to speak to a lady in the front row. He smiled, closed his eyes and returned to his reverie.

He was desperate to see Elena after a whole year of separation, but the ocean of problems drowning him dampened the happiness of their encounter. Unstoppable, nagging thoughts pierced his heart.

The shocking news that Anita was pregnant devastated him. How could this have happened? It had been just one night of weakness and now this. He would never forget that fateful evening six months ago when Francisco Guzman, a business acquaintance, had called offering him a special deal. Roberto went to meet him at one of the brothel's he owned. Guzman was seated at a table with an incredibly beautiful red head.

"My friend! I'm so glad you could join us. Let me introduce you to Ana," Guzman said exuberantly.

"Señorita, at your feet", said Roberto, brushing his lips lightly on her hand. Ana blushed, and smiled shyly.

"Ana just joined our little family and she was dying to meet you, isn't that right sweetheart?"

Roberto understood immediately. This beautiful young woman was Guzman's "gift" to him as a way of convincing Roberto to go into business with him.

"I'm sorry Francisco, I'm not in the mood tonight, I've had a long day. I promise to come back another day."

"Roberto you don't understand. This is your only chance at untainted goods, if you know what I mean. Tonight is Ana's debut, you know. If you come back tomorrow you won't be the first."

Roberto was no prude; he liked brothels with their perverse ambiance and sinful atmosphere, but a virgin prostitute! There was something wrong with this picture.

Roberto pushed his chair back to leave but Ana placed her small hand on his and gave him a soulful look, her gray eyes piercing him. "Sir, please . . . I'd like to get to know you better."

"O.K. that's it! Let's go Ana!" He grabbed her hand and pulled her up. How much Guzman?"

"Roberto, we are all gentlemen here, you try the goods and then tell me how much they're worth. I trust you'll be fair, and gentle . . ." he added with a wink.

"Now where to?" Roberto asked Ana.

She led him to a second floor and entered a room.

When they were alone Roberto turned her around brusquely and asked. "Why are you doing this?"

"Why do you think?" she retorted, with fire in her eyes. "If I get raped here I will at least get paid, if my step father gets his way, I'll have nothing but my shame. Is that reason enough for you?" Ana yelled, tears streaming down her cheeks.

"My God! How old are you?"

"I'm already fifteen."

"Fifteen! You are a child!"

"I'm a woman, and I know what I'm doing. When Señor Guzman told me you were going to be my first customer, I agreed. At least you're good looking and not too old."

The stewardess returned with his drink. He had a few sips; but the image of Anita's determined face intruded again into his thoughts.

He would be lying if he told himself he hadn't been tempted that night, but then thoughts of Ruth's smiling face appeared, strengthening his determination to resist Ana's appeal. The thought of a man pawing his sister enraged him. He would kill the son-of-a-bitch.

He smiled at the memory of Ana's pout when he refused to touch her.

"Listen Señor, this is going to happen one way or another, why don't you help me out here?"

"I am helping you. This is a big mistake. There has to be another way out for you."

"Oh really? Mind telling me how? I am a minor like you just pointed out, but I'm not a child; I've had to grow up fast. My mother is drunk half the time and the other half she's yelling at me and blaming me for being alive. If I tell her what her new husband has been trying to do to me she's going to kick me out of the house, so anyway I look at it I end up on the street, a whore!"

Roberto pulled himself from his memories, ran his fingers through his hair and looked around. The stewardess was taking orders for dinner. When she stopped by his seat, he chose chicken with rice instead of pork roast, respectful of his Jewish tradition. But he could not keep his thoughts in the present; they reeled back to the past.

"Ana, I need time to think of something, but for now, I am going to pay for you to stay with me all night. I want you to stay in this room with the door locked. I will tell Guzman that I want you just for me tomorrow too. This should give me time to come up with a plan to help you out."

Why on earth had he felt obligated to take a stranger under his wing? He had placed Anita under the care of his mother's chauffeur and his wife, a childless couple who lived alone in a cottage on the grounds. Marina and Emilio swore not to tell a soul the truth about Ana. Roberto provided enough money for expenses and made plans for her future.

With the best of intentions, he visited Ana occasionally to make sure she was okay. One evening when he stopped by to see how she was doing, Marina asked if he could stay with Ana for a bit as she had errands to run and she didn't want Ana to be alone too long. She seemed depressed and hadn't come out of her room all day. Roberto agreed.

He knocked gently on Ana's door but there was no answer. He tried again. "Ana. Are you okay? Can I come in?"

"What do you want?"

"I just stopped by to say hello."

"Go away."

"What's wrong?"

"Nothing. Why should anything be wrong?"

"Marina thinks something is troubling you."

Ana opened the door. She was wearing a pastel cotton robe. She looked stunning.

"So, what do you want to talk about? Are you checking on your social project? Do you need to pat your back because you are such a great guy?"

Roberto stood motionless, not comprehending the anger and lust he saw in her eyes. Ana came closer, her robe parting and revealing part of her body and shapely legs, as white as porcelain.

She stood in front of him, so close that he could smell her sweet breath. She placed her hands on his chest and began to undo the buttons on his shirt.

He grabbed her hands. "Don't do that . . ."

"Why not? Let me ask you something Roberto. Are you gay?"

"What! How dare you?" Roberto shouted enraged, pushing her roughly away from him. Ana fell back on the bed, the robe fell open revealing large, well-formed breasts and a luscious mound of copper hair between her generous thighs.

"I dream all the time about you making love to me," Ana cried into the pillow. "Am I that ugly to you?"

Roberto sat on the bed by her side. "You are beautiful. So, so beautiful," he said leaning towards her and kissing her gently on the lips. He felt his manhood awakening and there was no way he could stop now. He wanted to possess this voluptuous child, hidden in the body of a woman. He surrendered to her passion, and the consequences would hang over his head forever.

The plane hit turbulence, and Roberto came back to the present. When it was tranquil again, he made his way to the plane's restroom.

Once there, he spat at the image reflected in the mirror. "You despicable imbecile," he said bitterly, knowing his future with Elena was at stake. It would all be over if she ever found out.

Back in his seat and unable to keep his mind on pleasant memories, he wrestled with another problem. There was one other part of his life he had kept from Elena. Well, there were a few more. How could he brake the news to this devout catholic woman, that he was Jewish?

The plane finally arrived in New York and all of Roberto's problems and turmoil did too.

CHAPTER III

Looking For Trouble

Elena went to work next morning giddy with excitement and paralyzed with fear. Today was her first day as the sole owner of the ABC beauty salon. She was the boss, she was independent and she was solely responsible for its success or failure. She could ruin herself, Vilma and the other employees. What on earth gave her the idea that she could run a business? Enough! She would succeed. She could make it.

The busy workday began as soon as Elena arrived. Today she would have to do without Vilma, since she had asked for the day off to run errands. Gina wasn't supposed to be there either! She suspected she'd miss Gina a lot more than she'd anticipated. So when Gina showed up late in the afternoon, Elena was happy to see her. She was in debt to her friend, to God, to life.

"How are things going?" asked Gina.

"Good! Everything's running smoothly. How about you?"

"I'm all packed for the move."

"Good for you, my friend!" said Elena.

"Keep in touch, will you? And don't hesitate to call if you need anything."

They conversed a while longer. When Gina left, Elena looked back at her busy first day as an independent woman. She was exhausted but filled with hope and satisfaction.

Elena pushed open the door to her efficiency. Vilma jumped up from the couch, a wide smile revealing white, even teeth. "I've been waiting for you!"

"What's going on? Why are you so excited?"

"Oh, Elena, you won't believe this . . ."

"Try me!" Elena threw her purse on a table and sat on a nearby chair. "First tell me, were you able to fix your immigration papers?"

Vilma blurted out, "Forget about immigration . . . Finally, a guy asked me out!"

"How exciting! Tell me about it. Who is he?"

"I went to Miles to buy shoes and a young man asked me out."

"Ohh! Are you going?"

"What do you think? Of course!"

"Vilma, you don't know this man . . ."

"I don't care. Look at my figure. I can't be choosy. I'm lucky he asked me out at all."

"You need to find out first who he is."

"Are you kidding? Nature gave me too much." Vilma looked at her large bosom, sadly. "If I wait to find out who he is, he'll be gone."

"It is obvious he was attracted to you, otherwise he wouldn't have asked you out. Wait until you find out more about him."

Vilma's expression turned bitter. "Por favor, don't spoil my joy. This is the first time a *muchacho* has asked me out."

"I'm happy for you, really, but I'm afraid. It's very dangerous."

"But you are coming with me . . . ."

"Am I? Who told you?" Elena asked, astounded.

"What kind of a friend are you? I'm asking you for a favor."

"I'm really sorry, Vilma, I'm still scared from the other night. I won't go out with a stranger and you shouldn't either."

"Everybody knows him at Mile's. He works there."

"Oh, yeah? What's his name?"

"Benny."

"Benny what?"

"Oh, who cares?"

"I don't like the smell of this," Elena insisted.

"There's safety in numbers. If we go together, we are safe. Do you want me to beg? Kneel?"

"Don't be silly . . ." Elena said, laughing.

"I told him you're coming with us."

"I am not," Elena said firmly.

"He's coming at eight to pick us up."

"Let him visit you here. Get to know him first."

"Elena, we'll go out," Vilma said with conviction.

"Don't count on me."

"Okay then, I'll go by myself."

They talked some more until finally Elena gave in.

CHAPTER IV

Rape

On the evening of the outing, Vilma's date arrived punctually at eight. After introductions, Benny, a clean-cut young man with thick black eyebrows and deep dark eyes, was eager to leave.

"Where are you taking us?" Elena asked, already bitten by suspicion.

Benny avoided the question as he sized them up. "Girls, you look very pretty." He led them to a white, four-door Packard, opened the back door for Elena, and then helped Vilma into the front. He stepped on the gas.

"Where are we going?" Elena asked again.

"We're picking up a friend."

"What?" Elena jumped. "No one told me anything about a friend. I just came to chaperone you two."

Benny burst into laughter. "You're cute! We don't need a chaperone. Don't worry, you'll like Peter."

"I don't have any use for Peter," Elena said, the knot in her stomach tightening. "Call your friend and let him know."

"Okay, if that's what you want. But, the problem is . . . you know, he's waiting outside. First we have to drive to where he is and let him know."

Good gracious, what am I doing here, this guy is cooking up something, thought Elena, panicking. Then, she told her friend in Spanish, *"Vilma, no me gusta esto. Convencelo que nos regrese a casa."*

"Cut it out!" Benny said. "I don't understand a word you're saying. Broken English is better than Spanish."

"Benny, my friend wants to go back home. Let's take her, please," pleaded Vilma.

"OK, but I must let Peter know first."

Benny picked up speed on his way toward the George Washington Bridge. He glanced at Elena in the mirror.

"You, back there, I forgot your name."

"Elena."

"Right, Elena, New Jersey is just over the bridge. Do you want to go there? Do you want go to Palisades Park first?"

"No thanks, I want to go home. My mother's very sick. I'm expecting a call from Cuba," she lied.

He turned his head and said, "Sorry, It's your loss."

Just before the Washington Bridge, Benny veered to the side of the road and stopped by a man standing on a corner. "There is Peter. Be nice to him, you hear?" He stopped and a well-built, good-looking young man approached the car.

"Oh man, it's about time," Peter said, as he slid next to Elena. "Pretty girl," he said, looking her over. "It's worth waiting. I'm Peter. Who are you?"

"I'm Elena. Benny is taking me back to my house."

"I don't think so," he said, the offensive smell of alcohol invaded the space between them. "I love Latin girls, and you look like my kind of woman."

"I'm expecting a call from Cuba. My mother's very sick. Please be kind and take me home."

"Hey, Ben, is she supposed to be my date or what?"

"Baby, let's have a good time and then we'll deliver you safe and sound. We won't hurt you, I promise," said Benny.

"That's if you behave and do what we say. Right Benny?" asked Peter with a half-smile.

"*Vilma, tu sabes lo que estos tipos tienen en mente, verdad?*".

"Hey, no Spanish, you hear?" said Peter, brusquely.

Virgin Mother, it's time for your help, I promise to say all the rosaries in the world if we get out of this, Elena prayed.

Benny drove for a while with an occasional conversation with Peter.

"There's a tavern," exclaimed Benny. "I'll stop for some beer."

"Good!" said Elena thanking the Virgin for her quick response. "I must visit the wash room."

"Sorry, Elena," said Benny, "I'm the only one getting out. Good try, though."

"You should take us in, buy us a drink, you know—to loosen us up, to get in the mood," tried Elena again, trying a coquettish smile.

Benny looked sideways and smiled back, as he pointed his index finger at her. "Not to worry, Cutie," he said, "drinks will take care of the mood all right!" He hurried and disappeared into the bar.

Elena tried to open the door to get out, but Peter grabbed her hand. "Where do you think you're going, baby?"

"Let go of me. I'm going to the bathroom."

"Sorry! You heard the boss."

Why isn't Vilma doing something? What's she thinking?

"Vilma, run. Get out." Elena said rapidly.

"I'm afraid."

Peter grabbed Vilma's ponytail and with the other hand held Elena's wrist. "Just as a precaution, girls!"

"Vilma, think fast! Do something . . ."

Elena gasped as Peter squeezed her wrist. "Pig, you're hurting me," she cried.

"Sorry!"

Moments later Benny reappeared carrying an armload of brown paper bags. Peter let go of Vilma and Elena.

The ache in her wrist brought to Elena's mind her mother's letters about the danger of big cities like New York. She'd included a number of clippings describing the rapes and killing of young women. *I'm as good as dead; I won't survive this, because if they don't kill me, I will kill myself. I can't go through this again.*

In her mind flashed the hurtful memories of her father's advances. And later, it was Rodolfo, forcing himself on her. She felt her heart pierced by pain. "No! No! Not again!" she heard herself pleading.

"What did you say, bitch?" asked Peter.

Elena jumped as if bitten by a snake. "Where are we going?" she croaked.

"Hey Benny, Elena wants to know where we're going."

"Curiosity killed the cat," said Benny laughing. "We're going to my parent's house, cutie."

"Please, I need to go to the bathroom right now! It's urgent," moaned Elena.

"Hold on, we're almost there."

Soon after, Benny turned left onto a dark roadway and parked at the back of an isolated ranch-style house.

"We are here," Benny announced. "Now, prepare yourselves for the ride of a lifetime."

The young men grabbed the girls by the arms and pulled them along into the house. Benny locked the front door and turned the lights on. Elena glanced around, surprised that the house appeared tidy and smelled clean.

Benny looked at Elena with a teasing smile. "The toilet is right there in the hall in case you still need to piss."

"Thank you," she whimpered. *There might be a way out,* she thought.

Elena hurried to the bathroom; a ray of hope encouraging her. Once there, she looked for a window or a connecting door to another part of the house from where she might climb outside, but her high hopes deflated at once—no window, no door! She fell to her knees and prayed as hard as she knew for the Virgin Mary to save her.

A knock at the door brought her to her feet.

"Hey Elena, have you drowned or what?" Peter asked.

Elena crossed herself and turned her eyes up as if searching for the sky. *Mothercita, I need your mercy now . . . help me.*

She opened the door.

"You're missing the party. Come on." Peter placed his hand on her waist and pushed her roughly to the kitchen where Benny and Vilma were drinking. Benny raised a can of beer, glancing at Vilma. "To my fatso," he said jokingly, bursting into laughter.

Vilma grimaced and Elena saw a tear in her eyes. She couldn't help it but feel pity, in spite of the resentment against her friend for placing her in this dangerous entanglement. To her surprise she saw consternation in Benny's eyes, as he noticed Vilma's reaction. He wasn't as much of a jerk as he was pretending to be. He was acting out for Peter's benefit.

"Here, this is to your happiness," said Peter, embracing Elena tightly and handing her a beer.

"No, thanks, I don't like beer."

"Sorry, your highness," said Benny genuflecting. "I don't have champagne." He returned his attention to Vilma.

We must find a way out of here. The doors are locked and the windows reinforced with bars. How on earth will we break free? Unless I tell Peter I have an infection or a contagious disease? Yes, I must try that or something else . . . anything.

"Hey, today's my lucky day . . ." Peter said. "Elena, you turn me on more than anything else." He grabbed her breast and Elena slapped his hand energetically. He laughed mockingly. "You don't have tits, but your ass makes up for it." He groped her backside and pushed Elena through the dining room, which was openly connected to the kitchen, and to the living room.

"Wait! Wait! I need a drink," said Elena, dying inside.

"You and I have things to do . . . right here, right now!" He held her chin and kissed her, forcing his tongue inside her mouth. Unable to hide her disgust, Elena pushed him away with all her might.

"Witch!" he shouted.

It was a wrong move on my part. I should pretend I like him, thought Elena. "Wait," she tried in a low voice. "Let's get to know each other first."

He cracked up. "What?"

Elena forced a little smile. "First I want to know a little about you . . ."

"You'll know me inside out. Okay?" he slurred, pulling her into his lap, then he yanked open her blouse and squeezed her nipples through her bra.

She jerked herself from his arms. "Stupid bastard! Leave me alone!"

He grabbed her wrist. "I will, but not before I fuck you!"

"OK, OK, I won't resist but let me cool off first," Elena said, braking loose and rushing to the dining room. From there she could see Benny in the kitchen, kissing Vilma. She wandered around looking at photos on the wall.

"Hey, you won't get away!" barked Peter.

Elena flinched, and she called out, "I'm not trying to get away. I need a drink.

"Oh, so now a beer is OK with your highness?"

"I don't drink alcohol, but I need a drink. Give me a minute OK? I'll make it worth your while."

"Oooo, sounds promising."

"Hey, Benny, are these pictures of your family?" Elena tried

"Yes. Why?" he answered without looking.

"Do you mind if I look at them?"

Benny's hands and mouth kept busy with Vilma as he muttered over his shoulder "Go ahead."

"For the blood of Christ! Not now!" shouted Peter.

"Peter, could you please give me a beer."

With great effort Elena tried to act normal. She picked up a framed picture of a pretty young woman on a cocktail table.

"Who's this girl? She looks like you."

"Damn! Who cares?" Peter hollered.

"Shut up, Peter! Be patient for a moment." Benny stood up brusquely and came to where Elena was holding the picture. "That's my sister Laura." He said as he put the picture back on the table face down.

Peter lit a cigarette nervously inhaling noisily and exhaling smoke.

"Benny, we aren't here to learn about your family tree! We're here to fuck the hell out of these chicks. Let's get going!"

"Relax, man. We got lots of beer and plenty of time." Retorted Benny, looking more ill-at-ease.

Peter frantically began to caress Elena, who in turn screamed at the top of her lungs, furiously trying to break loose. Peter tightened his grip. With a clenched hand Elena struck his chest, then got loose and ran to Benny.

"Benny, you're not this kind of person. Help me!" she pleaded as she grabbed his hands.

Vilma hugged Elena, and with tears in her eyes said "I'm sorry my friend—very sorry!"

"Benny, don't forget Elena is my part of the deal!" Peter shouted.

"Shut up, Peter! We're here to have good time. Not rape them."

"Vilma, *sacame de aquí antes de que me violen*."

"Benny, let's take Elena home and I'll come back with you."

"Benny, you are a kind person, help me," Elena pleaded.

"I said, Elena is my part of the deal!" Peter shouted.

Elena fell to her knees. "Peter, my mother may be dying. I have to go . . ."

"Well good!" shouted Peter. "Let's have a quickie! Then we'll find out about your mother."

"Please Benny, think of Laura. What would you do if a man raped her?" Elena said guessing Benny had a weakness for her sister.

"Peter, what do you say?" asked Benny. "Let's take Elena back."

Benny helped Elena to her feet. "A drink will help. Yes, a drink." he insisted softly.

"You have my future in your hands. I'll kill myself!"

"Don't say that!" Vilma placed her arm around her friend and wiped away her tears. "Benny, listen to her. You have to help my friend. You must!"

Elena sobbed some more, then blew her nose and went on, "Benny, I can tell that your family instilled good values in you. Don't destroy my life when you and Peter can find easy women that will entertain you without being forced; plus, if you do this you will be committing a felony."

"Enough with this shit!" yelled Peter.

"Shut up!" roared Benny.

"Don't tell me that this bitch's tears softened you."

"We're taking the girls home . . . that's final!" Benny said firmly, pushing Vilma aside and placing something in her hand. "Call me," he said in a low voice.

"You pansy son-of-a-bitch!" Peter barked.

"Whatever."

They left. On the ride, the two men sat in front. Elena sat in the back with a sorrowful and repentant Vilma next to her.

CHAPTER V

Roberto`s Arrival

The flight from Spain arrived early Saturday morning. Michael, Roberto's business associate, was at the airport waiting for him. Together they drove straight to the office. Before anything else, Roberto called Elena at Gina's house hoping that Elena, not Gina, would pick up the phone. He got a recorded message: "The number you have reached is out of service. Please check the number and call again."

"Well, that's odd," he said to himself as he dialed the beauty salon and got the same thing: the telephone was disconnected. Now he was really worried. A year of not hearing from her, and apparently now everything had changed.

Where's Elena, for heaven's sake? Does she still love me? Is she waiting for me?

He decided to go to the beauty salon.

He arrived at the building and hurried inside, anticipating his meeting with Elena, but dreading to find Gina. The possibility of seeing Gina again was a thorn in his heart. Would she still be an obstacle between him and Elena? Their agreement had been that no matter what turn Gina's life had taken, they would continue with their plans to marry when he returned.

He approached the beauty salon and was shocked to see the plaque outside: ELENA STYLIST. He opened the door and went in, puzzled at all the changes. The receptionist was unfamiliar as well.

He walked to the desk. "Good afternoon. Is Elena in, please?" he asked, with an uneasy feeling in his gut.

"She's not here today. May I ask who's looking for her?"

"Roberto. But why isn't she working today? Is she all right?"

"I really don't know."

"May I have her phone number, please?"

An embarrassed silence followed.

"I'm sorry, Sir," the woman said finally. "I can't do that."

"I understand. Can you call her and let her know Roberto Carvajal is here. I'll wait." *Well, I'm sure she'll talk to me. Won't she? It's only a week shy of our agreed time.*

The young woman turned to him.

"I'm sorry, Sir, if you leave a number for her, I'm sure she'll call you soon."

"Soon! When is soon?" he shouted. "I'm sorry. Here is my phone number." Roberto took a pen from the counter and wrote his private phone number in the back of his business card.

"May I talk to Gina then, please?"

"Gina isn't here anymore, sir."

"She's not? Where is she? Oh-forget it. Thank you. Have a good day!"

Roberto left. Did Elena forget him? What was going on?

Back at his office he couldn't concentrate on business and waited in vain for Elena's call. Feeling his blood boiling and tired of the whole thing, he decided to leave. He grabbed his coat and hat, turned off the lights and was locking the door when the phone rang. His heart leaped. He dropped everything and ran to the phone.

"Hello," he answered eagerly.

"May I speak with Roberto, please?"

"Speaking. Who is this?"

"I'm Vilma, Elena's friend. We got your message . . ."

"Is something wrong with her?" he interrupted. "Please, tell me . . ."

"No. She doesn't know I'm calling, but I believe you should know she's not well. She doesn't want to talk to you on the phone, nor see you; but if you come to see her, she won't have any other choice."

"Please tell me at once what's wrong with her."

"When you get here I'll tell you everything, I promise," said Vilma timorously.

"I need to know right now!"

Vilma cleared her throat and paused a little.

"I'm listening," he urged.

She spoke haltingly. "I'll tell you because she's going to anyway . . . knowing how understanding you are, it's better if you know . . . ."

"Know what, in the name of God? Speak! Who are you, anyhow?"

"I'm her roommate. I took a course in cosmetology with her, and then we moved in together. I also work for her. She told me about you and how much you love each other. She's been waiting for you anxiously. She works hard and dreams of you—that's her life. You'll know the rest when you get here."

"I want to know it at this moment! Right now! What's the matter with Elena?"

A pause.

"It's not easy. I don't know where to begin. Well, you see, I am not like Elena, you know. Elena's very popular, everybody likes her . . . which isn't my case. So when a *muchacho* finally asked me out, I was thrilled. Elena didn't want me to go out with him because he was a stranger and all, so I . . . kind of convinced her to be our chaperone. She told me very clearly that she didn't want to be my chaperone, but I begged until she accepted." Vilma blew her nose. "I'm ashamed to tell you the rest."

"Please! Go on!"

"Elena was right all along. The bastard picked up a friend and they tried to rape us."

"What?" he shouted. "Is Elena OK? Was she . . ."

"Clever Elena came up with a ruse and saved us, it was rough, but we're OK."

"I'll be there as soon as possible. Give me the address, please."

Feeling as if a sharp stake had pierced his heart, Roberto grabbed a cab and gave the address to the driver. *If I get that hijo-de-puta in front of me, I'll beat the hell out of him,* he vowed.

When he arrived at the apartment, Vilma let him in.

"Where is Elena?" he demanded.

"She's in her room. Let's think about how we're going to do this. Should I let her know you're here or do you just want to go in?" Vilma wiped away a tear.

"Go and tell her I'm here and won't leave until I see her."

"I don't know how Elena is going to take this. I don't want to lose her friendship."

"You won't lose her. You're a good friend. You did the right thing."

With an expression of hope, Vilma left and soon came back with a smile.

"Reluctantly, but she'll see you," she said patting his shoulder.

He rushed toward the half open door and swiftly ran to Elena, who was sitting on the bed, sobbing. She fell into his arms, her body trembling. They embraced until her body steadied and her sobs had quieted down.

"Elena, my love," finally he was able to say. "Are you OK?"

"My precious Roberto," she murmured. "Now I'm safe! Thanks to my *Mothercita Virgen Maria* . . . ."

Roberto couldn't help but flinch when she mentioned the Virgin. How would he ever find the courage to tell her he was Jewish and didn't believe in the virgin? She looked so vulnerable now! He would find the right moment . . . another day.

She looked up at him, tears in her eyes. "I'm not worthy of you," she said. "I feel filthy."

He placed a finger on her lips. "Shshsh! Don't say that! Nothing can touch your pure soul, ever."

"You don't know what happened to me last night."

"I do know. Vilma told me everything. You are not to blame, my love, you're a victim and a very brave one. I'm so proud of you . . . the way you got out of it."

"Oh Roberto, it was horrible. Even with all the bathing and cleansing I've done since, I still feel dirty."

"You're okay now. You're safe."

"I'm so glad you're back. I don't know what I would do without you."

He helped her to a rocking chair. "*Mi cielo*, sit here. We have a lot to catch up on! Tell me about Gina and the changes in the beauty salon." He sat across from her on a little stool, trying to distract her.

Gradually, Elena became animated as she filled him in on all that had happened. He listened, dumbfounded, when Elena told him that Gina was married and gone and that the beauty salon now belonged to her.

"This is amazing Elena! Congratulations!" He jumped to his feet and took Elena in his arms.

Elena winced at his touch.

"I'm sorry, did I hurt you?"

"No. Roberto. It's not you. It's me."

Roberto let go of Elena reluctantly. "Come on *mi amor.* Let's pack some things and come with me to my apartment."

"Not today, please. I can't. Pick me up tomorrow, *por favor.*"

"I don't want to leave you here alone. I want you with me. We've been apart too long."

"Tomorrow, Roberto."

"Why Elena? You should not be alone at a time like this."

"I don't want to be touched."

"Darling, I won't touch you until you are ready."

"Give me time. Be patient . . ."

And Roberto was patient but relentless.

Reluctantly, Elena walked out of her studio with Roberto. He guided her to the cab, helped her inside, sat beside her and reached for her hand. She turned and forced a smile.

"*Querido* Roberto," she said. "More than anything I want to make you happy." She squeezed his hand. "I'm afraid of failing, but I'll try hard."

He wiped away the tears running down her cheeks. "My love, you don't have to try. Just looking at you makes me happy. Together we'll find peace—the peace we both so desperately need. Relax, *Niña mia*, relax."

Finally, she said, "I'm bringing a lot of issues into your life. It isn't fair that you have to endure this . . ."

He folded her hands into his and kissed them. "With or without issues, you are my life. I prefer to live burdened by your problems than to lose you. My love, I don't think I could live without you."

"Is it okay if I leave you here instead of going all the way around, sir?" the cab driver asked, stopping on the opposite street to the apartment building.

"Please, take us up to the front."

"It's a one way street—I'll have to drive around."

"Thank you for your concern. Take us to the front of the building, if you will."

"No problem."

The cab driver drove around the block and a few minutes later parked under the canopy of the apartment building. The uniformed doorman rushed towards Roberto.

"Welcome back, Mr. Carvajal. How was Spain? Did you have a good trip?"

"Yes, very good, Joe. Thanks. How are things around here?"

"Under control." The doorman looked around, troubled. "But, where's your luggage?"

"It will arrive tomorrow."

Roberto paid the cabbie and took the overnight bag from his dispirited Elena. He was eager to get to the penthouse to observe her reaction, hoping she would be pleased. As they got off on the eleventh floor, Elena said wistfully, "*Mi amor,* I was afraid I wasn't going to see this place again."

"I never doubted that we would both be here again. Seeing you here now made me feel like I never left."

Elena walked through the door while Roberto held it open. She stepped into the living room and froze. With tears in her eyes, Elena raised a hand to her mouth and murmured, "I can't believe this!"

Dried red roses were everywhere. Crinkled petals, like potpourri, scattered under the vases. Colorful balloons hung airless from their ribbons; the same balloons that a year ago had enhanced the farewell party for two that Roberto had improvised for them. The signs, discolored by time, hung as they had been then. She read out loud: "I love you." "Welcome!" "Thank you for coming." "Until we meet again."

She burst into laugher and Roberto was pleased that he'd kept the decorations intact as a sanctuary to their love. As she laughed, the aura of magic filled the room again. He didn't know what to do or say. He didn't want to break the illusion. He stood still . . . did nothing . . . said nothing.

After long moments of wonderment, Elena ran into Roberto's arms and they embraced tightly. "Roberto, thank you, my darling, for being here for me! Thanks for your support, your patience. I am so grateful that God has made you part of my life."

"Let's celebrate and thank whoever made all this possible."

"Oh, Roberto, *mi Virgencita* heard my prayers."

Here we go again with "her Virgencita," thought Roberto, remorse creeping into his conscience. Was he a coward for not speaking out? No. He would tell her—but later.

He opened a bottle of champagne; they toasted. He struggled against the urge to kiss her and take her to bed. He didn't want to spoil the moment, as this was the first time she seemed happy since his arrival.

"Why is everything the way it was a year ago?"

"On my return I wanted to relive our first time together, with you by my side. The memory of you in my arms never left my heart."

"Nor mine," she said coquettishly, a spark from her old self returning to her eyes.

They began the night in a tight embrace with Roberto fighting against his longing to be inside her. No matter how hard he tried, he couldn't put out the fire in his loins. He needed to wait until she had recuperated from her nauseating experience. But even tired and jetlagged, he was unable to sleep. Finally, he pulled himself from her arms, took a cool shower and found refuge on the sofa. It was close to dawn when he returned to his bed and lay next to Elena, admiring her delicate features and grateful to see her resting peacefully.

Early the next morning, Elena rose first and left quietly to buy the things she needed for a small breakfast.

Upon her return, she made fresh orange juice and coffee. She took it to Roberto on a fancy tray that she decorated with ornaments she found in the kitchen, left over from last year's party. She sat the tray on the night table and woke him up with a kiss.

"Am I in heaven?" he asked, taking her in his arms.

"We are in seventh heaven," she said after a long kiss. Then she went on. "Thank you for being so considerate."

"What did I do now?"

"You took care of my needs, forgetting your own."

He laughed. "But, *mi Niña*, your needs are my needs. Your happiness gives me happiness."

Elena smiled and placed the tray on the bed and they drank the juice.

"Love," she said. "Do you want to go to mass with me?"

Roberto choked, spraying the juice all over Elena. "I'm sorry!" He grabbed the napkin and wiped her face and dress. I'm so very sorry!"

She laughed. "That's a subtle way of suggesting I shower! Are you okay?"

"Just embarrassed," he said with a half smile. "Do you mind if I take a rain check? I'm jet lagged and really need some more rest."

"It's fine with me." She ruffled his hair playfully. "But, just this time. I'll pray for you in church, and after mass I'll grab some lunch for us to eat here."

Elena left and Roberto couldn't go back to sleep. For how long was he going to keep this lie? It's true that she seemed to be feeling better now, but not enough for a blow like this one. He would keep Anita and the baby a secret, but Elena should know that he was a Jew! Today.

He showered and spruced himself up, ready to confess.

When Roberto heard a noise outside, he rushed to the door. On seeing Elena, grocery bags in her arms, his good intentions fled, as the urge to possess her grew stronger. He threw his arms around her shoulders, smashing the bags against their chests.

"You look marvelous," she said. "You smell so good! I thought you needed rest."

"The thought of you took my sleep away." He helped with the bags and cradled her in his arms for a long time, loving her so and hating himself for deceiving her. Then he kissed her ever so tenderly. With great effort he tried to restrain his passion for the moment. With soft strokes he caressed her back, her arms and slowly kissed her neck, which caused giggles and little moans of pleasure.

"Roberto, don't stop!"

He had waited for those three words for so long . . . . Now his knees began to shake and he felt his heart jump to his throat. Roberto carried her to the sofa, avoiding the bed because its connotation might alarm her. In spite of his urgency, he took his time—waiting until she wanted him as much as he wanted her.

Roberto hunted for the radio and searched for soft music. For a long time he caressed her arm tenderly, then slipped his hand around her breast. He stopped, but soon began again, this time playing with her nipples.

She begged, panting, "My love, let's make love!"

He carried her to the bed.

Hurriedly, he undressed her. She lost herself in his arms and totally submitted to his passion. The bedspread hit the floor followed by the pillows. Roberto took her in his arms, the warmth of her body fused to his and her ardent breath on his neck. Sweat built rapidly with the movement of their bodies.

After a sublime time of total surrender, Elena pulled up the sheets up to her chin.

"Are you trying to hide from me under those sheets?" Roberto murmured in Elena's ear.

"Come hide with me."

Once out of hiding, they had lunch amidst phrases of endearments and playful moments.

"Roberto, there's something bothering me," she said some time later.

Roberto froze. Not wanting to mar this perfect happiness he pleaded. "Can we talk about it later. I'm enjoying this time with you too much."

"Please, let's talk about it now."

"What is troubling you my darling?"

"For sure your family wants a big church wedding for you."

"Excuse me?" Roberto almost choked with relief.

"Parents want their children to marry in the church. I spoiled that for you and for them, because I'm a divorced woman."

"Elena, believe me when I tell you that my parents don't want a big church wedding for me. I promise you this." *No, what they want is a big temple wedding right in Beth Shalom Synagogue,* he thought. "We'll have a private ceremony in City Hall. Alright?"

She tried to say something, but he covered her lips with his and said while kissing her, "If we are happy . . . my family will bless us." He kissed her passionately and went on, "Now let's pick up where we left off . . ."

CHAPTER VI

Club "21"

Early Monday morning Roberto hailed a taxi to take him to his office, and drop Elena home to get ready for work. Elena was so happy, but at the same time she felt guilty. Roberto possessed all the qualities that would make her deliriously happy. He was so good to her, but was she good enough for him? Did she have the right to be selfish and think of her own happiness? True love was important to her; she had been pursuing it ever since she could remember. She had found the ideal soul mate in Roberto—she was tempted to grab it and leave scruples behind.

But Elena had grown up listening to her sister Alma lecture her about selfishness. At the time it had bothered Elena; now it haunted her. Alma considered selfishness one of the worst sins. If Elena were to ask Alma's opinion, she would have told her to not marry Roberto, to not allow a good young man to be ostracized from the church and to not marry a virgin.

At her arrival home, she dismissed her reveries. The door opened and Vilma appeared in the doorway wide-eyed.

"My friend, how are you?" Vilma said, with a concerned look on her face. "I was expecting a call from you all day yesterday. Are you okay?" she asked, throwing her arms around Elena.

"Thank you, Vilma. I'm fine. Sorry, I should have called. How about you?"

"Couldn't be better," she answered with a joyful, wide smile.

Elena tossed her night bag on the sofa.

"Good! I'm going to get ready for work. Are you coming along?"

"Of course . . . I'll be ready in a minute."

"On the way you have to tell me why you look so radiant."

Half an hour later they were walking down the wide West End Avenue towards the IRT subway line. Elena asked, "So, tell me what's going on?"

Vilma smiled and coughed nervously. "Benny called yesterday and I'm going to see him tonight."

Elena stopped and shouted, "What?"

"Elena, I don't hold anything against him."

"After what he did to us you don't hold anything against him? You must be nuts."

"He saved you from Peter because he has a good heart."

"He was the one who arranged a blind date for me in the first place. They intended to rape us. He's a pig! *Un hijo-de-puta!* How can you go out with him?"

"You are my only friend . . . please, try to understand."

"I thought you had principles! You mean to tell me you enjoyed him pawing you? You think that what he did was okay?"

"I'm sorry, Elena, but you're wrong. You have no right to judge me. You don't know what it's like to be ignored by everyone! To never be invited out by a man! You have no idea what that is like! Now for once in my life a man likes me. What is so wrong about that?"

"How can you be like that? Don't you have any fear of God? Don't you feel any shame?"

"Shame of what? Love? Don't priests tell their parishioners that God wants his children to be happy and to love each other? That's exactly what I'm going to do. Benny and I are going to love each other and be happy. With this, we hurt no one."

"But you're sinning, for God's sake."

"Do you sin when you sleep with Roberto?"

"That's different. We are in love. He's going to marry me."

"I'm going to do it for love, and who knows, he might marry me."

"At least make him wait. Men don't marry easy women."

"You can say that because you're pretty and well-liked. Men do what you want . . . So they wait—or they leave. With me it's not the same. I have only one and I'm not letting him get away . . . I'll give him what he wants, and I'll be thankful for what I get." Vilma grabbed Elena's arm and squeezed it. "Can't you see how much I want him?"

Elena released her arm and shook her head in disbelief. "I can't believe this! You're talking like a street woman!"

"I'm just being honest for once."

"For heavens sake, be careful! Imagine if you got pregnant."

"A baby?" Vilma's expression softened. "A little bundle of joy that would be all mine forever! All mine! I wouldn't be lonely anymore. God should hear my prayers."

"Vilma, please, a baby needs to have a home with a father and a mother. Pregnancy and childhood are very costly. What would you do?"

"For heavens sake, I haven't slept with Benny yet and you are ready to baptize my child! Don't run, my friend . . . walk. Let me enjoy my farewell to virginity . . ."

The shock of discovering a lustful Vilma went deep through Elena's being. "My God! This can't be you! How could you hide your true self from me for so long?"

"I want to be liked and loved, where's the sin? I want to live and be happy . . . then I can die in peace."

Elena's face clouded with concern. "Here comes our stop, but we have to talk some more. I want you to reconsider."

"No, Elena. Don't waste your time. I've made up my mind."

It was a busy Monday at Elena's Beauty Salon. Many customers showed up without an appointment, but Elena managed to have the ladies attended and satisfied. The image of Vilma being fondled by Benny flashed in her mind now and then. She couldn't find a free moment during the day to talk to her. Although she didn't like to meddle in anybody's life, now she felt the urge to do so. Vilma was going too far in dating an almost-rapist. She felt obliged to intervene; she had promised Vilma's mother that she would look after her.

"Elena, can I leave now?" Vilma stood behind her, while removing her uniform.

"Sorry Vilma, but we're still very busy."

"Oh, Elena, Benny will be here any moment."

"Can you at least wait until Carmen is dry? Then you can take out the rollers and leave." Elena patted Vilma's shoulder "Maybe he'll be kind enough to wait for you?"

Vilma rolled her eyes. "Okay. I'll wait."

So Vilma helped clean up while Carmen's hair dried. When Benny arrived, he made himself comfortable in the waiting room. Elena greeted him sternly and thanked him for agreeing to wait for Vilma. His presence made her uneasy, reminding her of Peter's lascivious face and alcoholic breath. The thought of his hands touching her still nauseated her. She sought refuge in the bathroom and composed herself. Once done she came back out to attend her costumers, showing the best of her smiles, using all her will power to shove Peter's odious image to the back of her mind.

When Roberto called later on, she was so busy that she couldn't talk to him. When he called again they talked for a little while about how their day went and other unimportant matters. Later, he picked her up and they had a quiet dinner. On the way home he announced that he had made reservations for Tuesday night at Club 21 where he had a surprise for her. No matter how much she asked for a hint about the surprise, he didn't yield.

"Just get dressed to kill and leave the rest to me. It's going to be your night," was his answer, and then he added, "Bring Vilma along, if you like."

She didn't feel like discussing Vilma now, but she thanked him, sent him a kiss and hung up.

Curious about what her surprise might be, Elena went to bed. Even with the concern that Vilma wasn't home yet, she sank in a deep sleep, exhausted.

Elena took Roberto's words seriously: "dress to kill." Since she no longer had access to the exclusive evening dresses Gina kept in the office, she went to Gimble's to buy one. She fell in love with it as soon as she saw it—emerald green tulle with long green gloves. It was fitted, strapless, and had a boned bodice with a gathered bust. Subtly shimmering sequins and prong set rhinestone embellished the bodice and extended below the waist. The gown had a full, floating double layer tulle skirt. It was fit for a princess, and so beautiful! She had to have it, even if she had to spend her last penny. She also bought a two string pearl choker with matching earrings, and a pair of high-heeled green brocade shoes.

When Roberto came to pick her up, he reached for her hands and exclaimed, "You look striking!"

"You look fabulous yourself," she exclaimed, returning his kiss wrapped in the aroma of his perfume.

Roberto wore a navy blue suit, white shirt and a dark blue tie extremely well. His brown shiny eyes were larger than ever, his usually wild bushy eyebrows were combed, and his wide happy smile displayed white even teeth. *Oh my God, I love this man so much!* She thought. "Am I still due for a surprise?" she asked coyly.

"Tonight will be a memorable evening."

"Every moment with you is memorable."

"I'd do anything to keep you thinking like that." He took her in his arms in a long, tight embrace, then helped her into the waiting cab. "I love you, mi Elenita," he said once she was seated, and kissed her hand gently.

The cab driver shook his head smiling. "I'm a sucker for young people in love," he said, as he started the engine.

Elena got closer to Roberto and whispered, "What did he say? What does 'sucker' mean?"

"That you have a soft spot for something or someone, like I have for you."

As always, Elena reveled in the ride through New York City. She found the Fifth Avenue stores so elegant and out of her budget; the skyscrapers were grandiose, making her feel insignificant. She didn't know what Roberto called memorable, but taking in this view next to a man she adored . . . it didn't get any more memorable than that.

Soon the cab stopped in front of Roberto's building, and she was astounded.

"Does your place have anything to do with my surprise?" she let out, without thinking.

"Let's say that it's a big part of it," he said with a mischievous smile.

Oh, my love, don't tell me that I spent all my savings on my outfit just to visit your penthouse. I love your place, but I didn't have to go broke to come here, she told herself.

"This is our first stop, my love," he said, while paying the cab driver.

"Now I'm more curious. Did you forget something, that's why we're here?" she said, hopefully.

"No, Elenita, this is only the first part of your surprise. Be patient, Chiquita."

"I'll try, but can't promise to wait patiently."

He just laughed.

When they reached the front door, he opened it. It was quite dark already but Roberto didn't turn on the lights, rather he placed his hands softly on her shoulders and guided her to the living room. "Sit here for a second," he asked. Roberto disappeared into the kitchen for a few minutes. *What's with the cloak and dagger,* Elena thought.

"Okay, you can come in now." Roberto went to her side and gently guided her through the dark apartment into the studio. The darkness lessened and the room appeared to glow. As they walked in she saw dozens of small candles on beautiful ornate candleholders, on the floor, spelling out the words "Will you marry me?"

Elena couldn't contain herself. Tears flowed down her cheeks. He embraced her tenderly. "What is your answer? Will you be my wife?"

Finally, sobbing with joy, she said with a faltering voice, "*Mi vida*, I'd be proud to be your wife."

He wiped the tears springing from her eyes. "Your make-up is ruined."

"Roberto, this is too much. This is incredible!"

"It isn't over yet. The best is still to come."

"Nothing can surpass this!"

"Just wait and see!"

They alighted at the restaurant. When Elena saw the four-story brownstone building that housed the "21" Club, her mouth fell open in awe. Adorning the balcony above the entrance, all in a line were numerous colorful painted cast-iron statues of jockeys. Elena couldn't take her eyes off of the lifelike figures.

"What do you think they mean?" she asked, curiosity showing on her face.

"In 1930 an affluent patron of the restaurant donated the first jockey painted to represent the racing color of the stable he owned," he said, his face animated with interest. "It was followed by 34 more statues from other famous owners of racing horses. One of them you might have heard of: Vanderbilt."

She wanted to say, *no, I never heard of him*; but opted for: "Yes, it sounds familiar."

She had her eyes fixed on the figures, so he nudged her tenderly to get going. They got inside through an imposing, large door decorated with Tiffany glass.

They turned to the right, where annexed to the building was a brick wall with a door concealed within it. Roberto pushed hard and it opened, giving way to a vault. The view of it took Elena aback. The vault was huge and bottles of wine covered the walls. There was a lacquered top dining table set for twelve. Each place had a vase with a single long stemmed red rose, as well as wine and water glasses.

"Oh, my goodness, Roberto, I didn't know there could be a wine cellar like this. Are we early? Nobody is here," she said anxiously.

Roberto placed a hand on her chin and gazed into her eyes. "Be patient. I wanted you to see the infamous wine cellar before going to our dining room." He took her by the hand and led her through the room, gesturing at their surroundings. "This place, once a glamorous speakeasy, provided liquor during the prohibition era to everyone who was someone. Here powerful people and the rich socialites of the Roaring Twenties spent wild nights evading federal agents. Although raided by police numerous times, the owner never got caught."

"How could it be possible? Did the owner have ties with the underground or big shots of the era?"

"That, *mi Chatita*, I don't know; but as soon as the raid began, a well-planned system was used to tip the shelves of the bar, sweeping the liquor bottles through a chute and into the city sewers."

"What a waste! Imagine all the money involved . . . so many bottles . . ."

"Think about it. Even now the private wine collection of many celebrities and presidents are kept here—like

Hemingway, Zsa Zsa Gabor, Mae West, Onasis, Sinatra, just to name a few. For Christmas time the regulars receive silk scarves decorated with a motif of various unique clubs' insignia. I read that Siggie Nordstrom had dozens of these she received through the years."

"And who is she?"

"Model, actress, entertainer . . . you name it. She just came back from Cuba."

"*Caray,* Roberto, if you ever find yourself without a job, you can earn your living as a guide. How come you know so much?"

"Well, the first time I came here for lunch was a business meeting. I was impressed with '21', so I set out to learn everything I could about the place." He grinned at her sheepishly. "I could tell you more, but I'm afraid I'd bore you."

"I'd love to know more—the easy, short way . . . and with someone as wonderful as you."

"Okay, I'll tell you all I know, but I expect a generous tip."

They laughed, amused.

"Our dining room is under the famous Bar Room."

"I'm sure there is another good story there," she said, still laughing.

On the way to the Bar Room they walked along a stately lounge with an oak bar, red leather armchairs, plush striped banquettes and some tables.

They arrived at the restaurant and were met by a solicitous hostess, who treated them as if they were the only customers she had to attend. Elena felt important. They followed the hostess to their table.

The restaurant was part of the so-called Bar Room. The décor was pure fun. The walls and ceiling were decorated with what the owner called toys: antique cars, sport memorabilia, trucks, tennis rackets, ballet slippers, airplane models and an endless array of other antique toys that were suspended from the ceiling and walls. Attached to each "toy" was the name of the donor. Among them were Howard Hughes, Vanderbilt, Humphrey Bogart and many more, including powerful politicians and statesmen.

A waiter in a crisp white jacket approached them and placed a pair of impressive menus on the table. "What would you like to drink, sir?" The waiter asked politely.

"May we have your trademark—rum and mint cocktail, please?"

When the waiter left, Elena asked, "Mi *amor*, I'm afraid rum will be too strong for me."

"Not at all. You'll have food soon."

"I thought you didn't drink."

"Only on special occasions."

The low lighting was intimate, and adding to the already perfect atmosphere was the musical background of the song *La vie en Rose,* sung by Edith Piaff.

Elena's big black eyes looked at Roberto with passion. She was delighted to see the same passion reflected in his gaze. "Thank you *mi amor,* this place is amazing."

Scanning the menu, Elena heard voices and she looked up. The voice belonged to a lady at a neighboring table. She was a vision of surreal beauty. Suddenly Elena recognized her—a movie star she had admired for years. Then the woman subtly smiled at Roberto, who had bowed his head at her in acknowledgement.

"Roberto, do you know her?"

"Well, yes."

"How come? Were you in show business?"

"No, *mi amor*, I know her through her former husband, John Loder. We were stationed together during the war. Would you like to meet her?"

"Oh, is that possible . . . ?"

With this Roberto took her hand and Elena found herself being introduced to the most beautiful woman in film: Hedy Lamarr.

"Hedy, may I introduce to you my fiancée, Maria Elena Alcantara?"

"It's a pleasure, Maria Elena, I am Hedy."

"The pleasure is all mine," Elena said shyly.

"We're celebrating our engagement," announced Roberto.

"Congratulations! Do you know that a few years ago Humphrey Bogart asked Lauren Bacall to marry him right here?"

"How nice! I didn't know that. Hedy, please, Elena would love an autograph." He handed her a cocktail napkin.

"Of course, with pleasure." She took a pen from her purse and wrote something, then returned the autographed napkin to Elena.

"Oh! Thank you," said Elena, smiling.

What have I done to deserve all this? Elena thought. *Roberto asked Hedy Lamarr for an autograph! That reminds her of the time he took Gina and her to see Tito Guizar, the famous Mexican singer, and Roberto generously bought all of Tito's records for them. Mi Roberto, I adore you!*

"It's my pleasure. Elena, I detect an accent . . ."

"Elena is from Cuba," prompted Roberto.

"She's a very pretty Cuban. I just came back from Havana; I got my tan there. Would you like to join us? My husband will be here soon."

"Oh, that would be . . ." began Elena, thrilled.

But before Elena could finish her statement, Roberto jumped into the conversation. "Thanks for your kindness, Hedy, but being our special night . . . you know."

Elena blushed, embarrassed and disappointed. She wanted to grasp this one-time opportunity to dine with Hedy Lamarr and hear her speak. Roberto must have a reason . . .

"Of course. I understand," Hedy said graciously.

When they returned to their table, the drinks had arrived. Elena sipped her drink, "*Salud, mi amor*, it's delicious."

"To your health and happiness, gorgeous."

Elena went back to her subject. "Oh, Roberto, she looked ethereal. I also detected a light accent."

"She's Austrian; she was born in Vienna. And yes, many critics and fans regard her as the sexiest Hollywood star, ever."

"In spite of her looks, I find her beauty spiritual, not sexy. She's utterly beautiful to look at."

"She's not only a sultry beauty but very intelligent. She's an inventor."

"Oh? What did she invent?"

"She co-invented a secret communication system; an early type of frequency hopping."

"*Caramba*! She's a beauty with a brain. How interesting. By the way, why did you turn her invitation down?"

He cleared his throat. "I think she used it to break the impasse."

"What do you mean?"

"Perhaps we stood there too long. It was either leave or dine with her."

"I'd have loved to dine with her, to get to know her better."

"There will be other opportunities . . . but tonight is our special night. I want you for myself."

Elena had to make an effort not to stare at the movie star, but when Hedy's husband arrived she tried not to be too obvious when peeking. Now because of Roberto she had met Tito Guizar and Hedy Lamarr! She needed someone to pinch her.

She immersed herself in the huge menu. "Oh, oh . . . this is going to be a problem," she said, smiling.

"What is?"

"To choose from this menu."

"No problem . . . I'll order for you."

They looked at each other and laughed.

He began to read: "Steak tartar, bouillabaisse, grilled Dover sole, black sea bass, truffle potatoes, honey roasted duck . . ."

She interrupted. "Wait a moment, Roberto. Take a look at the special treatment they give to the hamburger. They called it the #1 at '21'. What could be so special about an ordinary piece of ground meat?"

"You'd be surprised. Forever that burger has been the specialty of the house, and famous around the world. If '21' were not so pricey, I'd be here more often for my burgers."

"I don't see any prices here."

"They don't want their clients to get indigestion before they eat. But tonight don't worry about prices . . . the evening is yours."

A tuxedoed headwaiter stopped by their table.

"Are you ready to order?" he asked politely.

"Yes. Bring the lady grilled Dover sole and the hamburger for me."

Soon the aroma of spices and herbs alerted Elena that their order had arrived. Her mouth watered in anticipation of the delicacies placed in front of her.

She used the fork to cut the fish. "Wow! I don't even need a knife . . . this meat couldn't be more tender, juicy or tasty. How about yours?"

"As good as I expected it. I never go wrong with my burger. A taste?"

"No, *mi amor*, thank you."

"Here. I insist."

Elena tasted it. She was surprised by the delicate flavor of spices she couldn't recognize. The piece of ground meat seemed to melt in her mouth.

"Roberto, you're right, this is delicious."

Once they were done and the table cleaned, the headwaiter appeared with a bottle of champagne in a cooler and filled their champagne flutes. Another waiter appeared with a silver tray holding a covered porcelain vase. He placed it on front of Elena, along with a long-stemmed red rose.

They began eating the cake slowly when Elena let out a small cry and took a hand to her mouth. "*Virgen del Cobre,* what's this?" On her fork was a ring with a big diamond. "I must be dreaming! I'm afraid I'll wake up."

"Your dream has just begun."

Roberto took the ring from her, then poured champagne in a glass, washed the ring carefully and wiped it dry with a napkin. He placed it on Elena's shaking finger. "May this diamond seal our love forever."

"Oh, Roberto, you promised me a memorable night, but I never could have imagined all this. I will take this magic night with me into eternity."

"I love you, *mi Elenita.*"

George Gershwin's music in the background reflected the moment perfectly: *No, no, they can't take it away from me.* She sighed. "Those lyrics are right; nobody can take this enchanting evening away from me."

They ended their magical evening with a horse-pulled carriage ride around Central Park. And, if it were not enough, she felt blessed to be bathed by a full moon.

CHAPTER VII

Will Roberto Tell?

A crumpled piece of paper lay on Roberto's desk. He grabbed it, straightened the letter out and looked at it with unrestrained hatred. Just now when he finally experienced happiness, the phantom of his past came back to haunt him. Now, when Elena would belong to him . . . yes, his Elena, the woman that brought out the best in him. What would happen if she found out about this mess? She wouldn't accept it, for sure.

Unfair to pay such a price for a one-night affair! To have a child with a woman who meant nothing to him, and have that baby shatter his future—changing his life forever! How on earth would he find a plausible explanation for this?

Worse than infidelity, it was proof of his lack of willpower. It was unpardonable, and if he couldn't forgive himself, would Elena?

After a long debate with himself, he decided to treat this part of his life as if it had never happened; a terminated and forgotten chapter . . . Could he do that with a child in the middle? Of course! He'd make sure that Anita and her baby didn't lack for anything their entire lives. He'd make that clear through Emilio and Marina. They would take care of everything.

Once this problem was in the background, he would deal with the issue of his religion. He didn't feel as strongly about that, though. How would Elena react to his being Jewish? He would wait until later to tell her, so she wouldn't have time to back out of their engagement. In the meantime, he would make his Elenita the happiest of all brides. Then perhaps it wouldn't be so hard for her to overlook their different beliefs. He was hoping their love would be stronger than their differences.

What a disappointment! Once again, Roberto gave Elena a good excuse for not attending mass, so she went to church with Vilma. Elena loved eating at the *Automat*, so after mass they went there for breakfast. It never ceased to amaze her how after inserting the coins in the slot the food she chose found its way down the chute in a glass case. She was always happy with her choice, even for food she normally didn't care for.

Elena spoke of Roberto incessantly during their meal.

"You are very much in love, aren't you Elena?" asked Vilma, grinning.

"I don't think I can live without him."

"I wish you the best."

"I have the best of the best, Vilma. I'm afraid of so much happiness."

That Sunday night Elena met Benny when he came to pick up Vilma at the efficiency the two girls shared. She was uneasy; she hadn't been able to make peace with the man. They had a meaningless conversation about the weather and such. Moments later, Roberto arrived. His expression changed when he saw Benny. After cold greetings, he asked Elena to hurry. A taxi was waiting.

He wore a frown to the car.

"It worries me to find that guy at your place. I don't trust him. Why do you allow Vilma to see him in your apartment?"

"I don't like it either, but it's as much her place as it is mine."

"You are moving to my penthouse tonight. When we come back you're going to pack."

"I'm not going to live with you until we are married."

"That doesn't make sense. We're engaged and soon you'll be my wife."

"*Mi amor,* don't insist, please."

"In that case, I'll move to a hotel. The apartment is all yours."

"Vilma is my friend. I'm not going to do that to her."

"Elena, please, be reasonable. Vilma brought that man to the house in spite of what he did. She's not respecting you." He paused for a few moments. "In fact, she's not respecting herself."

"I don't agree with what she's doing, but she's an adult."

"As a friend you should advise her."

"I did. But, I can't force her. She's older than I am, you know."

"This is serious, Elena. I can't leave you alone at his mercy. What if he comes back with his friend to finish his unfinished business? What would you do?"

"That's not nice of you to alarm me that way."

"I'm trying to make you understand for your own good. You need to get out of that apartment."

"I understand your point. But, I'm sorry, Roberto, I'm not changing my mind."

"Of course you are," he shouted.

"You can take me back home if you like, because I won't yield," she said calmly.

"Stubbornness is a new trait in you. I don't like it at all," he said sternly.

"Not even loving you the way I do . . . I can't change my mind."

Roberto was silent for a few seconds and Elena could tell it was taking a great effort for him to calm down.

"There should be a way to solve this problem without ripping ourselves apart." He paused for a moment. "I love you, *mi Elenita preciosa*," he said, amorously.

Elena kissed his cheek tenderly and Roberto took her hand and brushed it with his lips.

"Roberto, I'll spend the night with you. Let's go."

"Thank you, my darling."

"In your house . . . not in your bed."

That night at Roberto's apartment, Elena settled in the guest room and Roberto, reluctantly, went to his bedroom. She was tense and couldn't go to sleep. She heard Roberto pacing around his room. Then, after a few hours of tossing and turning, she finally fell into a restless sleep. She must have been asleep for a short time when a loud crashing sound and muffled voices woke her. With a pounding heart and weak legs she got out of bed and stood by the closed door, shaking with indecision. What was going on? Should she check or lock herself in the room? She placed her ear on the door and listened. It sounded like Roberto's voice. She opened the door slowly and peeked. The lights were out, everything was dark but Roberto's voice was clear now.

"You leave him alone," he said.

Was somebody with Roberto?

Elena walked cautiously through the dark hallway and stopped by Roberto's door. She heard a muffled cry.

"I can't do this. I can't, I can't!"

Elena knocked gently on the door.

"Roberto?" she asked softly. She couldn't even hear her own voice. She swallowed and tried again. "Roberto. Are you okay? May I come in?

Moaning came from the other side of the door.

Elena opened it. Darkness. She turned on the light and gasped. Too stunned to scream or to move, she stared at Roberto's tear-streaked face and in his right hand a gun pointed at her. Her whole life flashed in front of her in a matter of seconds. And out of nowhere she heard the voice of the old woman outside in the hallway of her apartment.

'You have many angels watching you. Looking out for you. But you are stupid child, and one day the angels can't protect you.'

Elena stood there, afraid that her guardian angel wouldn't help her now. She waited for what seemed an eternity, but must have been just a few seconds. Finally, she found her voice and said,

"Roberto. What are you doing?"

"Stay away from him!" He shouted between sobs.

"Away from whom?"

"From Carlos. You can't take him yet!"

Roberto's empty gaze, made her heart skip a beat. He was looking in her direction, pointing the gun at her but he wasn't seeing her. He wasn't seeing anything.

"Roberto. Wake up! It's me, Elena."

"I can't do it!"

Elena took a gamble that Roberto didn't want to use the gun and stepped, carefully, closer to him. Her legs felt like noodles but she kept talking in a soothing voice.

"No one is going to take Carlos. Roberto, don't worry *mi amor*. Please put the gun down."

Roberto brought his hands to the sides of his head, gun and all, and sobbed openly. Then, she got closer and took the gun gently from him, and placed it on the night table. She hugged him, and then shook him gently. "Roberto, wake up! Wake up!"

She held his face in her hands, and as if someone had turned on a light, his vacant eyes changed into the loving, brown eyes she loved so much.

"Elena. What happened? Why are you here?" Roberto looked around the room, perplexed. He saw the gun on the night table.

"Why is that here?" He said looking at he gun. He rubbed his face and eyes and noticed the wetness on his cheeks.

"I think you had another of your nightmares Roberto, but this time you were sleep-walking. When I came in the room you were pointing the gun at me. *Mi cielo*, you must get rid of that gun. It frightened me so . . ." Elena began to cry herself. All the fear and hurt that she kept at bay during the crisis, came out in torrents.

Roberto went as pale as his sheets and hugged Elena.

"Of course, my darling, I'll get rid of it. Oh, *mi Elenita*, forgive me. I would rather die than hurt you. I would never, never harm you, my love." He took the gun and disabled it.

They sobbed in each other's arms. Then Roberto spoke,

"I . . . I remember the dream. I must tell you why I have these nightmares hunting me." Roberto sat on the edge of the bed, placed his elbows on his knees, and covered his face with his hands.

"I had a very good friend in Tangier, Carlos. We were neighbors. He was two years younger than me and saw me as his big brother. When I joined the Royal Air Force during World War II, Carlos wanted to join too. When I came back to Tangier after a year of being in the Air Force, Carlos told me he had joined as well and that he was coming with me."

Roberto had to swallow a few times before being able to continue. Elena could see his jaw clenching and unclenching in an effort not to cry.

"Carlo's mother came to my house and she cried and pleaded with me to take care of her only son. 'You are like a brother to Carlos. He looks up to you. Please, please bring my boy back safely. Take care of him as if he were your baby brother. Swear to me, Roberto.' "Those words are engraved in my heart. I will never forget them."

Elena fought back tears. She could guess the outcome. How dreadful, she thought.

"On our first mission together we got hit. Our plane came down. I don't know how I survived. The first thing I did when I came to, was to look for Carlos. At just a few feet away from me . . . he was still alive. His legs were gone." Roberto began to weep.

"Roberto, my love. You don't have to continue."

"Yes, I have to. Now that I started I have to tell you everything. That's the least I owe you after what I've put you through."

"You don't owe me anything, my Roberto,"

"Please, Elena. Let me go on . . . Carlo's abdomen was torn apart and his guts were spilled out," Roberto croaked. "And he was in so much pain! There was nothing I could do! He begged me to kill him. I refused. I told him I would take care of him—that I had promised his mother I would bring him back home and I was going to bring him back home."

Roberto stopped for a few seconds and Elena remained silent with an arm around his back.

"The enemy was approaching. I heard them. Carlos heard them too. He looked at me with pleading eyes. I took my gun, bent over and kissed his cheeks. I told him. '*Te quiero, hermano.*' He smiled faintly. I shot him between the eyes."

Roberto and Elena sobbed in each other's arms for a long while, then she said, "I'll dedicate a mass for the peace of his sole."

The next Sunday, again Roberto had an excuse for not attending church. Elena was left not knowing what to do, when Benny showed up at the door to pick up Vilma for mass. Not wanting to hurt Vilma's feelings, she joined the couple and the three of them went to Saint Patrick's Cathedral.

After mass, they returned home where Vilma prepared lunch. Elena was uncomfortable around Benny. The idea that she was betraying Roberto hung over her. She didn't want to leave the house, so she opted to stay in the kitchenette helping Vilma cook the meal. Benny waited, reading the newspaper. The black beans were already cooked, so it wouldn't take too long; Vilma just had to make the *sofrito* and add the sausage to finish; cook the rice, fry the plantains, and grill the Cuban style steak.

"Girls, the food smells great," said Benny from the sitting room.

"Do you like black beans?" asked Vilma.

"I never had them, nor fried plantain."

"I hope you like them."

"If I don't, I'll learn to like them."

The table was set. They ate in silence, interrupted at intervals by the exclamations of praise from Benny for the two cooks. When Vilma went to the bathroom, he quickly addressed Elena, his brow raised.

"Elena, if you don't mind, I'd like to talk with you."

"What is it?"

"I know my presence is difficult for you."

He waited in vain for any reaction.

Finally, he coughed nervously and went on. "Well Elena, I'm very sorry for the way we met."

"I prefer not to talk about that."

"Pardon me if I insist."

"I'm really not interested. I have been trying to forget."

"If you listen to my side, I think it will help you to forgive and forget."

She bit her lip and scanned the room. "Some memories cannot just be rooted out like weeds."

"I know. But . . . ."

"Why don't we talk about something else instead?"

The lines around his mouth deepened. "I care a lot for Vilma, so for her sake, I'd like your approval for our relationship. Neither of you have family in the United States, so you need each other. I don't want Vilma to lose your friendship on my account."

Then, leave her alone. Elena wanted to say but instead she couldn't help but be happy for her friend. Benny sounded sincere and it took guts to apologize for his mistake.

An embarrassing short pause followed.

Then Benny said, "At least you should know how things happened."

"OK Benny go on." Elena said with resignation.

"To begin with, Peter isn't my friend. We don't have much in common. We used to go to school together and would see each other at parties. I ran into him after not seeing him for a long time and we agreed to go out. When I met Vilma, she told me she was bringing a friend. Peter came because I figured it would be an opportunity for all of us to have a good time. My family was out of town, so I thought of going to my place."

Beads of sweat began to form on Elena's brow. "It was clear I didn't want a date and you forced me into it!"

"In the beginning I didn't pay attention, I thought you were playing hard to get, and I was busy with Vilma." He paused, looked around and toyed with his tie, then went on. "Peter and I wanted to have a good time. He was crazy about you the minute he laid eyes on you; and selfishly I wanted to enjoy Vilma's company. I had never dated anybody like her. I hadn't dated in a long time, and I must admit that I wanted things to work out for everyone." He got to his feet and paced the floor.

After several seconds, he stood in front of her. "This is really bothering me . . . not only because I care about Vilma, but because I know it was wrong and I was too blind to see it then." His voice trailed off as Vilma entered the room.

"Oh, don't stop on my account," said Vilma. "What are you two talking about?"

"I'm apologizing to Elena for the circumstances in which we met."

"I'm so glad that you finally did. I know how much it weighs on you."

"Elena, can you find it in your heart to forgive me?"

"I understand many things now and I appreciate the courage it took for you to talk to me about this. I can't erase what happened nor the way it makes me feel. I can't promise you we'll be friends but I will try harder. That's all I can promise you."

"Thank you, Elena," said Benny eagerly. "I appreciate your understanding."

Elena smiled at both Vilma and Benny and left for her room.

For the next two weeks Elena felt as if she were living on a cloud. Perched on that cloud, she saw Manhattan in its entire splendor with its million twinkling lights. Though known as a cold and insensitive city, Manhattan had brought her much happiness.

She was grateful to God and to Roberto for the exciting life she was experiencing. Back in Cuba, she had hoped for a better life and independence, but she never dreamed of the happiness she was living now. The night Roberto proposed was etched on her mind as the happiest day of her life. The way he pampered her! The gentleness and passion in his lovemaking made her toes tingle. *Virgen del Cobre, don't let anything end my happiness,* she urged the Virgin.

What was Roberto leaving for their honeymoon, if now every night he showered her with new surprises? One night it was dining and dancing at Morocco's nightclub among movie stars. Another evening it was a ride under a starry sky on a horse-drawn carriage in Central Park, followed by dinner at Tavern on the Green. This exquisite place impacted her even more than "21" Club. Well, each one had its unique charm, but Tavern on the Green was more to her liking.

Another place beyond her imagination was Radio City Music Hall. The alignment and exactitude of the endless line of Rockettes, and the Spring Spectacular Easter Pageant, were too much for her mind to assimilate.

She almost fainted the night Roberto took her to Broadway to see the award winning musical, *South Pacific*. She had goose bumps during the whole show, but when Ezio Pinza sang to Mary Martin *Some Enchanting Evening,* Elena couldn't stop the tears running down her cheeks.

This particular Sunday night she went to bed reveling in her good luck. It was a night of several awakenings from her light sleep. When finally it was morning, Elena got up and dressed to go to work. It was going to be a special day: she was having lunch with Gina. Elena decided that the time to tell Gina about her engagement to Roberto had arrived. She thought it was safe to do so, now that Gina was happily married. She took along some of the pictures taken at luxurious places where she had been going lately to show them to her.

"Well, Elena, there's a saying that you can't hide money or love," said Gina, while waiting for their lunch at a luncheonette close to the beauty shop. "I've got the impression that you're trying, in vain, to hide both."

Gina gazed at Elena for a long time and said, "You've learned how to dress and how to profit from your own natural gifts. You look outstanding! Every little detail in your outfit matches." Gina burst into laughter.

"Are you laughing at me?"

"Of course not, silly. I'm laughing with you. You haven't changed at all. You still blush at compliments."

"Oh, Gina, you're overdoing it."

"No, my friend. Remember when I tried to change your look? The makeover I gave you when you first arrived?"

"I'll never forget."

"It was nothing compared with what you've done with yourself now. But most of your change comes from within. Are you in love?"

"Oh, Gina, I'm crazy in love with a wonderful man."

"That's terrific! How? Where? Do I know him?"

"Yes, very well. Your approval is very important to me."

"Anyone able to erase the usual sadness in your face has my approval automatically." Gina beamed. "Go on. Speak up!"

"Gina dear . . . I'm in love with . . . Roberto. We are in love."

Gina's eyes widened and her mouth was open for seconds before she could utter, "What? Were you the other woman in his life at the time he left me?"

"NO! It wasn't like that at all. It all started shortly after his return from Spain."

"Elena, if this began when we were together, I couldn't forgive you."

"Gina, listen to me. Our friendship is invaluable to me. If I started seeing him, it's only because you had a new life. He's so easy to love. He's sweet . . . I need him."

Gina remained silent for a few moments, looking at Elena, obviously, with mixed feelings.

"I guess it's okay. Anyhow, just be careful. Do your parents know that he's Jewish? My mother is so religious that I kept it from her."

Elena felt her knees weaken. Her heart jumped to her throat. "That can't be true."

"He didn't tell you?"

"There's nothing to tell. He is Catholic—all Spaniards are," Elena was not so sure now.

"He was born in Malaga but raised in Morocco," said Gina. "His father was a Greek Jew."

"But he said he was raised here, in the US."

"You know what? You'd better ask him. But, first analyze your own faith and find how rooted and important it is for you."

With a big effort, Elena hid her hurt feelings. After lunch they went back to the shop and spent some time with Elena's accountant, balancing checkbooks and straightening out her payments on the salon. Elena couldn't concentrate. She felt a tight knot at the pit of her stomach. Gina was surprised to see how well Elena had managed the business and was pleased to receive a good portion of what Elena owed her.

"Elena, I'm very happy you got the knack of the business so well and so soon. At this pace, the salon will be yours in no time at all. Congratulations."

Elena heard Gina talking but nothing she said registered in her mind. Was she telling her the truth about Roberto? Why would she lie? Was it possible that Roberto had been lying to her all this time? Why would he keep his religion from her? Or the place he was born and where he was raised? What else was he hiding then? She had to ask him! He would tell her the truth. No doubt!

To Elena's mind flashed the day she had asked him how many languages he spoke. He answered spontaneously, "Spanish, English, French, Hebrew, Portuguese, and Italian. Also some dialects like Catalan, and . . ." Then, she remembered asking, "Why Hebrew?" He grinned, and said, "In Morocco you grow up with all these languages . . ." And just there, he changed subject. "By the way, my love . . ."

That Monday evening, Elena waited anxiously to meet Roberto. Finally, he arrived with a red rose and a bottle of wine. He gave them to Elena and kissed her on both cheeks, and then on her lips.

She placed the rose in a vase and served two glasses of wine. "You're spoiling me. Why wine again?"

He looked at her mischievously. "Spending one more day with you merits celebration, my darling."

Sitting next to each other on the sofa, they raised their glasses.

"To our happiness, my darling," Roberto said, clicking her glass.

"For us!" she replied.

They sipped the wine. "You look stunning, dear. How was your day? Did you have lunch with Gina?"

"Yes."

"How did it go?"

"I told her about us."

"You did? What was her reaction?"

She sighed. "At first I thought she understood." She paused.

"And . . . ?"

"I don't think she's happy about our relationship. She lied to me about you . . . I think she's resentful."

"What did she say?"

"She told me that you are Jewish! Isn't that silly?"

Roberto turned white as the snow; he took a deep breath and asked, "What if I were?"

"No, you are not."

"Why not?"

"You would have told me if you were. That's why I know!"

They locked eyes for a moment. Then, he asked, "So, is being a Jew that bad?"

"Of course not. What's bad is lying about it! So it's true?"

"First of all, you never asked."

"Oh really? Now that I think about it, all the excuses you came up with never to go to church with me didn't constitute lying? Once you even said that you had gone already. Why didn't you say, *'honey I'm sorry, I can't go to church with you because I am Jewish',* instead of inventing ailments and meetings that never happened? And . . ."

". . . You and your sister are so religious . . . so Catholic . . . I panicked . . . Elena, my love! I want . . . I need you! I was afraid to lose you."

"So in order to keep me you lie to me? Because you love me you deceive me? What kind of love is this?"

"For you I would do anything! But, I didn't really lie to you. I just withheld information. That's all."

"That's all? How could you do this to me? I trusted you! You were my hero!" Confused, Elena stared at him in disbelief.

"Forgive me. I was about to tell you."

"Really? When? Before or after the wedding?"

"Every time I saw you I wanted to . . ."

"Just stop talking! You are making it worse . . ." She got to her feet and fixed her fiery eyes in his. "You laughed at me. You deceived me. How sad! It happened to me once; it seems to be my destiny."

"It's not the same Elena . . . I love you with all my heart. What I did or didn't say for that matter was out of fear of losing you. You are my life! Can't you understand that?"

"Liar!"

"I didn't choose to be Jewish. That shouldn't be an obstacle . . ."

"Don't you get it? What hurts and disappoints me is not whether you are Jewish or not . . . it's your duplicity. You purposely hid it from me." With a tone of defeat and a faltering voice, she said, "You leave now. I need time to think . . . I don't want to say something I will regret later."

He tried to stroke her cheek, but she turned her head. "My love, please, let me do something to redeem myself. What do you want me to do?"

"Get out! I don't want to see you!"

"Elenita," he said almost crying, "I want to be here by your side . . ."

She shoved him to the door. "When I'm ready to discuss this, I'll let you know. Good night."

She slammed the door after him and ran to the bathroom. She struggled to hold back the tears. *I'm not going to cry, I hate tears*, she told herself while pouring cold water on her face the way she used to do in Cuba, when dealing with her frustrations and her inability to do anything about them. Luckily, she wasn't in Cuba now; now she was independent, but so alone. She had to be strong to get through this. The time when she cried for everything belonged to the past. Now she had to think coolly about Roberto's deceit. Oh, if she could talk to Father Gil or Doña Pilar, her confidantes in Cuba, they would help. Alma was too religious and narrow-minded.

"Elena, I'm here." Vilma tapped her accordion door. "Are you okay?"

"Yes. I'm trying to sleep. See you tomorrow."

"Is there anything I can do for you?"

"I just want to sleep."

"I understand. Good night."

Elena pressed the pillow against her head; as if it would stop her grief from swallowing her being. But it was too late. The unwelcome pain had already slipped in, so she surrendered and cried hopelessly for the devastating fall of her phony idol.

CHAPTER VIII

Restoring An Idol

It was impossible to sleep. Elena read, prayed, drank linden tea, counted sheep, but to no avail. She couldn't take the image of Roberto from her mind. She regretted not paying attention to all the clues that were there, that she had chosen to ignore. For a long time he had found excuses not to go to mass with her . . . once he even told her that he had already gone. Liar! She lamented having put all her faith on him.

Either he was a master at lying, or she was naive gullible. Maybe both. But why put herself down? She was trusting and he was a schemer—that's why he took advantage of her blind love. Why on earth had she thought he was almost perfect?

He was a scoundrel.

After a fitful night, she had no other choice but to get up and go to work. Walking with Vilma on the way to the subway, she found herself growing annoyed as Vilma repeatedly asked what was bothering her. Elena's answer was always the same: "I don't feel good." She used the same excuse at the shop when clients and co-workers asked what was bothering her.

The day seemed longer than ever. Not that she wanted Roberto to call, but she expected he would, and he didn't.

His silence concerned her—it was out of character. To her chagrin she realized she missed him terribly.

None of the girls spoke on the subway ride back home.

"Elena, do you have plans for tonight?" Vilma asked, as they walked up the stairs to their studio.

"No."

"I'll cook for you then. Oh, look, there's something at the door."

"It must be from Roberto!" exclaimed Elena, before she realized she had spoken the words out loud. She ran to the door. Lying on the floor was a long stemmed red rose with a card. She ran to the kitchen and read: "This is the first day without you."

"Roberto isn't coming tonight?" asked Vilma.

"No."

"Is there anything wrong?"

"Yes. Very wrong, Vilma."

"If it helps, tell me. I'm listening."

Elena plunged herself into the sofa, followed by Vilma; then she updated her friend on the latest happenings.

"I am so sorry," Vilma said, concern written on her face. "What are you going to do?"

"Wait until I can confront it."

"Will you break off the engagement?"

"I don't know. I need time—"

"We should have suspected something was wrong when he refused to go to mass with us." Vilma scratched her head, and added, "Yet, most Catholic men don't go. I thought he was one of those."

"I don't know if I can face a life without him in it, but I know I can't live a lie."

For the next few days Roberto sent roses daily. The second day he sent two; the third there were three. Friday there were five. The cards reminded her of how many days he'd suffered her absence.

Each night Elena cried her way to sleep. Tears were such a relief that she didn't care if they meant weakness, because they helped to release the heaviness in her heart. On Saturday morning she couldn't wait any longer and called her mentor in Cuba, Doña Pilar. After short greetings, Elena emptied out her heart and told the lady in detail of her anguish.

"You keep calling it 'Roberto's betrayal,'" Doña Pilar said. "I see it as a little white lie to save a great love. It's not easy to find real love in the course of a lifetime. Grab it! Don't let it go . . . ."

"But I can't trust him anymore. My love for a man feeds from admiration—I don't respect him anymore." She sighed and went on, "Who knows how many other things he's keeping from me?"

"Ask him; give him the chance to unburden himself. He didn't want to lose you, that's why he kept things from you." Doña Pilar cleared her throat. "Elenita, there was a time when you lied to Rodolfo and to your mother-in-law . . ."

"But I was trying to save my marriage and my life."

"They were lies all the same: With a good reason, and for a good cause. I think you mean *life* to that young man. He also wanted to save his life and your relationship, same as you. Elenita, I would have given my life to have lived a love story like yours."

Doña Pilar's argument began to sway her.

Elena felt a heavy weight lifting from her life. She was finally calm enough to talk to Roberto.

So she called him.

Before the rooster crowed, Roberto was at Elena's apartment. She opened the door and was stricken by the sight of Roberto struggling to hold a huge bouquet of red and white roses, which covered his whole face. To her mind came the first time she saw him. She was leaving an elevator when this man rushing to catch it took her hand and placed a bunch of red roses in her arm, and then disappeared, leaving her perplexed. But they had locked eyes and she thought he was the most handsome man she had ever seen. She would have given anything to see his dark, dreamy eyes again.

Roberto stood by the front door, and neither of them moved. He was still strikingly handsome, with beautifully sad, brown eyes, straight nose, sensuous lips and strong jaw. But he was gaunt. He'd lost a lot of weight in a few days. Before she realized what she was doing, she threw herself into his arms, crushing the roses. He let go of the flowers and held her tightly against his chest, losing his face in her neck and hair. Roberto stepped into the sitting room and with his foot pushed the door shut, then carried her to the bedroom and closed the accordion wall hard. Without words, the silhouette of two bodies became one, as they conveyed to each other the love they had been withholding for so long. Elena was relieved that Vilma was out with Benny, so she could express her feelings openly.

The couple let time pass tightly embraced. Reluctantly, Elena broke the magic moment.

"*Mi amor*, I hate to bring up the subject, but we need to talk. I understand why you lied. But I can't forget it. My love for you is unwavering, but my trust in you is faltering. Love without trust . . . it's not the same."

With the expression of a starving orphan hopelessly begging crumbs, he looked at her. She felt sorry for him.

She wanted to forget everything and take refuge in his arms, but she couldn't.

He struggled for an answer. "My beloved Elena, I have known deep sorrow in my life. I saw things during the war I wouldn't wish on my worst enemy. I faced pain and death every day, hell many times a day. Yet none of those experiences compares with the prospect of you leaving me. Simply put, I can't face life without you."

"That sounds beautiful, but again, Roberto . . ."

"Don't say it, please." He combed his hair with his fingers and said sadly, "I'll do anything in my power to win your trust again. You won't regret this, I promise. Why don't we get married right away?"

CHAPTER IX

A Simple Wedding

"Yes, *querida Doña Pilar*," said Elena into the phone. "We don't want a big wedding, because of the difference in our religion. Just City Hall and the paper to prove we are married . . . oh, and a honey-moon in Acapulco."

"Great, Elena! Is your mother going to the wedding?"

"No. Later we'll organize a party for family and friends."

"But I don't want you to be alone on your big day."

"I will be fine, don't worry."

"No, dear, I'll be there. In fact, I'll bring your mother with me and I'll take care of her visa. That will be part of my wedding gift."

"*Doña Pilar*, I don't know what to say. To see both of you will be the best gift—it'll make me so happy!"

"Do you have accommodations for your mother?"

Elena was silent for a moment. "I don't. My apartment has only one bedroom with a single bed and Vilma sleeps on a sofa in the living room. But I can move into a hotel with both of you."

"I'm staying with Thomas Alexander and your mother is welcome to stay there with me. By the way, he's happy for you and sends you his regards."

"I'm very grateful . . . I owe both of you for helping me to be where I am now."

"We are very proud of you. Thomas would be happy to lodge your mother in his house."

"I think my mother would be overwhelmed by the wealth surrounding the Alexander's."

"Nonsense. You know they are down-to-earth people and will give Magdalena the best treatment."

"True, but I know my mother. She'll feel intimidated. And also there's the problem of language; I want my mother to feel comfortable."

"Stop fretting. Your mother will be fine, and so very happy for you. Now before you and I make all these plans, I need to see if she is willing to travel. As soon as I know, you will know."

"Okay, I will wait for your call. I don't dare hope that Mother will accompany me on the most important day of my life."

They hung up the phone, and Elena recalled the way she met Mr. Alexander. When she left Cuba, Doña Pilar had given Elena a letter of recommendation for Mr. Alexander. From that moment on, the nice gentleman took Elena under his wings. In fact, he took her step by step to the place where she was now.

Five minutes later Doña Pilar called again with the news that Magdalena accepted to stay at the Alexander's.

Elena called Roberto.

"What great news!" he said. "I really was concerned that your mother wasn't going to be with us on our big day. Now everything has fallen into place."

"I'm really happy!"

"Elenita, you should stay with your mother at my apartment."

"*Gracias, mi amor*, but it's not necessary."

"Why not?"

"Mother and Doña Pilar will be staying at Mr. Alexander's home in Long Island."

"You couldn't find a better family; they will know what to do to make your mother feel at home."

"I know . . . we are so blessed to have them in our lives. Most of what I have accomplished is because of Mr. Alexander."

"What you have accomplished is because of you, my love, and no one else. You are smart, beautiful, and you have great taste in men." Roberto added, winkling.

"You think so, eh?"

"I know so."

"*Mi amor*, I could talk with you all day, but I'm afraid I have to go now to continue with the preparations. I love you. Bye."

The ladies arrived from Cuba a week before the wedding. To Elena's relief, her mother and Roberto took a liking to one another at once. In the best of humor, he drove the ladies to the Alexander's place. The family shared coffee and cookies with their host before retiring.

"*Mi amor*," Elena implored in private. "Let me stay with my mother tonight. I want to help her break the ice; this is such a different environment for her—look, she's so pale, and her knees are shaking."

Roberto agreed.

At the Alexander's mansion, the three ladies shared a large, elegant room. They spent most of the night catching up with past events in their lives. Most of the time they spoke about Roberto, and both Doña Pilar and Magdalena seemed to be crazy about him.

The next day Elena brought the group to see her new business. Elena sent tender glances to her mother, who seemed to be in awe of the beauty and elegance emanating from the salon. All of it meant happiness for Elena and she could hardly contain her elation.

None of the clothes Magdalena brought were suitable for New York's climate. The following day Elena took her shopping.

"*Hijita*, what a different world this is. Not even with your detailed letters explaining all this, could I have imagined such abundance and beauty." She looked around and sighed deeply. "Thank God you found this when still young enough to take advantage it."

Her mother's pride in her success overwhelmed Elena. In a burst of joy, she held her mother in a long and tight embrace. "I love you, *mamita linda.*"

The long awaited day finally arrived.

"*Querida mia*," Roberto said over the telephone. "When I went to pick up the rings the inscription wasn't ready, and I couldn't wait for them to complete the work. Do you mind picking them up on your way to City Hall?"

Elena was happy to help and thrilled that he'd asked her to. It made her feel loved and important. "Of course, *mi amor*," she said cheerfully. "Mr. Alexander is taking Mother and Doña Pilar directly to City Hall. I'll see you all there."

"I don't want you to be late. Ask the cab to wait for you."

"It's a waste of money. I'll find another one."

"Elena, please do as I say. It's too important of a day to take any chances."

"If you say so, *mi general.*"

Still, once at Tiffany's, Elena was made to wait, so she dispatched the cab. By the time the rings were ready, she had difficulty finding another one and was an hour late getting to City Hall. Roberto was furious.

"Where the hell have you been?" he shouted, nostrils flared with anger.

Elena had never seen an expression change Roberto's face so much, nor had she experienced such a fit of rage. With a knot in her stomach, she struggled to contain her tears, but when she looked at her mother on the brink of crying, she couldn't hold the tears and burst into sobs.

"Roberto, what's the matter with you?" exploded Mr. Alexander. "Watch your language . . . and manners."

A long line of people was waiting to get married. A number of heads turned, eyebrows raised. Some stared openly.

"We lost our place in line and now we'll be the last," Roberto said, trying to recover his composure.

"That's no reason to act like that in front of the ladies. You need to apologize."

"Of course, you're right," he said, chagrined. "I'm sorry, ladies," he said, obviously mortified by Alexander's stern rebuff. "Thank you, Mr. Alexander, for reminding me of my place. It won't happen again."

Roberto walked to Magdalena and kissed her hand. "*Señora,* it won't happen again, I promise," he said firmly, and then he kissed Doña Pilar's hand. "Pardon me, Doña Pilar." Then he approached Elena. "Elenita, I hate myself for shouting at you. *Perdoname, mi amor.*"

He was obviously bothered by his outburst, but Elena was reticent to let Roberto near her. "Stop, Roberto" she said when Roberto tried to embrace her. The hurt look in his eyes made Elena want to hug him, but those same eyes had distilled something very different a few minutes ago. "Roberto, you scared me. I don't know if we should go on . . ."

"Elena please, stop! Don't say it. I can't bear the thought of losing you. I swear to you, this won't happen again. I love you more than you'll ever know."

He sounded sincere. Elena thought for a moment. Roberto had overreacted and had been rude, but only because he loved her so and feared losing her. After all, he had told her to keep the cab waiting so she wouldn't be late and she had ignored him. Nobody is perfect, nobody has it all in life . . . why would she? She turned quietly to her mother. "*Mamita*, I'm sorry you had to witness this. Roberto is not like that. He's sweet and he loves me."

"*Hijita*, I can't tell you what to do. I'd hate myself if I gave you wrong advice. Pray to God and trust your heart."

Elena turned pleadingly to Doña Pilar, hoping to hear the wise old lady assure her that everything was going to be all right.

"*Querida Elenita*, no one can tell you what to do, you must listen to your heart, but also listen to your head. Love is blind and forgives everything, but your brain won't lie to you."

The violence she lived while married to Rodolfo, rushed to Elena's mind. But, again, Rodolfo didn't have the education and worldliness that Roberto had—Roberto could control himself.

Now he was looking at her and the anger was gone. The spark of violence had disappeared quickly and was replaced by sadness and love. She heard him saying in a small voice, "It is our turn."

"Let's do it."

After the short ceremony, the guests gathered at Club 21 for dinner. Elena made a big effort to appear happy by forcing herself to remember the joyful memories experienced in this restaurant. But Roberto's outburst hung over her heart, throwing shadows over her treasured memories. Had she made a mistake by marrying Roberto?

In the short time Magdalena had been away from Cuba, the change in her spirit had been remarkable—her eyes seemed alive, and joy had replaced her perennial gloom. Elena had rejoiced at her mother's transformation: thank God for this respite from life!

As the time for departure neared, Elena noticed her mother's face begin to cloud over. When she glanced at her she saw the usual hurt expression on her face; the borrowed pleasure of the past few days was gone. The emptiness and the knot in Elena's stomach grew deeper with Magdalena's imminent return to Cuba. Obviously, her mother was going back, concerned that her daughter's marriage might not be as solid as she first had thought. Elena wanted her to leave convinced that her daughter's second marriage was a happy one. So, Elena hid her uncertainty.

Back at the restaurant, Elena held Roberto's hand, and said, "Did you all know this is the restaurant where Roberto and I got engaged?"

Roberto turned and held her chin with trembling fingers. "Yes, it was here that she made me deliriously happy." He brushed her lips with his. "Dear, forget what happened today and let's look forward to a future full of love and understanding." He looked at Magdalena, and with conviction said, "*Mamá*, don't worry about Elenita, I will dedicate my life to making her happy." Obviously, Magdalena was relieved to hear the conviction in Roberto's voice and the adoring look in his eyes.

He looked directly at Doña Pilar's eyes, holding her gaze. "Thank you for your support. And you, Mr. Alexander, again, forgive the outburst of this afternoon. I'm indebted to you."

"Don't mention it my boy. Doña Pilar and I will keep looking after Elena." He pointed a finger at Roberto, and smiling, he said, "I'll be checking on you, young man, you better make our Elenita happy or you'll answer to me." Then he turned, and with a kind, but firm voice, he said, "Don't be concerned, Señora Magdalena, your daughter has a protector here."

"God bless you all," Magdalena said, happiness returning to her face.

The warmth of gratitude ran through Elena's body. Following an impulse, she got up and hugged and kissed each of her friends.

Elena managed to enjoy the rest of the evening, the nagging in the back of her mind almost forgotten. When the time of farewell arrived, the ladies shed a few emotional tears, and the guests went their own way.

The newly-weds hailed a cab and went to Roberto's place, where Roberto carried his bride over the threshold and straight to the bedroom. He placed her gently on the bed and bent to kiss her, but Elena turned her face from his.

"Darling, what's wrong?"

"You know what's wrong."

"Yes, darling, but I thought you forgave me . . . ."

"You scared me and embarrassed me on the most important day of my life. I'm just not in the mood tonight."

"So . . . so you don't want me here tonight?"

"If you don't mind, I prefer to be by myself and think things over. Tomorrow, in Acapulco, we'll begin our honeymoon."

"Well . . . if that's what you want."

They embraced. He kissed her on both cheeks, then grabbed a pillow and a blanket and walked away.

Unable to sleep, Elena tossed and turned, torn by her love for Roberto and her unease at his outburst and previous lying. Had she done the right thing marrying him? A desperate scream pierced the silence, "Nooo! nooo! I can't do it!!! Elena flew out of bed to the living room, heart pounding. She turned on a lamp and found Roberto desperately trying to untangle himself from his blanket. His face flushed; a mask of agony contorting his handsome features. Elena rushed to his side.

"Roberto, wake up!" she cried, shaking him with all her strength. He was sweating profusely, and yelled over and over again, "Nooo! nooo! Please don't!

Elena fought with the blanket, trying to free him. "*Mi amor,* you're ok. It's your nightmare again. Wake up Roberto, wake up."

Roberto opened his eyes but he didn't seem to see her; he was looking beyond her to something that terrorized him. Elena held his sweaty face in her hands and kissed him gently, looking into his eyes. Slowly she could see him coming back and terror turned into relief and love.

"Thank God," he said, sobbing. He jerked her into his arms, holding her tightly against his chest.

"Roberto, don't worry, you'll be fine."

"Elena," he moaned, "I'm so glad you're here with me. I don't want lose you."

"Of course you won't, ever!"

"I . . . I . . ." Roberto pulled away from Elena and covered his eyes with his fisted hands. "I can't tell you. It is killing me. But, I can't. You'll leave me. I can't talk."

Elena had never seen Roberto like this. She was used to the larger-than-life image of Roberto: strong, handsome, successful, the world at his feet, towering over everyone and everything. *There's something he wants me to know, but it frightened him. I wouldn't force him to talk. This broken, sobbing man filled her with tenderness and pity; she didn't know what to do.*

"Elena, give me some time. Please. One day I'll tell you . . . promise you won't leave me when you find out."

"Take it out of your chest. Talk!"

"I'll take care of you, always."

"Of course you will, I have no doubt, my love. Don't worry."

"I'm fine."

"Then, talk to me."

"I will, my darling. I will. But not yet! Can you be patient, give me a little time."

"You can have all the time you need. I'll be here when you are ready." Elena kissed his forehead and guided him to their bed and held him tightly until his muscles relaxed. They fell asleep.

CHAPTER X

Honeymoon In Acapulco

The newly weds arrived at their hotel in Acapulco on Saturday afternoon, after a long and exhausting flight from New York, via Dallas. They rushed to their suite and changed into summer clothes. Elena couldn't wait to walk on the beach. When Roberto took her hand to help her into the pink rental jeep, she placed her arms around his neck, playfully.

"My love," she said, grinning. "Thank you for choosing Acapulco. I love it!"

"I know your taste, *mi chiquita.*"

He drove along *La Costera*, which follows the shoreline of the Bay from one end to the other. It provided a magnificent view of lofty mountains and majestic cliffs. The city in Southern Mexico captivated her: the dark blue of the Pacific Ocean meeting the infinite blue of the sky made her praise God's artistry. Nothing made by man could come close to the beauty of nature. Her eyes followed the outline of the mountains against the slowly fading sun, and the numerous sailboats gliding on the water. The lush greenery contrasted with the showy red bougainvilleas and jacarandas. It was a sight to behold. The active waters and rough mountains reminded her of the *Bahia de Nipe,* in her natal *Santiago.*

Could all this be real? Could all this be happening to her? She had never experienced so many extremes as she had the past few days, from immeasurable happiness to deep sorrow.

Evening had not yet given way to night when Elena and Roberto found themselves dining on the outside terrace of the hotel *El Mirador* after an invigorating walk along the beach. The smell of seafood made Elena's mouth water. The soft crashing of waves pulled her into a dream world. Every now and then, the waves created a mist that touched her face. She played her tongue around her lips, savoring the salty water.

"*Chiquita mia*," Roberto said, grinning mischievously. "If you keep doing that I won't be held responsible."

She threw her head back and burst into laughter. "Oh . . . Yes? Show me what kind of consequences?"

"I'll forget where we are and will make love to you right here."

"You wouldn't dare!" She laughed and held his gaze daringly.

"Try me . . ."

Elena half opened her mouth and with her tongue outlined her lips slowly. He jumped to his feet and stood in front of her. Then, holding her chin in his hand he kissed her, his tongue searching for hers passionately.

Embarrassed, Elena tried to free herself. "No, Roberto, don't."

"You dared me, remember? If you want me to behave stop doing that tongue thing."

"Ok, ok, I promise. Now stop it! People are watching."

People at other tables craned their necks for a better view.

"You're crazy," she teased.

"I am. I'm crazy about you! We better eat fast and leave . . . I don't think I can wait." He kissed her again, this time softly, and to her relief, he returned to his seat.

For some reason, Roberto's boldness reminded her of his nightmare. She shivered, remembering his sobbing and vulnerability. Totally different man, yet the same.

The food arrived. The fish was delicious. They ate their fill, and left the restaurant to walked along the beach holding hands.

As they walked, the sound of waves crashing on the beach, and seagulls screeching mixed with one of the most beautiful baritone voices Elena had ever heard.

"*Tuyo es mi corazon, o sol de mi querer . . .*" the voice crooned the lyrics to *Maria Elena*, a popular song at the time.

Elena turned to comment on this beautiful song to Roberto when she realized it was he who was singing. He stopped and grabbed her hands and sang directly to her, his powerful voice carrying over the beach and sea. People started gathering around them admiring the handsome couple and the talented singer.

She loved his voice and she loved the song. But her face turned hot and her cheeks reddened with the awareness of the crowd around them.

"Roberto, please," she said. "People are watching."

He ignored her and kept singing, drawing applauses and praise form the crowd. She wanted to disappear, to sink into the warm sand beneath her feet.

Realizing her embarrassment, he stopped for a moment and kissed her.

"Shhh . . . Everyone's looking!" she pleaded.

"Isn't she a sight for sore eyes?" he asked the crowd, who cheered and applauded in agreement. "I'm the luckiest man alive! I'm married to the most gorgeous woman on earth!" Roberto told whomever would listen. The crowd congratulated them.

Earth, open up and swallow me, Elena thought. "Darling, can we leave now. Please?"

"Anything for you." He winked mischievously. "I hope you'll be more amenable later on?"

"Thank you," Elena said to the dissipating crowd as she and Roberto made their way back to the hotel.

"So, you kept another secret from me." Elena said as they approached the hotel.

"What secret?" Roberto asked.

"That you are such a good singer. You sound like a professional. Are you?"

"The only reason I'm a good singer is because you are my inspiration, my muse."

"You inspire me too but I guarantee you that if I started singing now, someone would call the police."

"You're too modest, my Elenita. I'm sure your voice is like that of angels."

"Thank you, for your confidence in me." She laughed, amused.

Once in their suite, Roberto began to sing again.

"My heart belongs to you, to you, woman of my dreams! Maria Elena, can you see, I love youuuu . . ." He held a high note while swirling her around; then, as if floating across the room, carried her to the enticing bed.

"Oh Roberto, sing to me," she pleaded, passion burning in her eyes.

"Sing? No! You told me to be quiet," he teased. "Now I'm going to punish you with my silence."

She burst into joyful laugher. "Punish me?"

"You didn't care about my song before. Now you killed my inspiration."

"So, you're going to deprive me of your magnificent voice?"

"Most definitely."

"Mmmmm, is there any way I could bring that inspiration back?"

"I can think of many. I'll whisper a few here," he said, while gently nibbling her right ear lobe, "and a few more here," he whispered in her left ear. He continued kissing her gently until she begged for him to take her.

Next morning, while shaving, Roberto said, "Today I'll take you to La *Quebrada.*"

"What's that?"

"An impressive jagged cliff," he said enthusiastically, "from where fearless young men hurl themselves from 148 feet to the sea below."

"My God . . . ! It sounds terrifying! But also fun . . . I can't wait."

"I made reservations for dinner. It will be more dramatic because at night the divers carry torches. It's quite a sight."

"Must be beautiful! Very thoughtful of you, thanks."

"Darling, I'm hungry. Let me finish shaving, and then we'll have breakfast."

She gave him a peck on the cheek. "I love you!"

Elena thought of her mother and her sister Alma. There was so much to see outside their little hometown! She felt guilty because she was the only one in the family enjoying such amazing experiences. She had been sending post-cards and letters to them, from all the remarkable places she visited, detailing the marvels of each one, hoping they would experience vicariously some of the joy she felt.

"I'm ready, dear," called Roberto.

He placed his arm around her shoulder and they left. On the way to the elevator, he said, "We will have brunch here; they have buffet and mariachis."

They entered the dining room where a long table held diverse fruits and an assortment of cooked eggs with sausage, beans and red and green sauces. A cook was heating tortillas and making tacos. Musicians were walking around the tables playing and singing Mexican *corridos.* To her mind came Tito Guizar, with his big sombrero, and his beautiful Mexican songs.

Roberto and Elena filled their big plates with all kinds of food and fresh fruits from the long table, Elena wondering if she ever could eat everything on her plate.

They were enjoying the food when one of the young singers approached Elena with a wide smile and asked if she had a request.

"*Rancho Grande*, please," she responded at once, grinning.

They began the cheerful song and Elena was transported to another world, so much that she didn't notice the twisted anger on Roberto's face. The group finished the song and everyone applauded. The singer, with a twinkle in his eye, asked Elena.

"*Señorita*, what else would you like to hear?"

"Not *señorita*, but *señora*," said Roberto, sharply.

"I'm so sorry, *señora*!" embarrassed, the singer said.

"Please, *Cielito Lindo*!"

Roberto stood up abruptly, placed the tip on the table and grabbed Elena's arm. "Come, we're leaving."

"What do you mean we're leaving? I'm not through eating."

"You are finished! What kind of imbecile do you think I am? Flirting in my face!"

"Me? Flirting? With whom?"

"With your cowboy singer, who I am sure reminded you of Tito Guizar."

By now, the cowboy singer had discretely moved away, ignoring Elena's request.

Oh no . . . Elena thought, *I'd better keep my mouth shut until we get back to the room to avoid a scene. But what in the name of God is Roberto accusing me of?*

In their room, with a look of disgust on his face, Roberto took off his *guayabera*, and slipped on his robe. Then, he picked up the newspaper, went out and sat in a rocking chair on the terrace. He scanned the pages first and then went back to the front page and began to read.

Elena didn't know what to make of his attitude. He was actually ignoring her in punishment for what? For requesting a song? This made her blood boil. She went to the bathroom and splashed cold water on her face, breathing deeply a few times, then marched out to face Roberto.

"We need to talk," she said moving a chair close to him.

"I'm listening."

"Do you want to tell me what's wrong?"

"You know what's wrong."

"You said I was flirting. What did you mean?"

"You insulted me. You flirted openly with that singer . . ."

"Wait a moment! I did not!"

"Of course you did. You were asking for songs and drooling at the sight of that ridiculous mariachi, just like a silly, little teenager. You were oblivious to your husband's presence!"

"Roberto, are you out of your mind?"

"You bet I am. To think I have married a . . . a coquette! I thought you were the best thing that happened to me . . . I thought you were different from other women."

"Even if it were true, you don't have the right to talk to me like this."

"The right? I'm your husband. I don't know for how long, but you owe me respect while I am."

"Oh really? What are you saying? I can't listen to this anymore."

She returned to the bathroom struggling unsuccessfully to hold back tears. Perhaps this was a punishment for stealing Roberto away from Gina.

Virgencita, here I am again begging for your help. I'm so angry I could just walk out of this marriage! But I can't hurt my family. It would destroy my mother. What am I going to do? He hinted at separation. Now everybody is going to think that it is my fault. They'll think the first divorce was my fault, too.

Elena heard the door slam and ran out of the bathroom. Roberto had left. Where was he going? Why was he doing this to her? Again, and as she had done so many times in the past, she sobbed until the tightening in her chest subsided.

Suddenly, a new thought occurred to her. What if she was really the one to blame? Roberto had been a gentleman always. Loving and considerate, he read her thoughts in order to please her, as if she were his queen. It was precisely because of these qualities that she had forgiven him his lies.

Should she forgive him again?

Forgive him? She paced the floor, biting her nails. Maybe this time he was right. Maybe she shouldn't have asked the singer for another song. After all, she hadn't allowed Roberto to sing to her in public, but she asked a stranger to sing to her.

Oh God! I should have paid more attention to my husband. While I was dreaming and having a good time, he was longing for my attention . . . . How could I have been so selfish? She was so confused . . .

A noise at the door made her heart skips a beat. Roberto! She ran to the door to meet him, full of hope, but it was only the maid, who had come to clean the room.

"Sorry, *Señora. Vuelvo luego.*"

She reached out a hand to stop her.

"Don't go. Make the room, please. I'll step out."

"I can come back later."

"No. I prefer you to do the room now."

She took her purse and went to the lobby, where a man was playing the piano. She was tempted to sit there, and she almost did. On second thought, she walked away. Nearby, she found a quiet room decorated with colorful paintings made by natives. She guessed they were pretty, full of bright colors and child-like images, but her mind was elsewhere. She finally settled for a magazine and read for a long time.

It was late by the time Elena returned to the room. She was disappointed that Roberto wasn't there, so, she sat on a rocking chair in the terrace overlooking the swimming pool, and the immense ocean beyond.

Why do people fight over such insignificant things? Why, waste precious time when life is so short?

Down in the swimming pool the happy noise of children playing and the laughter of adults made her long to join them. She wondered where Roberto was. Elena felt it was her fault their honeymoon had been spoiled.

Time passed and Elena's feeling of guilt deepened. When the sun began to set, the knot in her chest tightened.

The outstanding red and orange intensity of the sky, which usually made her senses explode with admiration and happiness, now plunged her into sadness.

Finally, the front door opened and Roberto walked in. She hurried to welcome him, but the expression on his face stopped her.

"*Hola* Roberto," she said hesitantly. "Where have you been?"

"I have been reflecting on how blinded I was by you. We will pack and fly home tomorrow."

"Why cut our stay short? The hotel is reserved for a week."

"I don't want to waste my time and emotions on a marriage that isn't working."

"What do you mean a marriage that isn't working? After one argument during our honeymoon you decide our marriage is not working?"

"It's not the argument or a difference of opinion. It's something more fundamental than that; the foundation of any relationship is respect. Without respect there can be nothing. My heart is broken because I still love you more than life itself. I can't change that. But love without respect can turn into something ugly."

His expression of anger shifted to one of deep sorrow, and Elena felt guilt and compassion invading her.

"I have been thinking," she said firmly, grabbing his hand. "Come with me to the terrace, let's talk."

He withdrew his hand. "I'm tired. I'm going to bed."

"Listen to me first. Then you can go to bed. Roberto, *mi amor*, I'm very sorry. I want to apologize. I see how you interpreted what happened the wrong way. I wasn't flirting. That young man meant nothing to me. You know I'm romantic by nature and I love music. This experience was totally new to me; being serenaded while eating brunch, with you at my side. I was just swept off my feet by the whole package. Can you see that? Part of the magic was having you by my side."

She placed her hand on his arm, and felt the desire to be held close to his chest. This time he didn't try to get loose, so she guided him to the terrace and they each sat on a chair. Elena turned hers to face him.

"There's nothing more important to me than you."

"You could have fooled me," he said sarcastically. "You made me feel as though for you, I was not there at all . . . you were lost in a stranger's song, yet when I sang to you, it was not romantic, but embarrassing!"

"It is not like that Roberto . . . *Mi amor*, please, understand. It was not the singer. It was the song."

"So I should have picked a different song?"

Elena held her breath for a moment, then noticing a small smile on Roberto's lips she flung herself on his lap and kissed him. "No mi amor, the song Maria Elena that you picked was perfect."

"Darling, you better get off my lap," Roberto murmured into Elena's hair. "If you keep this up we'll miss our reservation for *La Quebrada's Sky Divers.*"

"So, you changed your mind?"

"I think we can give it a try."

That evening, Elena took extra care choosing her outfit and makeup. She wore a green summer dress that Roberto had bought for her at Gimbles. The fitted blouse outlined her natural curves, giving way to a flared skirt that reached below the knees. Her high-heeled green sandals matched the dress perfectly. She scrutinized herself in the mirror and approved of what she saw, filling herself with confidence.

She finished it off with a spray of Taboo eau de toilette. She didn't like it; it was too strong.

"You look sensational, and smell divine!" said Roberto when she emerged into the sitting room.

"Well, you just earned the full-time job of dressing your wife." She threw her arms around his neck and they embraced for a long time. Tenderly, he disengaged himself from her arms.

"I'd prefer the full-time job of undressing my wife. But alas, we have to go."

"Do we?" she asked suggestively.

"Listen Chiquita, I know what I'm talking about." He took her arm and picked up her purse, playfully pushing her out the door. "This show is unique. You'll love it."

"Oh Roberto! What a spectacular place!" said Elena, as Roberto helped her to her seat. "This is fascinating."

"Look at the divers . . . they're climbing the cliff." He pointed to the left. "See that little shrine? It is where they go to pray to the Virgin of Guadalupe before the big plunge."

"Do they jump from there?"

"No, they go higher up to the peak."

The table was set with crackers, olives, anchovies, cheese and peanuts; also two glasses and one bottle of Sangria. Roberto poured sangria into the two glasses.

"To your health, dear," he said, gazing at her adoringly.

"*Salud!*" she said, clinking her glass with his.

Soon after, a waiter came with the menu. "Do you need anything? Would you like some snacks? Appetizers?"

"Thank you, what we have here is more than enough."

"Are you ready to order?"

"Give us a few minutes, please."

"Take your time."

Mi vida," said Elena, "why would the divers risk their lives like that?"

"It's a family thing. One can say that they are born divers, and they train from childhood. As young children they dive from the lower peaks, studying the currents and waves carefully. There aren't as many accidents as you might think, but it's still quite dangerous. It's a living I guess."

"Do they make a lot of money?"

"They used to work only for the tips of the onlookers, but now they are organized and have a salary and scheduled shows . . . I don't think there's much money involved, though."

Elena shook her head and sighed. "Poor people, I feel for them."

"It's a hard way to make a living, but they enjoy what they do." He turned his attention back to the menu, and running his fingers through his hair, said, "Always the same problem in Acapulco. I don't know what to order because everything is sooo good!"

"Have you come here often?"

"Several times. Usually, when I schedule business meetings, I choose Acapulco or Mexico City. The restaurants here all have the same great, fresh seafood."

"You're very lucky, traveling so much."

"I'll bring you on my next business trip if you'd like."

"I'd love to come, *cariño mio.*"

He pointed to an appetizing, full-color picture of a lobster on the menu. "I think I'll order flamed snapper for two. What do you say?"

"Flamed?"

"It's delicious and quite a spectacle! The waiter brings a cast iron skillet to the table with a variety of freshly cooked seafood of choice; the chef comes along, sprinkles it with brandy and fires up a match. The flames flare up and voila! Flaming meal that elicits a delicious garlicky aroma."

"My mouth is watering already . . . . I love *mariscos.*"

"Dear, we can't eat shellfish. I'm ordering us fish."

"Why's that, *mi amor,*" asked Elena, half smiling.

"It's against the Jewish religion."

What a pity! Now that I can afford lobster, I can't eat it.

"Well I'm not Jewish," Elena dared. "Can I have lobster and shrimp?"

"Elenita, honey, please respect my beliefs."

Elena reluctantly agreed.

Roberto placed the order, specifying that shellfish not be included.

An entourage brought the food to the table. She couldn't help but jump when the chef lit the match. The aroma of fresh fish and the whoosh of the flames startled her.

"I'd say the fish had been taken out of the water a minute ago," said Elena, closing her eyes and breathing deeply.

Sometime later, while enjoying dessert, Roberto told her, "Pay attention, darling, the divers ended their prayer. They're walking away from the shrine . . . ready to jump with torches."

"What a view! Look at the illumination!" exclaimed Elena, and then murmured, "*Virgen de Guadalupe*, be with them."

The three men crossed themselves. Elena crossed herself after them.

The jagged cliffs jutted out high over the Pacific Ocean. The divers looked as tiny as ants standing on the peak staring solemnly at the sky and meditating for what felt like ages. Then, they circled their arms a few times with torches in each hand. Finally, they dove, shooting straight down the 148-foot drop to the narrow inlet, where huge waves entered and crashed over the rocks. Their timing was crucial. If they missed the waves, they would surely lose their lives. They did catch the waves on time. The three smiling *clavadistas* emerged victorious under thunderous applause from the enthusiastic crowd.

Back in their hotel, Elena hurled her shawl and purse onto the chair in the sitting room. "*What an Enchanted Evening,*" she sang.

"It's not 'What an enchanted evening' but '*some enchanted evening*'," *Roberto* corrected. "And that *enchanted evening* is about to begin, mi Chiquita Linda". Roberto came to where Elena was standing and kissed her gently on the lips. He undressed her slowly. He scrutinize her naked figure for a few seconds and said, "I can't say what part of your body I like best." He cupped her small breasts in his hands and kissed them ever so tenderly, running his tongue around her nipples; then, eased his way down to her bellybutton. He lowered himself to his knees, and moved passionately downwards, ending with his face between her legs. She clasped his head with both hands, moaning with pleasure, arousing him still more.

"*Mi vida,* I can't take it any longer," she pleaded in ecstasy.

Roberto took off his pants and hurled them across the floor. He cradled Elena in his arms and took her to the bedroom. She sat on the edge of the bed and removed his underwear, came to her feet and took off the rest of his clothes. She kissed all his exposed skin . . .

"My love, I'm afraid I'll be finished too soon. Let's take it slowly," Roberto said, taking deep breaths.

Elena lay back onto the bed; Roberto caressed her body, leaving no inch untouched. Elena fondled him as if she had never touched him before. They made love for what seemed like hours, only ending when both had come several times.

"I've never felt anything like this before," whispered Elena.

"Elena, making love to you awakens a side of me I thought was dead" said Roberto, tightening his embrace. "I could stay like this forever."

CHAPTER XI

Back To Reality

"Home, sweet home!" said Roberto, placing the two suitcases on the floor.

"*Hogar, dulce hogar*," echoed Elena, as she kicked off her high heel shoes. "I am happy to be back. I love your place."

"Our place." Roberto hung his Panama hat on the hook by the door. "I'm happy wherever you are. I'll go check the mail; the box is bound to be overflowing."

"Forget the mail and let's go to bed. I'm so tired!!!"

"Me too. I suppose it can wait one more day."

Next day they each went their different way to their jobs.

Elena was surprised to find so many wedding gifts at the shop, even though she hadn't invited any of her clientele. She felt blessed.

Vilma approached her with a beautifully wrapped package, which she left on the desk.

"*Felicidades, mi amiga*," she said, embracing her tightly. "I hope you enjoyed your honeymoon."

"Thank you, Vilma, I did. It was heavenly."

"How was Acapulco?"

"Fabulous . . . if and when I find the words to describe it, I'll tell you," Elena said with a smile. "But now, tell me how things went while I was gone."

"Thanks to Mrs. Taylor's help, everything went fine."

They examined the log to see what appointments Elena had.

"Shoot, I have a long day. I better get ready."

It was a busy day indeed. Elena didn't have time to daydream or relive the wonderful moments of her honeymoon. Vilma had booked one customer after the other, and by mid-day she was exhausted. When it came time to leave, she realized that Roberto had not called her at all.

She summoned a cab and went home. Immediately, she called Roberto at his office.

"Mi *amor*, are you well? How come you didn't call?"

"It was a crazy day. I'll tell you about it later. Do you want to meet me for dinner? We need to talk."

"Anything wrong?"

"Not really. Just a little problem we need to solve together."

"You worry me. What is your problem?"

"A situation we need to deal with."

"Roberto, tell me already."

After a long pause, she asked again. He cleared his throat and kept quiet.

"Roberto, I'm waiting."

"Well, Elenita, my mother and sister are coming."

"What?"

"A cable was waiting for me at the office this morning."

"You should be happy."

"I don't need my family's visit right now."

"*Mi amor*, that's not a problem, but a gift. Why isn't it good?"

"Well . . . you see, it just so happens they think you are converting to Judaism."

"What are you talking about?"

"They don't know you are still a Christian."

Elena fell silent in shock. Convert to Judaism? She was drained after a full day of work . . . and now this! She felt as if her legs were made of straw.

Not again, she thought. *Why is Roberto doing this to me? I was under the impression we were through with the religion problem. Why did he misrepresent the whole issue?*

"Elena, are you there?"

"What do you want me to do?" she stammered.

"It would make everything easier if you could start the process of converting before they arrive," he said, a sense of urgency in his voice. "Please, *mi niña!*"

"You're not making sense . . . are you out of your mind? When did we discuss the fact that I was converting to your religion?"

"I'm sorry *cariño*, but I have to hang up now. Think about it, will you? Let's meet at *El Chico* at seven. Remember that you are my life."

Elena took a shower and allowed the water to run for a long time over her head and through her hair, hoping it would help to clear her mind. She was astounded. How was she going to tackle this one?

"Calm down, Elena," she told herself, "This isn't the end of the world. Not yet, anyhow." Fortunately, she had an hour to sort out the new mess they were in.

Virgen de la Caridad, por favor, I need your helping hand.

It was past seven when she arrived at the restaurant. Roberto's table was close to the entrance and his eyes were fixed on the door. He was sipping from a glass when he saw her. He left the glass on the table and rushed to her, kissed her on both cheeks, and escorted her back to the table.

"A glass of sangria, my love?"

"Okay."

He signaled the waiter. "Marcos, the same for my wife, please."

"At once, *Señor*."

They remained silent while they waited. The waiter brought the sangria, and addressed Elena.

"Madam, are you ready to order? What would you like to eat?" he asked.

She shrugged. "Whatever."

Roberto handed the menu to Marcos and ordered *arroz con pollo* for two.

"*Mi Chiquita linda*, I don't like to see you with that face."

"And I don't like you acting as if nothing were happening."

"Elenita, I just want the waiter out of the way so we can talk about our problem."

"*Our* problem?"

"Okay, *my* problem!"

They ate in silence. Finally Roberto said, "I don't think we should talk here."

What's wrong with him? Is he avoiding discussing the problem?

She asked, "Were we not here precisely for that reason?"

"I thought it would be easier. I was wrong."

"Then ask for the check and let's go."

At home, they sat next to each other at the kitchen table. Elena sat with her arms crossed, and tapped her foot against the floor.

"My dear Elenita," he said, kindly. "I need your support once more."

"Do you mind telling me exactly what you told your mother about me?"

"Well, I told her I met the most beautiful, kind, smart and caring woman in the world. I told her I was madly in love and wanted to marry her."

"Dammit Roberto! I mean about me not being Jewish."

"I'm getting there. My mother was thrilled that I had finally met a good Jewish woman to set me straight. Her words. She was so happy that I didn't have the heart to tell her the little detail about you not being Jewish. I thought I'd let her get to know you and see how wonderful you are, before revealing the other detail."

"And how did we get from *you'll tell her later* to me converting to your religion? How about my religion? How about my mother wanting me to find a good Catholic man? Why don't you convert to my religion?"

"It's different Elena. Your mother knows the truth and it doesn't bother her. Something like this could kill my mother. Besides, you are my wife. You swore you would follow me, respect me, and obey me. Remember your vows?"

"My vows Roberto? Or our vows?"

"Elena, you don't understand! I am begging, not for me, but for my poor blessed mother. She lost my father under terrible circumstances and she is devastated. Try to understand, my love, I can't add to her misery."

"But you don't mind adding to mine."

"My adorable Elenita, our happiness is in your hands. I want us to be together after we are gone. Imagine! If you are of a different faith, we cannot even be buried in the same cemetery. The thought is killing me!"

For heaven's sake! Why didn't you think of that before you asked me to marry you? I don't want to do what you're asking. Oh Jesus! It's always about him. As if I didn't have a mother and sister to think about.

"Elena, if your love is as strong as mine and you want us to be together now and after . . ."

"That's enough. You know I love you. Now you're just trying to manipulate me."

The intensity of his gaze deepened. "Of course not! How can you say that? I'm opening up to you, revealing my pain and my fears in an effort to touch your heart!"

Elena bent her head, as if gathering strength to go on. Finally, she let out a sigh, "Well Roberto, you did."

He looked at her quizzically. "I did what?"

"You touched my heart . . . I don't want our love to cause a rift with your family. I don't want to be the reason for you and your mother to become estranged."

Roberto's eyes filled with tears and he buried his face on Elena's shoulder.

"Elena, you are the best. I'm the luckiest man walking this earth. How can I ever thank you? You won't regret it."

But I already regret it Roberto. I want our marriage to succeed but I don't know if I can live with this decision.

He covered her face with kisses. "So, first thing in the morning we'll go to see Rabbi Jonathan. You'll like him! Yes, my love?"

"Okay, after lunch," she said, releasing herself from his arms. "I'll work in the morning and will cancel the afternoon appointments."

"I am at your command, *mi reina*."

My command? Yeah, that would be nice.

In bed that night, gently but firmly, Elena refused her husband's arms around her. She fought against her anger towards Roberto. Past midnight, she heard painful screaming and bolted out of bed. She turned on the lights, and saw Roberto wrangling with himself. He hurled his pillow and sat up in bed, shouting, "Nooo! Go away! Go!"

Scared and anguished, Elena embraced his trembling body.

"You're OK Roberto. It was just a dream," she whispered in his ear. "I'm here with you."

Slowly, his trembling subsided and Roberto threw his arms tightly around his wife's body.

Next day, at three in the afternoon, Roberto and Elena arrived at the Synagogue for her appointment with the rabbi. Rabbi Jonathan wanted to talk to Elena alone. Roberto fought to hide his disappointment and watched her disappear through a door.

"Please, sit. Be comfortable," said the rabbi, pulling a chair in front of a large desk. She sat and he did the same behind the desk, across from her.

He was a sturdily built man with rugged, attractive features. She refrained from running back to Roberto and from biting her nails. But, she soon felt comfortable as his soft voice spoke of mundane things. He wanted to know about her family, if it was hard to adapt to a new country, how she got into the beauty business. He congratulated her for learning English so well in such a short time. Finally, he eased his way to the point of the meeting.

"I understand you want to convert to our faith."

Elena's heart dropped. "Yes . . ." she caught herself on time before saying "Yes, father." Roberto hadn't told her how to address a Rabbi and she was used to calling priests "*father*".

"May I ask you why you want to do that?"

Roberto, why do you place me in this situation? I want to kill you. What am I going to answer?

"Elena, why do you want to do that?" she heard the Rabbi asking again.

"I want to be of the same faith as Roberto and his family."

"Does his family have anything to do with your decision?"

Goodness, the way he looks at me . . . he's reading my mind. I better stop thinking.

"No. I want to learn everything you can teach me about your God and your customs."

Rabbi Jonathan cleared his throat and smiled openly.

"God isn't mine, but ours. We don't have customs, but rooted traditions that we follow as if they were law."

"Oh . . ."

"My little daughter," he went on kindly, "God is only one. What we profoundly study and anticipate is the delivery of His son. Do you think that our Savior is to come?"

Without thinking, she said, "No, He has saved us already." Then with fervor, she added, "He died on the Cross in order to save us!" And then, she wanted to add: "Jews put Him on the cross, they killed him!" But, she swallowed her words.

The rabbi shook his head sadly.

"Jews do not think so."

Elena's face turned crimson. For a moment she fidgeted with her purse. *Virgencita, Roberto and his family are Jewish.*

They don't believe in Christ. I won't know how to respond to that. I don't know how to refute my beliefs.

"Are you aware that after you read all the books you see there," he pointed to a book case, "you'll be requested to change your beliefs and embrace ours? We're still waiting for the Messiah."

She was shocked. Those words burned her like the fire in hell. She wanted to shout at him that he was wrong and then she visualized Jesus on the cross, the huge nails piercing His hands, dying to redeem our sins. She could never renounce Christ! "God, forgive the rabbi; he doesn't know what he's saying," she murmured to herself.

Elena couldn't hold back the tears rolling down her cheeks. Of course she wanted to help her husband, but not at this price! Her emotions threatened to choke her.

She took the soft handkerchief the Rabbi handled her. She wiped her face and blew her nose. "Thank you Father . . . Pardon, please, Rabbi," she murmured.

He looked at her sympathetically.

"My dear child, you are not ready to change faith. Not yet, if ever." He stood and tapped her shoulder. "Come with your new family to the synagogue and get acquainted with our congregation. There is no hurry. This doesn't happen in a matter of days . . . it takes a very long time. Shalom, Elena."

She placed the handkerchief in her purse, and got to her feet. "I'll clean this and return it the next time we visit. Thank you again for your time and your kindness."

As soon as Elena and Rabbi Jonathan disappeared through the door, Roberto had plunged himself into a brown leather armchair and prepared to wait. He grabbed a book and began to read. Minutes later he tossed the book back on the table. Jumping from his seat, he paced the room, like a father awaiting the birth of his child.

He suddenly stopped pacing and looked at the sky through a tall window. *Oh dear God, enlighten Elenita, please!*

He was so lucky to have found a girl like Elena. For him she was everything he expected in a woman. But he was sure his family would not agree. Elena's conversion would take months . . . maybe more, because she wasn't doing it out of conviction. He knew how to appease his mother. His sister was another story.

He sat on a chair, only to get up and pace and agonize. Elena would win over his family when they watched her visit the Synagogue; it would also help when she joined them in their prayers on Friday nights and kept the Sabbath with the family.

Well, maybe Elena would object to observing the Sabbath, because she wouldn't want to rest all day on Saturdays and neglect her business. But who knows, she might stay home with them.

Caramba! It will also be a problem to keep a kosher home, which my family will expect. Why was he in this mess? Why did he place Elena in such a situation?

He hoped the rabbi would explain their faith to Elena in a convincing way. She knew nothing of Judaism; she only knew the false interpretation that Jews put Christ on the cross.

All too soon, the door opened and Rabbi Jonathan and Elena appeared. Roberto hurried to join them.

"How did it go?" he asked with trepidation when he saw Elena's tear-streaked face.

"Elena will explain," said the rabbi, kindly.

"I'm anxious to hear," said Roberto, as he held his wife's hand and looked the rabbi in the eye. "When do you want to see Elena again?"

"Be patient, my son; everything in its own time. Speak with your bride and listen to her."

"I will. Thank you for everything."

"Thank you for your understanding, Rabbi," said Elena.

"It is my pleasure." Then, he turned to Roberto. "How's your mother?"

"Given the circumstances, she's coping all right. Did I tell you she's arriving with Ruth next week?"

"I didn't know. Bring her to see me. Shalom, Roberto."

"I'll be glad to. Shalom, Rabbi."

Out on the street, Roberto insisted, "*Chiquita, por favor,* tell me everything, word for word."

"Please, be patient. Let's go home first."

"*Mi amor*, don't torment me. I can't wait."

"I'm really sorry, Roberto, but you have to."

"At least tell me when your next appointment is."

Roberto hailed a taxi. He helped Elena in and slid in after her. He gave the address to the driver, and then turned to Elena. "When will Rabbi Jonathan see you again?"

"It isn't that easy. I cannot say next week or next month. You need to hear the whole story."

"I'm all ears."

"I want it to be for your ears only. At home we'll talk."

"Do you like him? Was he nice to you?"

"Absolutely. He's brilliant."

Roberto smiled. "Oh, good! There's no reason to worry then. Right?"

Elena grabbed his hand. "That's my wish," she said emphatically.

Roberto and Elena arrived home and made themselves comfortable. They sat on the sofa. Roberto placed his arm on her shoulders and rubbed her arm lovingly. "I love you," he said, kissing her head. "Now, will you please fill me in on what happened?"

"Roberto, my dear, please understand that things can't always go the way we anticipate." She sat on his lap and held his face, looking lovingly into his eyes. "I hate to disappoint you, *mi vida*, but you must understand."

"What?" he shouted, and then lowered his voice. "I'm sorry. What are you trying to say?"

"I like the rabbi. I admired his compassion and his faith. I swear to you I was ready to go through with it, I prepared myself mentally to accept the teachings of the books he would want me to study. But then, as I heard him speak, I realized that I could renounce my religion and adopt yours, but I could not change my beliefs."

Elena stood up and began wringing her hands.

"Go on, for God's sake!"

"I'm sorry! I cannot force myself to believe something I don't believe anymore than you can change your beliefs for me or anyone else."

"What are you saying? Are you backing out?"

"I told you I would convert to your religion and I would! But I refuse to lie to God or the Rabbi. Just because I agree to convert to Judaism for the sake of our marriage, doesn't mean I stop believing what I've believed all my life!"

He pulled her back to his lap and caressed her face tenderly.

"I understand Elena. I don't think I would have been as selfless as you were if I were asked to convert to another religion."

"Roberto, you're not mad at me?"

"How can I be mad at you? I'm just worried about what my mother will do. She will no doubt disown me and I won't be allowed to work at the office."

"She would do that? But you are her own son . . ."

"I'll figure something out. I'll have to look for a job far away from my family's reach."

"It can't be all that bad. Surely you're exaggerating." Elena said with consternation. Roberto seemed truly worried.

Once in bed, Elena was unable to sleep; she unfastened herself from Roberto's arms every time he cuddled with her while sleeping. Could he be lying to her just to scare her into doing what he wanted? She didn't think so. He appeared to be really worried and had seemed understanding, yet . . .

In her mind appeared the image of *Doña Pilar*. God bless her, she was always ready to help. First thing in the morning she would call her, as she was wise and would understand her dilemma. Just the thought of speaking with her made Elena feel better. Soon she fell asleep, and slept the remaining hours until morning.

The next morning, as soon as Roberto left for work, Elena placed a call to *Doña* Pilar's estate in Cuba. After pleasantries, Elena gave her friend a detailed report about their problem.

"My dear Elenita, at your young age you've been married twice. The first time, I admit you didn't have another alternative but to flee from your husband's house. Nothing was in your favor. But, this time, young lady, you better weigh your choices carefully. Roberto is a good man and he loves you. We humans are not perfect. We must learn how to cope with the cross that God sent for us to carry. We all have to carry a cross in life, but sometimes it's heavier than others, and if we're very lucky, we have a choice. *Do I carry this cross that weighs one kilo, or this other one that weighs 10?* Now, my dear, think hard. God doesn't ask if you want to carry a cross or not, just which one you'd rather carry."

"*Doña* Pilar, are you telling me I should lie? To the priest, rabbi, to God?"

"No Elenita, don't be simple. We women have ways to get our way."

A heavy silence reigned for a little while, and then *Doña* Pilar broke it. "Give lots of time to his mother and work on her. Now is the right moment since she's suffering so much from the tragic death of her husband. Comfort her, bring her to your side, win her sympathy." The lady cleared her throat and went on. "I haven't yet met a person who will turn her back to kindness. When that lady realizes that you are the ideal woman for her son, she'll relent."

"But what if she rejects me?"

"Keep trying and don't tell anyone."

"How about my pride?"

"Choke on it."

"Is that advice one of those things: Do as I say not . . . ?"

"It is not. I preach by example. Some day I'll tell you how I still hold the respect and love of Baron Morales and his family after thirty-five years."

"I am sorry if my question upset you, *Doña* Pilar, it wasn't my intention."

"It is okay. I suggest that you be extremely sweet and understanding with your mother-in-law. Learn from her everything about Judaism. Both of you will profit from it, and that will create a bond and a comfortable atmosphere."

"I'm afraid she won't give me the chance . . ."

"Look Elenita, you don't look for the chance; you make the chance. Learn to love her, and then wrap her in the warmth of that love. Remember the saying: Love conquers all?"

They were silent for a moment.

"Elena, do you hear?"

"I hear." Elena was thoughtful for few moments; then, spirited, she exclaimed with a deep sigh, "Of course, I'll do it! Thank you again, *Doña* Pilar. *La quiero mucho*! Soon you will be proud of me."

The next evening, during supper, Elena and Roberto talked about their day. Then, over dessert, Elena brought up the problem shadowing their happiness.

"Roberto, my love, what have you decided to do about our problem?"

"There's nothing we can do. Wait until my mother meets you and see what happens."

"This really puts a lot of pressure on me. I'm terrified of meeting her. What if she hates me?"

"No one who gets to know you can hate you."

"But will she give me a chance?"

"I'm sorry, *mi amor*. I hate putting you on the spot . . . I'm nervous because I've always worked for the family business."

"Roberto, you're smart and talented. Heck, you speak many languages. You won't have a problem finding a job.

I'm more worried about a break in your relationship with your mother."

"Well, it's out of our hands now. There's nothing we can do about it. They're on their way so we'll soon know, either way."

"If you want we can go shopping and stack the pantry with the things they like."

"Thanks. You're sweet." He reached for her hand and kissed it. "We have to wait for them to buy their own groceries at a kosher store."

"But we need to have dinner ready for them when they arrive."

"They'll eat only tuna fish until they go to the kosher butcher and the kosher grocery store. They are very strict about food preparation. They will transform the kitchen."

Elena took a long, hard look at the kitchen. "But we have a beautiful kitchen."

He grinned. "We have a beautiful non-kosher kitchen. But I don't mean a physical transformation, *mi chiquita*. They'll make a kosher kitchen by washing everything with sea salt water and separating the utensils and dishes meant to be used for meat or dairy. You shouldn't mix them, ever."

"And what if I make a mistake?"

"Let's hope you won't."

Elena felt a knot in the pit of her stomach. "Oh, Roberto, you scare me. Is it really that important to know what dishes or silverware to use?"

"Yes, my darling, very important. I'll go over everything with you. You'll be fine, don't worry."

CHAPTER XII

Family From Spain

The family from Spain arrived on Holy Tuesday. Roberto went straight to the airport from his office. Elena stayed home in order to have everything ready to welcome them.

The only food the family ate when kosher food was not at hand was *atun*. So, Elena was limited to tuna fish; she made tuna salad. When the salad was done, she wrapped the platter in waxed paper and slid it into the refrigerator.

Then she went on to the bedroom that would host the guests. When the room was to her liking, she stood at the doorway examining the last details. Dominica, the young Italian woman that came once a week to clean the house, had rearranged the furniture until everything looked its best. There was a basket of fresh fruits and two colorful bouquets of flowers, one for each lady. The bedroom looked cozy. Elena hoped they would be comfortable.

Next was the dining room. Elena took great pains in setting the table. She used the Wedgwood china from England, a wedding gift from one of Roberto's business associates. The fine Waterford glasses and the silverware went perfectly with the starched, white tablecloth and napkins monogrammed with the family's initials. A floral centerpiece gave the dining room a lively look. Elena felt confident. She hoped to impress her in-laws.

Yet, she was very nervous. Every noise startled her, thinking it was the guests' arrival. She had rehearsed several ways to greet them, but couldn't agree on one. Roberto suggested she kiss them and say "shalom," but she didn't feel comfortable with that.

Finally, Elena heard the front door open. She didn't know whether to run to greet them, or wait until Roberto called her. To mind came Doña Pilar's advice: 'It's hard to turn your back on kindness. Never hesitate to be the first to smile.'

Although kindness hadn't worked with Rebeca, her ex-mother-in-law, she pledged to try harder with Roberto's mother. She ran to welcome them.

"*Bienvenida, Señora* Aisha," she said, giving the lady a warm, sincere embrace. Then she turned to her young sister-in-law, hugged her warmly, and kissed her cheeks. "It's nice to meet you, Ruth."

Although Señora Aisha hadn't responded to Elena's embrace, her body remained relaxed, contrasting with the stiff rejection Elena felt from her brand new sister-in-law.

"Let me help with your suitcase," Elena said to Aisha enthusiastically, reaching for one of the bags. "You may want to rest until dinner time."

"Leave it alone. We can do it ourselves," said Ruth, grabbing the suitcase from Elena.

An involuntary shiver enfolded Elena. The unkindness in Ruth's voice shattered her hope of a friendly, cordial visit with her husband's sister.

"Excuse me," Elena said in a low voice. "I just wanted to help."

"Sis, I suggest a little politeness," said Roberto, tapping Ruth's shoulder.

"Elena," Aisha butted in, "would you, please, help me with my overnight case?" Then, she added with a smile, "Let Roberto and Ruth carry the heavy ones."

Surprised, Elena looked at the woman and was relieved to find her expression full of tenderness. She liked her mother-in-law.

While Aisha and Ruth rested from the long trip, Elena went to the kitchen to supervise dinner's last touches. From the refrigerator, she took out the platter with the tuna salad.

She sighed, "It looks as if done by a professional," she said aloud to herself.

She had made the salad with a variety of al dente steamed vegetables, blended into the tuna and topped with a layer of mayonnaise. Then, she ornamented it with sliced tomatoes, hard-boiled eggs, red and orange peppers, and pimento stuffed olives. It looked exactly like the ones her mother used to make for festive days.

Before long, running water alerted Elena that the guests were up and about. She called Roberto, as he had requested.

Soon, he showed up and together they went to meet Aisha and Ruth. Roberto kissed their cheeks, and Elena did the same.

"Did you rest well?"

"Very well, thank you, Elena," answered Aisha.

"Are you hungry? Dinner is ready." And Elena signaled the way to the dining room.

"We brought our own food," prompted Ruth, walking ahead to the kitchen carrying a grocery bag, which she placed on the counter. Then, she took out of the bag two large tuna fish tins, paper plates, plastic utensils, and plastic cups. Hurriedly, she proceeded to open the cans with a can opener that she took out from the bag.

Elena didn't know what to make of all this and thought it best to keep her mouth shut.

"Elena, the table looks beautiful," said Aisha, glancing at the dining room from the kitchen.

Oh, yes, but you aren't going to use it.

"Thank you, *Señora,*" she answered. "I prepared a tuna fish salad for dinner."

"We eat only kosher food," said Ruth, curtly.

"That's why I prepared tuna fish."

"I can tell my brother didn't instruct you about our customs," said Ruth, in a rasping voice. "Food has to be cooked and served only in kosher dishware."

"Elena, don't fret about this," Aisha intervened. "We brought everything we need for our first meal."

"Mother, Elena is willing to learn all about our customs," said Roberto. "Please, will you help her?"

"Of course, if she wants."

"Oh, *Señora* Aisha, how kind of you! I'll appreciate your help."

"Good luck, mother!" sneered Ruth, with a smirk.

Well, well. I thought I was going to have problems with my mother-in-law, not with my sister-in-law. But, really, if I have to choose one of the two to be against me, I rather have it be that young ignorant snot. Aisha has been really nice.

"Mi *amor,* this tuna platter you prepared looks beautiful. Would you mind serving me a plate?" Roberto asked, not without some trepidation.

"Of course, Roberto. Here, hand me your plate."

Aisha and Rebecca stole a glance at Roberto.

The only ones to eat from the large platter of salad were Elena and Roberto. Elena was pleased that Roberto had supported her in front of his family. After Elena was done with the first serving, she went for seconds, to show the family what they were missing. Ruth served their tuna, which she mixed with the mayonnaise she brought. She served it on plastic plates and placed the plates in front of her mother, her brother, and then herself, without even offering any to Elena.

Next day, Holy Wednesday, Elena rose early. Her guests were in the kitchen. Elena decided to skip breakfast. So as not to inconvenience them, she went to the kitchen and grabbed a glass of juice.

"Good morning, ladies. How did you sleep?"

"I was so tired, I didn't even miss my own bed." Aisha raised a hand in greeting and smiled kindly.

"I'm glad to hear that." Then Elena forced herself to ask, "How about you, Ruth?"

A heavy silence followed, and Elena saw Aisha nudge Ruth.

"Okay," Ruth said.

"Roberto will have breakfast with you, and if you need anything urgent, he'll take you grocery shopping. He's only working a half day."

"Thank you, Elena. That will be nice," said Aisha.

"Because of the holidays, there's no work on Holy Thursday or Friday. We can do whatever you ladies want then."

"Oh boy! How generous of you, thanks," Ruth said, twisting a lock of long, red hair.

"Not at all," answered Elena, in the same sarcastic tone. Then she took a bottle of orange juice out of the icebox and poured a glass, turned her back and left, calling out, "See you later."

"Virgencita, help me swallow my impulse to give that insolent snob a piece of my mind. But she might not stop bothering me if I don't do something to straighten her out. Talk to Roberto? It might work against me.

At the shop, the day went by like a whirlwind. Many customers were getting ready for the holidays. When Elena was at the peak of activities, Roberto called. The family was at the kosher store and ready to leave. He asked if she wanted a ride home.

"*Amor*," she said. "How sweet of you, but I'm not ready."

"It is close to six, my darling; you must be ready to close for the day."

"But there is a lot to do yet. Remember, we'll be closed for Easter.

"Well, *mi vida*, if you must, but don't be too late."

At the grocery store, as Roberto, Aisha and Ruth were pulling away from the parking lot; Ruth remarked.

"Your cute little wife is very independent, isn't she?"

"She was independent when I met her." He arranged the mirror so he could watch Ruth in it. "She was working then and loved her job."

"If she were clever, she would be working with you, not for somebody else. That would be the smart thing to do. Don't you think?"

Roberto didn't like Ruth's insinuations, but decided to ignore them. Instead, he said calmly,

"Except that she owns her own business and loves being her own boss."

"Oh, I see. She owns her own business. Did you pay pretty money for her whim?" She covered her mouth with a hand. "Sorry! I meant business?"

Roberto's hands tightened on the steering wheel and he ground his teeth. He was sure now that his sister didn't like Elena at all.

"Listen Ruth. Elena and I are married and everything I own is hers. If I had given her the money to start her own business, she would have been entitled to it. But it so happens that Elena bought her own business before we were married."

Ruth twisted her hair languidly around a finger and lifted her eyebrow. "She did? Well, that's interesting." she said, petulantly. "You are my brother and I care what happens to you. That's all. I'm looking out for you."

"Thank you sister, but don't. I can take care of myself."

"When you're thinking straight you can, but . . ."

"What is with you, Ruth? Stop it," broke in Aisha.

"Since when does the truth bother you, dear mother?"

"The undertone of this conversation is what bothers me. You are being unkind and unfair to Elena."

"My wife is the best and purest thing in my life. She's given me happiness and hope, and I would appreciate it if you would stop criticizing her." Roberto glared at Ruth in the rear view mirror.

Ruth lifted her lip in a sneer.

"No wonder they say love is blind," Ruth spat.

"You're being so unfair, Ruth," Roberto said. "After Elena tried so hard to please you both—"

"There you are! You admit it. The way she's throwing herself at Mother makes me nauseous. She only wants to gain her approval, and of course her money."

So that is what's going on. Roberto hit the brakes, realizing he had missed his turn.

"Sis, stop this nonsense," he said energetically. "Stop building walls and start building bridges. You'll be less bitter."

Aisha turned her head to see her daughter. "Your brother is right." She pointed a finger at Ruth. "You're going to end up alone, child, if you don't change . . . Look for the positive in people, instead of digging up dirt."

"Mother, I'm surprised. At first you were against this shiksa—this little nobody," Ruth snapped.

"I'm still not happy, but only because she is not Jewish. But, Ruth, that doesn't give us the right to judge her."

"Now, don't tell me you're accepting her into our family?"

"You heard her say she's interested in our religion and culture. After she learns a bit, then we'll see." Aisha, pensive, looked out the window, and then said, "For now she makes your brother happy and seems to genuinely love him."

Roberto felt a surge of hope. He guessed his mother was less intolerant than he thought.

"Now everybody seems to be against me," exclaimed Ruth angrily. "We are blood family, you know?"

Aisha again turned her head to look at her daughter. "Your lack of feelings makes me sad, Ruth. You're deliberately hurting your brother."

"Mom, remember? He lied to you when he told you that his newfound wife was on the way to converting. Now we see she knows nothing of our customs or traditions. She's a common gold digger, and of course she'll read a book or two if this will let her enjoy our money!"

Roberto fought against the urge to smack his sister. "I hope you choke on your own vileness," he snapped.

"I don't want to hear another word about this matter from either of you. Did you hear?" Aisha said heatedly. Roberto inhaled a couple of times, trying to calm himself.

On the rest of the trip back home, silence reigned.

Once they arrived at their building, the porter took care of the boxes and brought them up to the apartment. Roberto tipped the man, and then he disappeared from the scene. The family went straight to the kitchen where they put away the groceries. Aisha prepared some of the ready to eat kosher meals she had bought. Ruth made herself at home finding a place for everything.

"Ruth," said Aisha, "I would like you to use the Day of Atonement to repent for your ill-will against Elena."

"Roberto is the one who should repent for marrying outside our faith."

"We all are going to pray more than ever for wisdom and guidance. Roberto isn't hurting anybody by marrying Elena. Besides, she is going to convert. You, on the other hand, are being judgmental and cruel."

"Sorry Mom. I should have known that the apple of your eye could do no wrong. I pray God spare you from pain when you find out that I am right."

What in God's name is happening with Ruth? Roberto wondered. *We used to get along well. What have I done to her? I don't remember her ever being so vindictive.*

When Elena arrived at seven, they enjoyed supper together. Roberto was pleased with the way the relationship between his mother and Elena was developing; more so because he knew they both were sincere. He watched with delight when his mother squeezed Elena's hand.

"Elena," Aisha said with a smile, "next Thursday is Yom Kippur, the most sacred Jewish holiday. The day before

Yom Kippur is called the Eve of Atonement. On that day we feast, thus preparing for the long fast ahead, we pray and meditate all day long. It starts thirty minutes before sundown and ends after nightfall the following day. We'll cook and eat quite a lot to be prepared for the severe fasting on Yom Kippur. Would you like to join us?"

"Yes, *Señora* Aisha, I'll be more than happy."

Ruth stepped in front of her, hands on her hips. "I'd like to see how long your enthusiasm lasts after twenty four hours of total abstention from food and drink."

Elena tapped her sister-in-law gently on the arm. "You know, Ruth? If those same words were uttered with a smile, I could take them as a friendly challenge. But your tone . . . how should I take them?"

"You're free to take them any way you wish. But think about it and tell us, with all sincerity, if you'd willingly go without food and water all day long. And to that you must add constant prayers, meditation and no contact with any electrical switch: that means no TV, no radio, no stoves, and no lights . . . period."

No response from Elena.

"It's tough, isn't it?" pressured Ruth.

"It certainly is Ruth. But you know what? When I was growing up in Cuba there were many days when we didn't have enough food to eat all day and certainly no electricity or running water. My mother kept us in bed, as the only way she knew how to lessen the pangs of hunger. Do you see Ruth? I'm no stranger to discomfort. One day shouldn't be bad at all."

Bravo! That's my Elenita! Don't let Ruth put you down, thought Roberto.

Ruth turned as red as her hair, turned around and stomped out of the kitchen.

CHAPTER XIII

Yom Kippur

The Eve of Atonement arrived. The long prayers and meditations throughout the day drained Elena. Her heart tore every time Aisha broke down and cried openly. The poor lady suffered so much Elena wanted to embrace and console her.

Meanwhile, Ruth seemed restless. She went to the bathroom often and every time stayed away longer, obviously looking for a respite from the dragging prayers. Every time she left and came back she kissed her mother as if out of habit. No emotion showed.

After a few hours of planning on how to approach her mother-in-law, Elena finally made her move. As soon as Ruth left the room Elena pulled up a chair next to Aisha, placed an arm around her shoulder and tenderly reached for her hand.

"Señora Aisha," Elena began. "It breaks my heart to see you suffer like this. It might help to talk. I'm a good listener. I'd do anything to lessen your pain."

"I appreciate it, but I don't want to burden you."

"I'm very worried about you," Elena said as she gently combed Aisha's hair with her fingers and then went on, "It might help if you let out all that is hurting you. I would be honored if you trusted me. I'm here for you."

"I've prayed and waited patiently for the passing of time to bring me peace and lessen the pain, but nothing seems to help. I'm losing hope."

Aisha made an attempt to continue, but swallowed her words. After a while she spoke. "It was my fault. That's what hurts the most." She began to cry, sobs racking her body. She jumped to her feet and paced the room.

"I had to lose my husband in order to understand his views. Why did it have to be too late? Why couldn't he have lived to see me change?"

"Señora Aisha, I'm sorry!" Elena said lovingly, handing her a handkerchief.

She took it. "I can't find peace, I'm responsible for his death," she said, wiping her tears.

"No, Señora, you are not. It was an accident."

"Jacob was a happy, optimistic, fair person. Friends and associates held him in high esteem. He adored Ruth and loved to spoil her." She paused and blew her nose. "He believed there was only one God for all; he saw no differences among people. None of his family shared his ideas. There was constant friction between them. He built his fortune dealing with business people of different faiths." She sighed and added. "For an Conservative Jew, he was very flexible."

"I'm sorry I didn't meet him," Elena interjected.

"He would have liked you, I'm sure . . ." She burst into sobs once more. "He died before his time. I'm to blame. I killed him!"

Poor woman! Here lies the key to her anguish, the sadness in her eyes.

"My dear Señora, don't torture yourself!"

Aisha shook her head. "For this to not be true, I would gladly give my life."

A long silence followed. Elena held her mother-in-law's hand and waited patiently. Finally Aisha was able to bring out the truth.

"That day, we were in the living room waiting for his chauffeur. We seldom fought, but that morning we had an argument that rapidly grew out of proportion. He wanted me to apologize on behalf of Ruth, who had insulted a gentile woman. I refused. I felt it was beneath me to apologize. I don't believe that anymore, but to my misfortune it is too late; he doesn't know it . . ."

"Of course he knows! I'm sure he's proud of you."

"He dashed out of the house," she mumbled. "I rushed to the window to call after him, only to see a truck run him over." She covered her face with both hands. "I ran to the street but I didn't have time to tell him how much I loved him. He took with him the image of a selfish, unloving woman. Now that he's gone, I strive to emulate him."

Aisha sobbed some more. Many things were clear to Elena now. For Ruth, the death of her father had changed her for the worse, while Aisha tried to purge her guilt by honoring her husband's ideals. Obviously, her acceptance of Elena was a result of that.

Elena didn't know how she would survive Yom Kippur. In spite of the terrible ache in her stomach and the weakness in her knees, it was Aisha's grief that hurt the most. The sight of the woman brought to mind the memory of her own mother always crying, always submissive. In both cases, with her mother then and with her mother-in-law now, the feeling of impotence made her angry. She wanted so much to do something for them! But other than her love and compassion, what else could she do?

Roberto had something urgent to take care of and was not back yet. If only he were here . . .

Around four, he finally arrived.

There was an instant change in Aisha when Roberto arrived. She came to life, her eyes shone when Roberto bent to kiss her. She threw her arms around him and they embraced cheek to cheek for a moment. Elena felt tears coming and fought to hold them back.

Roberto greeted Ruth and kissed both cheeks, then approached Elena and did the same. They conversed for a while.

Elena whispered, "*Mi amor*, sit next to your mother, she needs you more than ever."

"You're right, my love, thanks."

Roberto sat next to Aisha and placed his arm around her shoulders. Some time later, when the prayers began, Roberto led them with energy and emotion. He chanted in Hebrew and Ruth and Aisha took turns answering his prayers. Roberto's booming, melodic voice contrasted with the women's equally beautiful alto voices in a magical give and take that was mesmerizing. Roberto winked at her when he caught her staring in admiration and he even managed to blow a kiss now and then.

To Elena's relief the time to break the fast arrived. It was done carefully and in steps. It began with half a cup of hot consommé, and thirty minutes later, they had the other half. Soon after, the water she craved for.

"Elena, you survived. I am impressed! Congratulations!" exclaimed Ruth.

I don't detect any sarcasm in her words. Is it possible? I think she's being sincere.

"Thank you, Ruth," Elena said. "It was definitely not easy."

On Sunday afternoon the family had tea and cookies in the solarium. Elena thought about how different her Sundays were now. She still missed Mass on Sundays. As an alternative, she looked for any opportunity to kneel and pray to God, in her own terms, in her own space.

When tea was over, Aisha asked Elena if she would like to spend some time learning more about Judaism.

"Yes, thank you, Señora."

Aisha asked Roberto and Ruth if they wanted to stay. They each had something else to do. Though Elena would have liked Roberto to stay with her, she said nothing.

Once alone, Aisha sat down next to Elena.

"Well," she asked, "do you know that Judaism is one of the oldest monotheistic religions?"

"Yes Señora Aisha, that I know." Elena answered, shyly.

"According to traditional Rabbinic Judaism God revealed his oral and written commandments to Moses in Mount Sinai, in the form of the Torah." Aisha paused to see if Elena had any questions.

"The Torah means learning and is the most holy, sacred book in Judaism. For us it's the law." She paused, cleared her throat and went on. "One important thing you must bear in mind is that one cannot be Jewish and also believe in Jesus Christ as the Messiah. We believe the Messiah has not yet come."

That exactly is what I am attempting to do: convert to Judaism while maintaining my personal belief in Jesus Christ. How can I not believe in Him when I was taught about Him at the same time I learned to walk?

Her mother-in-law went on, "Our belief is that there is only one God, who created and ruled the world. He is all-powerful—all knowing, and is in all places at all times. God is just and merciful."

Elena wanted to shout that it was exactly the same as what Catholics' believed, but she only said, "I agree."

"Each person is created in the image of God; all are created equal."

Yes? If created equal, how come a Jew can't marry out of his religion?

Suddenly, Aisha paused. "I've had a nagging headache since this morning," she said, frowning. She took the pins out of her chignon. Her gray hair cascaded down and nestled over her shoulders.

"We can go on with this later, or tomorrow," Elena suggested.

"Aisha rubbed her head. "I've been getting these very often."

"I'll give you a good massage."

"No, please, don't bother . . ."

"No bother at all. I used to do this for my mother. It used to work with her very well," said Elena remembering her stoic mother. She positioned herself behind Aisha and began to massage her head.

Shortly after, the lady exclaimed with a sigh:

"Ah, that's so much better! Now let's go back to our conversation." she gazed at Elena for a moment and then said, with conviction, "We should live by the Commandments."

"Oh, yes, I know the *Diez Mandamientos* by heart!" said Elena, feeling proud of her knowledge.

"Good! You know, the Torah contains five books and six hundred and thirteen Commandments, which are considered the most important of the whole book."

Six hundred and thirteen? Elena thought, and then said, "I don't understand. I thought there were only ten."

"Those are God's revelations. The Ten were written on stone and given directly to Moses to be delivered to the people of Israel at Mount Sinai. It happened just after He had delivered His people from slavery in Egypt."

Aisha spent some time telling how, why and where Moses received the commandments, and explained the New and Old Testaments. She explained how Jews had been waiting for the Messiah since the beginning of time while Christians believe that Jesus, a mortal Jew, was the awaited Savior.

Also, she told Elena Catholic theologians had rearranged the Ten Commandments and manipulated the word of God in order to change the day of the Sabbath.

Then Aisha summarized:

"Now there are three different versions of the Ten Commandments: Jewish, the original; the Catholic version and the Protestant version. To me this is a shameless attempt to change the Law of God.

Aisha got up and paced the room, and then stopped in front of Elena.

"Do you see, Elena? I think that no one has the right to re-write the commandments."

I suppose that what she's saying is true, thought Elena. Then, choosing her words carefully, she said, "I didn't know anything about that."

"I tend to respect all religions because they lead to God. But throughout the years people have manipulated the Holy Books to suit their agenda. That's inexcusable and disrespectful."

Elena cleared her throat. "What exactly has been altered?" she asked in a low voice.

"Several of the commandments—for example the second, which forbids idolizing carved images. Only the

Lord, our God, you venerate. Catholics have their churches full of icons of virgins and saints, which they glorify and bow to when passing by each one of them. 'You should not make for yourself a forge image' reads the second commandment. But it was changed by Catholic theologians to: 'You should not take the name of the Lord, your God, in vain'."

Why in the name of God hasn't anybody told me anything about this? I can't even begin to defend my religion. I don't have the tools for arguments. If this were true, Catholics are dead wrong.

"Elena, are you okay?" her mother-in-law asked. "You look pale."

"No, I'm fine. Please, give me another example . . . about the Sabbath . . ."

". . . Certainly. Our fourth commandment reads 'You shall remember the Sabbath and keep it Holy'." Aisha grimaced and went on, "Sabbath means rest and Jews rest and pray all day on Saturdays at home or in the Synagogue. Catholics moved the rest and pray day to Sunday."

Elena stood up. She wasn't ready to hear anymore about the religion she thought of as perfect. How could any human being dare challenge the words written in fire by Almighty God?

"If you don't mind, let's continue some other time," she said, and hurried from the room.

When she crossed the hall, Roberto approached her.

"Mi *amor*, what's wrong?" he asked, holding her arms.

"*Nothing.*"

"You look pale."

"I need to go to the bathroom, that's all."

Roberto looked worried.

"Okay, go ahead."

Elena went straight to Roberto's office and the phone. She needed some clarification. It was awful to feel let down by her church. She prayed with all her heart that Aisha was wrong and that all her ideas derived from her own perceptions and not from facts.

She placed a call to Cuba—once more she needed to unburden herself with her dear friend and mentor.

After greetings, Elena got to the point.

"My dear Doña Pilar, I need your help once more. I have some doubdts. My mother-in-law has begun her instruction about Judaism. Among other things she said that Catholic theologians have rearranged the *Diez Mandamientos* to fit their own needs." Elena paused for a moment waiting for a negation, but it never came. Apparently, Doña Pilar knew about it. So Elena went on, "Is this true?"

"My dear child, it's a very touchy subject. We're taught to have faith and believe. Never doubt."

"Oh, no, Doña Pilar . . . Not you! You are the only one that can, and will, help me understand. How could simple mortals dare to tamper with God's law?"

"Our faith is so strong that we don't have to see to believe. Everything happens for a reason—we don't question. I'll share with you my beliefs. It's my own version though." Doña Pilar coughed a few times and continued, "Jesus found miraculous ways to communicate to Christians what He wanted them to do after the Crucifixion. I think that the fact that the Messiah had already come, gave way to adaptations to the scriptures for the new world. Church councils adapted the New Testament with different perspectives of the same object. I prefer the word adaptation to alteration."

"Oh, Doña Pilar, I don't know what to believe now."

"Your doubts are normal but there are things we'll never understand. Nothing could last almost 2000 years without solid roots. That is where blind faith comes in. If you question too much your emotional state could end up in shambles."

"I still want to find out the truth," Elena said with a deep sigh.

"This subject is very difficult and endless. I think you should talk to a priest, and also to a Rabbi."

"That's a great idea—but I think Aisha is right. No one, no matter what, has the right to change God's sacred words," said Elena, not convinced anymore of what she was saying.

"I'm sorry if this time I couldn't help you."

"You did help, thank you so much *Doña* Pilar."

In spite of her religious doubts, Elena felt good about her faith, and at the same time she felt more respect for her in-law's religion. Now she began to understand Judaism better. Still, for the time being, she wanted to forget about this and enjoy Roberto and his family, wishing at the same time that the visit wouldn't be prolonged.

CHAPTER XIV

My Own House?

On a rainy Sunday afternoon, Elena and Roberto returned home from Idlewild Airport. At last, after a long month, the family from Spain had gone back home. Elena got along great with Aisha and grew to love the tormented woman. During the stay Elena and Aisha held many private sessions, Aisha explaining Judaism to her daughter-in-law, which drew them closer. Both women were broad-minded and Aisha was smart enough not to impose her ideas on Elena, thus helping her feel free to voice her doubts.

With Ruth it was different. Elena didn't know what to make of her outspoken sister-in-law, who was cold and occasionally rude. Elena resented the indifference from the young woman and had eventually stopped trying to win her over. If animosity was what Ruth wanted, let her have her way. All and all, deep inside, Elena was happy to see them leave and to have Roberto to herself.

Back from the airport Roberto embraced his young wife tightly.

"*Gorgeous lady*, may I entice you to go straight to our love-nest?"

"Try me . . . I think you have a good chance . . ." she said, pushing him away playfully.

"Imagine!" He pulled her back to his tight embrace. "No more worries about who might hear us!"

"Nobody has ever made me a better proposition, *querido Señor.*"

They kicked off their galoshes and tossed their raincoats onto a chair. Roberto swept her into his arms, whistling *The Nuptial March* all the way to the bedroom. He placed her on the bed and began to caress her, his hands moving deliberately across her body.

"Mmmm, taking your time, I like it."

"I've been waiting to do this for so very long. I'm going to enjoy every moment. I want to see your passion build and then overflow out of control . . ."

"Sadist!" She laughed. "Help me undress now, *mi amor,*" she said, unbuttoning her blouse.

"*Chiquita preciosa,* let's take it easy." He pulled down her blouse. "While you lay down naked, I'll find out how many beauty marks there are on your body."

"Oh no—there're too many!"

"The more the merrier," he said as he unbuttoned her brassier with great care, then pulled down her skirt. Lovingly, he removed her nylons and panties.

Early the next morning the happy couple had a light breakfast. "Darling, I can't wait for later," he said with a wink. "I want you to know now."

"Go ahead, tell me . . ." Elena drew Roberto into her arms.

"Well, my mother's buying a house for us."

"Goodness! She's doing what? I can't believe we're going to have our own home."

"Like my mother said, 'that's the best way to start a family'."

"God bless her a thousand times!" she said, whirling around.

Roberto drew his wife again into his arms and looked at her mischievously. "But, she has a condition."

"Oh, it was too good to be true. She wants something back."

"Darling, don't worry, it's something easy and we both want it anyway."

"Don't sugar-coat it, please. What's the condition?"

"Oh, well . . . My precious doll, we have to give my mother a grandchild."

A knot formed in her throat. She remembered how crazy for a baby her ex-mother-in-law had been. Elena was married to Rodolfo for almost three years and never . . .

"What's on your mind?" Roberto interrupted.

"You can kiss our house good-by then," she said spiritlessly.

"Why, I thought you wanted children?"

"I'm not sure I can have babies." She recalled Rodolfo calling her a barren woman.

"Of course you can!" said Roberto. "We'll work over-time . . . day and night, night and day. I'll try all the positions there are. Don't even think you cannot."

"Well it won't be for lack of trying," said Elena, hoping for that little bundle of love that could change her life forever.

I will pray with all my might. After all Diosito always listens to me.

True to their purpose, the couple worked at their goal almost daily. After each session of baby-making Elena remained in bed with two pillows under her hips. Their disappointment grew worse each month when Elena met with her period.

Time went by with no sign of a new life. On the bright side their passion grew and with it a better understanding between them. Elena was able to forgive Roberto's lies. More and more she felt that both of them became one person—and she loved and appreciated it! Also, miraculously, the nightmares that had relentlessly haunted Roberto for so long seemed to lessen.

One evening Roberto arrived home very excited. He handed her a bouquet of roses.

"*Mi querida esposa*, I have a tremendous surprise for you."

"Good! I love surprises! Thanks for the roses, *mi amor*. Is there another surprise?"

"One able to surpass any other."

"Enough suspense . . . Tell me already."

"I've found the perfect house for us."

"What?"

"I'll call Mother tonight to let her know."

"Don't rush things. I'm not pregnant yet, and that was her condition."

"My mother will understand . . ."

"What will she understand? That I can't conceive? We need to be sure before accepting her gift."

"Remember that Doctor Moreno told you about a simple surgery to clear up your tubes?" He took her face between his hands, looking at her tenderly. "*Mi Chiquita linda*, do you want to make an appointment and do it once and for all?"

"I'm afraid. I want to think about it longer."

"There's no reason to be afraid and we are both dying to have children . . . but we'll do this when you're ready."

Sighing deeply, Elena replied, "Roberto, I don't want to disappoint you or your mother . . ."

"This is not about my mother. It's about you, me and our baby."

"Yes but I also feel pressure about the house!"

"Elenita, I promise you I'll buy you a house. Maybe not right away; I need to get more established in my business, but soon, I promise. Meanwhile, my mother's gift is not really contingent upon you getting pregnant. She just wants to have a grandchild as badly as we want to become parents. And the truth is that I loved the excuse of having to "work" at getting you pregnant every day and night." Roberto said ardently.

"Roberto, you are incorrigible. Tell you what. I'll make an appointment to see Dr. Moreno on Monday," she said, "but there are no guarantees about anything. I'll just agree to talk to him."

On Sunday they went to see the house. It surpassed Elena's expectations: a two-story brick house with attic and a finished basement. The huge basement was a dream, with a red mirrored bar, a sauna and a luxury bathroom.

"Roberto, this is too much . . ."

"Nothing is too much for my princess. This is the incentive we need to work over-time placing that *especial* order for our baby."

Was it possible that a house like this could be hers? Elena loved the large kitchen. It was furnished with modern, comfortable, and practical appliances. With a kitchen like that she wouldn't mind slaving over baking and cooking meals.

"We have a guest room, plus four more bedrooms to be filled with babies—and a tremendous basement for their birthday parties," she exclaimed, but then frowned. "Can your mother afford this?"

"Together we can. Don't be concerned and enjoy her gift."

"What if I can't have babies?"

"Don't worry about it my love. The babies will come when God sees fit."

The days that followed were a blessing. Elena thanked God constantly for her happiness—she wanted everybody in the world to be as happy as she was, but knew this was not how things were. She felt guilty at having so much when so many had so little. With the promise of a new home and the thought of a dozen children running around making heart-warming noises, her happiness was even more complete—if that were possible.

Roberto showed up one evening brandishing papers.

"Elenita, guess what I have here!" he said playfully.

She wanted to share his mood, but nothing witty came to mind. "I'm not good at guessing. What is it?"

"Hang on tight. Here, on these papers, is the ownership of your first home!"

"You're kidding me!"

"No, Chiquita, I'm not. The house is yours."

"How? When?"

"Just now. I'm coming directly from the title company. I signed all the papers and they gave me the key." He said, dangling the key in one hand."

Elena was stunned, a combination of excitement and dismay, happiness and anger that she couldn't hide.

"What's wrong?" Roberto asked with concern? "I thought you'd be happy."

"Roberto, you bought a house for me, without me? I don't understand. Don't I have to be there and sign papers?"

"Not necessarily, darling. Everything I own is yours."

Elena was sizzling. *'Everything I own is yours'. Does he think I'm stupid?* Somehow she managed a smile.

"So my house is in your name? When did we discuss this?"

"My darling, what's the problem? As husband and wife we share everything."

"Please, Roberto, don't underestimate my intelligence."

"What are you talking about?"

"What is yours 'legally' is only yours. You are very generous, though. Thanks for sharing your home with me." She retorted, trying to hide her anger.

"Elena, you are being unfair."

Oh, gosh! I am being unfair! I shouldn't mind. After all, it's his money. I don't want this discussion to get ugly . . . . My ex-husband and his mother made me work at their rooming house without pay, and I had to beg for the bus fare to visit my mother. I shouldn't forget my past. I should be grateful of my present. I should avoid greed.

"Roberto, forget I said anything. I don't want to mar our happiness. If you feel better having the house in your name . . . I really don't mind."

"Tell me the truth . . ."

"Roberto, why don't we leave things as they are? I'm grateful to God and to you for my blessings . . ."

"You should be, Elenita. I love you with all my heart and my life and everything I own is yours."

After the joy of the past few months, which had bonded them more than ever, his attitude today, disappointed her. She remembered headlines that spoke of women depriving their husbands of their wealth after a painful divorce, some of them after only a couple of years of marriage. Elena chose to believe that that was what had caused Roberto to exclude her from the ownership of the house, and realized that her problem was not really a problem. There were worse things in life and her memories of Cuba proved it. Besides, God might punish her for complaining about having much more than she needed. Elena decided to erase the whole thing from her mind and concentrate on being happy. Hope should never die.

The day of her surgery arrived and Doctor Moreno was very supportive and patient. Vilma did a remarkable job in the beauty salon while Elena recuperated.

They moved into the new home and things went as well as expected. They continued to work as they adapted to their new surroundings.

Soon after the move, Elena's happiness soared. She was finally pregnant. Was it possible that a new little person began already to grow inside her? Images of a tiny baby girl in her arms occupied her mind for hours and she started to plan for the nursery, the clothes she would buy, possible names—What a gift! And dear Aisha, the happiness she was about to receive!

But what was she going to do about the religion problem? Now that she had so much more to be grateful to Jesus for. He had answered her prayers and she was supposed to forsake him?

Meanwhile, Roberto acted as if he were the first man in the world to have fathered a child. He treated Elena as if she were breakable: no more work, no high heels, no tight clothes and no anything he thought dangerous for "his" baby. They celebrated the happy occasion with virgin drinks, which was not hard since neither of them liked alcohol. Elena thought Roberto was going overboard; nevertheless, she was delighted with his constant attention. And she was amused! She couldn't help but compare her actual situation with the one in Cuba with Rodolfo and with her mother-in-law. She'd prayed for a baby then, but God knew which was the right moment to grant her wish.

Elena chose a room for the baby, and full of enthusiasm, she decorated the nursery. One day she went to the bathroom and panicked. There was blood in the toilet. A chill ran down her spine and a knot formed in her throat: God, don't allow anything to happen. She rushed to the phone.

"Roberto," she said, frantically. "I'm losing our baby. I'm bleeding."

"Oh, no!" he shouted. "Call a taxi and go to the hospital at once. I'll call Dr. Moreno."

"Will you be there?"

"Of course!"

After a thorough examination, Dr. Moreno, gave Elena a shot to help prevent a miscarriage. She returned home the same day with a treatment plan to be followed. It included complete bed-rest.

Roberto didn't waste any time in suggesting she should sell the beauty salon.

"I thought about that," she prompted, as she sat on a sofa in the living room. "But Vilma can manage it until I'm well."

"No, dear, forget working again," he said as he sat next to her. "Let her manage it until we find a buyer."

"Not that fast! We need to think about this and not rush into anything."

"Elena, you are going to be a mother now. Our baby needs a mother all the time not just part time. Parents that bring children to the world have to take care of them and dedicate themselves to them completely and not have strangers take care of them."

"In that case I'll sell my business to Vilma."

He shook his head. "Very poor choice, my love . . ."

"Why?"

"Vilma doesn't have a penny to her name."

"I didn't have a cent to my name either when Gina helped me to buy her business."

"Don't compare yourself to anyone, least of all with that girl."

"What do you have against Vilma?"

"Have you forgotten what Peter did to you?"

"What I can't forget is that Peter saved me from being raped and what does that have to do with Vilma?"

"They both placed you in that situation."

"You know Roberto, I never fight for my rights to avoid arguments, but this time I won't give in. I feel so much happiness that I want to pass some along to those close to me. I want to give her the same opportunity Gina gave me."

He patted her hand. "Elenita, you don't need this stress. Do whatever you want! But, understand this: I never want to see Vilma or her bastard husband in my house."

"*Your house*? How soon it's no longer ours! You have just said I need peace." She smiled sadly.

"Don't drive me to . . . Don't bring them here, that's all." He grabbed her hand and guided her to the bedroom where he helped her into bed. "Señora Elena, I welcome you to the beginning of your bed rest."

"Gee, thanks."

"Don't worry about a thing! I'll hire a nurse at once."

"No! That's too expensive." She thought for a moment. "Doña Pilar knows a lot of people from her church who are anxious to come to America. I'm sure she'll be able to arrange something."

"Then don't waste time. Call her at once."

Ten days later, Sandra Perez, a vivacious twenty-six-year-old girl, arrived at the home of Roberto and *Elena*. Doña Pilar had done everything in her power to push her papers through. The fastest way to enter the country was a twenty-nine day visa with the understanding that once in the States she could apply for an extension.

Sandra was a hard worker, a good-natured young lady eager to help. Soon she understood the situation and took the reins of the house. Elena was thrilled to have somebody from her own country. In no time at all they became very close.

An image of a baby girl was constantly in Elena's mind. Not for a second did she think it could be a boy, and was upset when somebody said it could be a boy. Roberto chose the name of Evita for a girl and James for a boy. Elena overlooked the fact that her husband didn't ask her what she thought about the names. For Elena it was plenty to have life and health to enjoy her daughter. Besides, she liked the names.

She used the time in bed to embroider or write Evita on every single item her tiny daughter was going to be in contact with: receiving blankets, diapers, crib's sheets, gowns, flower pots, toys, everything had the baby's name on it. Clothes were pink. She even filled up the announcement cards leaving blank only the date and measurements. Life was wonderful.

Thank God, she was alive, and able to conceive!

CHAPTER XV

Telegram From Barcelona

Roberto descended from the autobus that brought him from New Jersey to Port Authority in Manhattan, he hailed a yellow cab and whistled a happy tune all the way from the taxi to his office. There he hurled his hat at the hat stand on the corner.

It landed exactly where he wanted.

On top of his desk, a lot of personal mail waited for his attention. A telegram lay on top of the stock. He stared at it, his face contorted with rage. It was from Spain.

The part of his life that he would like so much to erase was here, haunting him like a black shadow. He told Emilio never to call or write to him, because he was done with that part of his life in Spain forever. Reluctantly, to mind flashed the memory of one carefree night in Barcelona shortly before his return to the States. He met Anita, the teen-ager with the voluptuous body of a woman who enticed him, and he succumbed to the temptation. On this one and only time, she got pregnant. To appease his conscience, he left her under the care of Emilio and Marina, with the understanding that they would not contact him ever. He promised to send money every month and take care of the child's future. Not personal contact.

Then, it must be something urgent for Emilio to send a telegram. So many things came to mind; he fought against the memories . . . they unsettled him too much.

He stared at the envelope and struggled against the impulse to destroy it. He yielded, and ended up reading it. As he read on, the color drained from his face. *Our daughter is sick. We need more money.* The telegram read.

He needed to take care of this problem. It was close to nine and Marcos, his partner, was about to arrive at work. He hurriedly dialed the operator and luckily was connected right away.

After Emilio explained the reason for the telegram, Roberto said in an abrupt and frustrated voice, "Emilio, tell Anita I don't want any link with her or the baby. I'm sending extra money this one time, but she must make do with the agreed monthly amount. This is the last time I make an exception to our agreement. She must forget that I exist." He slapped the top of the desk. "My life is here! Now my wife is pregnant, and I don't want anything from my past to spoil my present!"

He hung up, visibly nervous, and immediately called the bank to make arrangements to send more money to Anita. Damn his bad luck! He feared that his sin would relentlessly follow him the rest of his life . . . He shuddered at the thought that Elena could find out. Was he supposed to suffer the consequences of his sin all his life?

Everything is going so well at home, and that's the way it must stay, he thought.

Soon afterwards, Marcos arrived with two packages.

"Good morning, Roberto. Here are the samples from Spain." He placed the packages on Roberto's desk and they began to open them.

"Oh good, the cargo arrived, eh?" asked Roberto, pulling tape from the boxes.

"It's at the port. We need to pick it up and sort it out for delivery."

"I like that!" Roberto said, as he pulled open a box and carefully brought out a delicate piece of ceramic. The white porcelain base had a lattice structure accentuated with petite roses of lively colors.

"Elena will love this!" he said, placing it back in the box.

Marcos inspected the pieces. "They are exquisite." He paused and then asked, "Since your first shipment to Spain went so well, are you considering sending another one soon?"

"Yes. But the problem is to find someone we can trust to take the cargo."

"Can't you just ship the trunks?" Marcos asked.

"No, after the merchandise arrives there and is safely delivered, I have to distribute it to the retailers. That part is too risky for somebody else to do. My contact in customs makes sure we encounter no problems but insists I oversee the delivery there. The next step now is to find who takes the trunks."

Marcos cleared his throat. "I've been thinking about taking it myself," he said.

"Why don't you?" prompted Roberto. "Go ahead, escort the shipment. Once the merchandise is in Barcelona, then I'll fly for the distribution." He slapped his forehead. "You could take Martha along and have a second honeymoon."

"I discussed it with her yesterday, but she doesn't want to take any risks. She froze with fear."

"To travel by sea in a luxurious ship, plus the chance to visit Europe is worth a bit of risk. Don't you think?"

"No risk, no gain . . . I know. But that's the way wives are. They spot trouble in everything. She insists on calling our work 'smuggling'."

"Ask her to look at this from a different perspective. I'm not only doing this for personal profit, you know. I also want to help people there get the essentials to live a better life." Roberto placed everything back into the boxes and went on. "The Spanish Civil War left the country devastated, people lack almost everything. I find very good prices for what they need here, and we all benefit. I'm not sending anything illegal . . . just medicine, batteries, nothing perishable. Some basics."

"My wife is close-minded and doesn't see the big picture. All she sees is that you are shipping over there something the Spanish government doesn't allow." He paused for a moment. "Do you know something? I might go by myself," Marcos said hesitantly.

"Go for it!"

By the end of the day Roberto's good mood had returned. He longed to see his pregnant wife, so he hurried things along in order to get home early. He preferred a boy but would never mention this to Elena, who was crazy for a girl.

He arrived home whistling the same melody he had been humming in the morning when he arrived at the office. He had succeeded at putting the negative thoughts of Anita and her sick baby out of his mind, so he could concentrate on business and his growing family. Using his key, he went straight to the bedroom and handed Elena a gift along with a kiss.

She opened the box impatiently.

"*Amor*, this is absolutely adorable. I love it! When did the shipment arrive?"

"Early this morning and it's sold out already."

"The *Lladro* too?"

"All of it." He kissed her forehead, and placed his hand on her belly. "How's junior doing?"

"Evita is doing just fine."

"Señor Roberto," Sandra said, arriving at the scene. "Would you like tea, juice, or anything else before dinner?"

"No, Sandra, thank you. How was your day?" he asked, as he sat on the love seat by the bed.

"Very good. *Gracias.*"

Roberto gazed at her, smiling. "You look very good, the United States becomes you."

"I feel very good. I think that sleeping peacefully at night knowing that you're helping my family in Cuba, works wonders. I'm in debt to you both, thanks."

"Sandra," Elena said, "I told you it works both ways. I don't know what I would do without you."

"My family sends daily blessings and good wishes for your health and happiness. Their lives have changed because of Señor Roberto's generous help."

"Sandra, you work for it," said Roberto. "We are here for you! Is dinner ready? I'm starving."

"*Si, Señor.* I'll set the table at once. *Con su permiso.*"

Sandra left and Roberto glanced at his surroundings. If this was not happiness, what was? Here was the life he had dreamed of forever. Thank you Lord.

He gazed at Elena, her hands upon her belly; obviously ready to shout to the four winds how proud she was of what she carried inside her. He was almost certain she was now ready to forget about her own personal pursuits of being a professional woman, and selflessly concentrate on raising their child and creating a sound family. On the other hand, he, as a provider, would satisfy all of his family's whims. He would shower his wife with gold and diamonds for the world to see what a successful business man he was.

Several happy months passed by. Elena took advantage of the long days in bed to embroider, cross-stitch, and knit Evita's name on everything she found around that the baby could use. Close to the baby's due date Roberto's business required his presence in Spain. Elena panicked.

"My darling Elena, I promise I'll be back in time for Evita's arrival. Don't worry, my love."

"It would be so nice if you would cancel this trip! I need you with me more than ever."

"Come on, *mi* Elenita. You're acting like a child. If I say I'll be back in time, I'll be back. Trust me."

"Of course I do. But, darling, so many things can happen."

He took her head between his hands, ever so tenderly.

"*Mi Chiquita linda,*" he said, sweetly. "Everything's going to be just fine. Have faith."

The next morning Roberto left for Barcelona.

There was a bad snowstorm on March 22, 1958. Several days after Roberto's departure and two weeks ahead of time, Elena's water broke. She panicked, then collected herself and acted. First she called Doctor Moreno and told him.

"Do you have contractions?" he asked.

"Not really."

"You have time. Get ready and go to the hospital. I'll see you there."

With shaking hands, she dialed her neighbors—an elderly, friendly couple that lived next door. Marcia's answer made the knot in her stomach tighter.

"I'm so sorry, Elena! My husband can't drive in this weather. He's not well enough and his eyesight isn't good either. I'm very sorry, dear."

Elena hung up and froze in terror. She stood for a long time staring at nothing, unable to think of an alternative way to get there. She thought of Roberto's partner, but he lived too far away. It would take forever for him to get here, more so with the bad weather. She jumped as the phone rang.

"Elena," said Marcia. "My son Phil is here. He couldn't go home last night because of the storm. He'll take you."

Oh God, thank you.

"He has a sturdy truck that handles well in snow," Marcia went on. "Phil's young and strong, able to help much better than Armand. He'll take good care of you."

"Thanks a million, Marcia. God bless you and your son!"

¡Virgencita de la Caridad, gracias!

Yet, in spite of the urgency, Elena felt embarrassed. Her husband was an ocean away in another part of the world against her wishes, and now she had to go to the hospital escorted by a complete stranger. She whisked away the tears running down her cheeks and raised her eyes to heaven. *Dear God, don't mind me for complaining. Thanks for sending help, so I can have my baby. That's all that matters,* she prayed.

She trekked to the nursery to survey her luggage; she needed to be sure everything was there. Oh, the package with the announcement cards and her address book . . . she almost forgot it. She included them.

To her mind rushed Sandra's words from not too long ago: "Elena, you're going to a hospital, not a cruise."

To which she answered, smiling, "To me this is the most important voyage of my life."

Now, tears fought their way out, but she was able to stop them. With unsteady hands she folded a knitted edged cloth diaper and placed it in the suitcase. She lifted out a nightgown bearing Evita's name embroidered across the front and back of the lovely, pink garment and stroked it against her cheek. The thought of coming back home with a healthy baby in her arms made more bearable the pain of not having her husband by her side.

The doorbell rang. Moments later Sandra came to announce that the neighbor had arrived.

"Elena, I insist," Sandra said. "I want to go with you."

"I feel better if you are here when Roberto calls. He needs to know."

"But you need me more," Sandra insisted.

"Nurses are there to help, Sandra. Besides, you don't speak English . . ."

"Sorry. You're right! Call me as soon as you can, will you?"

"*Te quiero*," Elena said. "Now, bless me, please."

The young woman crossed Elena and then kissed her. "God bless you. Good luck to you and Evita," she said, as tears shone in her eyes.

Phil, an agreeable, good looking young man, helped Elena to the truck, settled her in the front seat, and then went back for the luggage. Soon, they were on their way.

Ice and snow clogged the roads. The zigzagging through the snow made Elena fervently invoke God for the miracle of arriving safely and on time to their destination.

The windshield wipers didn't have the power to clear up the accumulation of snow on the glass. Despite the situation, Elena admired the gorgeous, breathtaking view of the snow. The thick white, whirling blanket of snow appeared unreal! To realize that such an imposing, treacherous beauty had the power to provoke an accident where Evita could lose her life made her blood run colder than the outside icescape.

God, I don't care anymore if it's a boy, just make us arrive safely, she implored.

The weather worsened as the truck crawled its way to the hospital. As the roads grew more dangerous, Elena's fear intensified.

Phil sensed her unease.

"It's not long now," he said with a soothing voice. "Besides I have new and very good tires, don't worry."

I hope you're right . . . . Everything must be okay; she thought and felt gratitude for his good intentions. Though she wanted to say something to this kind man, she couldn't utter a word.

He was quiet for a while, and then he spoke again.

"It was good fortune that I was at my parents. I was supposed to head home yesterday, but the Turnpike was shut down. I live in Morgantown. Not since 1904 have we seen a storm like this. Your baby chose a bad day to arrive."

"Yes, and she also chose to come two weeks early. That's why my husband isn't here." Then she fell silent, as she felt her first contraction.

Finally they arrived at Saint Claire Hospital, where Elena was wheeled in to the waiting room. Phil brought her luggage and set it nearby while Elena answered a nurse's questions.

"When did your water break?"

"About three hours ago."

"Any contractions?"

"Yes, on my way here, several little ones."

After the questions, Elena signed a lot of papers.

"Your doctor isn't here yet but an intern will examine you."

"Should I take my suit-case with me now?"

"Yes, I'll help. Where is it?" asked a nurse-aid, searching the surroundings.

"Right here," Elena answered, turning her head. "It was here a moment ago." She looked around in confusion. "I saw Phil dropping my luggage here."

The nurse asked everywhere. No one had seen it.

Suddenly, a band of pressure contracted around her stomach and without meaning to, she screamed. The first real pain of labor had begun. Elena, protesting her lost luggage, was rushed away to the examining room. There she was prepped for delivery under the surveillance of a very young intern. Tall and gaunt, he gave her the impression of a vulture, impatient to rip his prey. Elena was terrified. No one had ever told her it would be like this. She was frightened to be exposed to a stranger—horrified to have some man other than her own doctor hovering over her.

An excruciating pain made her bite her lips, so hard that they bled. As soon as the contraction passed, the man bent over her and she felt his gloved hand checking her dilation. She was incensed.

"Don't you touch me! I want my doctor . . ." she cried.

Oh God! What if Doctor Moreno was busy with another patient and placed me in the hands of this young, inexperienced intern. God . . . what to do without Roberto! Without Mother and Alma, who had been there for me at time of crisis? She had endured hardship before, but this physical pain overwhelmed her . . . she wasn't prepared . . . she wanted to die . . .

A nurse came and caressed her head. "Be calm, honey, your doctor is on his way. This nice doctor is just helping you to get ready, so doctor Moreno won't lose any time when he arrives."

Elena couldn't endure the agonizing pain and no one could calm her. By the time Dr. Moreno showed up she was hysterical, and he stared at her in shock. "Elena, please, calm down. You can be heard at the other end of the hospital."

"I don't want a baby! I can't take this anymore."

The doctor told the nurse, "Prepare her for epidural."

"Epidural? Epidural?" Elena cried, "What's that?"

Doctor Moreno turned to face her and looked into her eyes. "Elena, listen carefully. The epidural is anesthesia. You'll feel relief right away. Lie on your side and curl up tightly over your abdomen. You need to be very still."

"How can I, with all this pain?"

"You can and you will! The pain is increasing your anxiety and muscle tension, which will prolong labor and put the baby's life in danger. This anesthesia will numb you from the waist down. We need it in order to deliver your child safely." He took her head into his hands. "Listen to me very carefully. You can't move while I introduce the needle between your vertebrae. If you move you could be paralyzed for the rest of your life."

"No! Don't do it . . ."

"I will . . . and you must cooperate. Keep still when I ask you to."

Immediately after the contraction, Doctor Moreno and the nurse acted. Elena feared the worse, but she cooperated and almost immediately, the pain of the contractions stopped. The Doctor and nurse helped her back to the delivery position. After some time, Dr. Moreno yelled, "The forceps. Get me the forceps!"

Soon after, she heard the cry of her baby—it was like the sound of tolling bells from heaven! Her baby had arrived in this world—her joy had no limits. Fear faded, replaced by bliss. *I hope my child will be very happy and healthy,* she wished fervently. Then she asked, "What is it, Doctor?"

"It is a beautiful little girl."

Elena threw her arms wide open at the doctor and exclaimed, "Gracias! Thanks! Let me kiss you!"

Doctor Moreno shook his head as if to stop her and said, smiling, "I had nothing to do with that! Kiss your husband."

After being cleansed, the brand new mother was taken to a private room. Some time later a nurse brought her tiny bundle, wrapped in a hospital receiving blanket. The baby had a pointed head covered with black hair down to the eyebrows.

Elena reached for her baby, eyes filled with tears of joy. Once in her arms, Elena tenderly took Evita's tiny hands and counted, one by one, each of her diminutive fingers. Then she did the same with the little feet.

"Oh, she's so beautiful!" she said admiringly, kissing Evita's dark-haired head. *"Virgencita de la Caridad, gracias por mi nenita!"*

Suddenly, she flinched, remembering her behavior during the child's birth. "My love, forgive my cowardice," she murmured into Evita's ear. "I promise I'll put you first the rest of my life."

Roberto called the hospital as soon as Sandra gave him the news. He was extremely sorry for missing the birth of his first child. After some excited chit-chat and plenty of pleasantries, Roberto gave her two choices: He could take the first plane to the United States and stay a few days to be with his family and then fly back to Spain to finish pending business; or he could stay in Barcelona until he could find someone he trusted to finalize the deal and be back with his family in a few days.

"You can bet that if you come home, I won't let you go back," Elena said. "I hate this . . . I was counting on you to take us home . . . But, do as you must."

That same day Elena's mother-in-law surprised her with a call from Barcelona. Aisha couldn't be happier. At last, she was a grandmother. Even Ruth, talked to Elena and begged her to take good care of her niece. Elena felt blessed.

Roberto called twice a day and Elena described little Evita as the most beautiful baby in the world. And for her she was.

"She has a tiny cleft in her chin—just like yours. She's so cute! I can't wait until you meet her," she said with emotion.

"I'm counting the days, my darling. Tell her about me."

"That's all I talk to her about. We love you, Roberto."

Without her suitcase, Elena went from having a surplus of everything, to have nothing at all. That afternoon she called Vilma and told her of the ordeal she'd been through and the loss of her suitcase. That same evening Vilma and Benny came to visit. Complying with Elena's wishes, Vilma brought cosmetics and toiletries, along with a box of announcement cards.

Elena wanted to ask her friend to pick up some of the pretty things that she has made for Evita. But she remembered Roberto's irate words: "I don't want that jerk in my house." Elena didn't ask.

The new mother was five days at the hospital. Vilma and Benny were present when Doctor Moreno discharged Elena.

"Since Roberto isn't here, we'll be here early tomorrow morning to take you home," Benny said, with determination.

"Oh, no, my neighbor will pick us up."

"Elena, you told us the man isn't well enough to drive in the snow. The roads are still very slippery."

"Please, Benny, don't worry. I'll manage."

Benny was adamant. He wouldn't listen.

Again, Roberto's words came to mind, piercing her heart.

When her husband called that evening, Elena was so confused she didn't know what to tell him about Benny and Vilma's offer. She didn't want to make him angry. In a good mood, Roberto filled her ears with endearing words, making her feel loved and needed, and she chose not to tell in order not to break the spell. But, when he asked directly who was taking her home, she felt obliged to tell, and his reaction was worse than she expected.

"I can't believe your stubbornness! How dare you defy my wishes?"

"There's no one else to take us. Benny will drive and Vilma will help with the baby."

"Why don't you put your mind to work? Call a taxi! Call a limousine! Hire a nurse! Walk if necessary, but don't even think of talking to that sonofabitch, let alone allow him to touch my daughter! Hire a chauffeured car . . ."

"That would cost a fortune!"

"Use money from your bank account! Why, then, do you think am I working like a dog? I want my family to have everything they need. Get it into your head and don't forget it: I'm breaking my back for you and my daughter! Did you hear me? *Do you?*"

And with that, Roberto hung up.

Elena's heart sank. A chill ran up and down her spine. Her head throbbed so viciously that for a moment, she couldn't see. Was this really happening? Was Roberto chastising her like if she were a minor with no right to make decisions of her own?

She felt so dizzy that she called for help. The nurse rushed in. "What's wrong, honey? You're so pale . . ."

"I feel faint . . . !"

Immediately, the nurse took Elena's blood pressure and found it to be very low. An intern came in, gave her an injection and raised the foot of her bed. Soon her headache faded and her vision cleared, as her blood pressure stabilized.

Elena thought if she had to stay another day, she could cancel Benny's offer of help. That would buy her enough time to find another way home.

"Do you think I really should go home tomorrow?" she asked, holding her breath.

"Doctor Moreno signed your discharge already. You shouldn't have any problem." The nurse tapped her shoulder. "Have a happy return home. Have your baby all to yourself."

Around midday next day, Elena and Evita left the hospital. On the way home Vilma and Benny tried to entertain her, but fearful of Roberto's reaction, she claimed to have a headache and avoided conversation. She regretted hurting dear Vilma, but the problem was Benny. Though he had proven to be a good husband and made Vilma happy, Roberto was so stubborn, he refused to understand. The couple just wanted to help. What to do? Later on, when she felt better, she would explain to Vilma.

The *bebita* slept all the way home. Upon their safe arrival, Elena found that Sandra had set the table attractively and had food ready. They all enjoyed a Cuban treat and café espresso after lunch. Elena thanked her friends with all the warmth she could muster, excused herself and retired to her room. The couple left.

Roberto called late that evening to make sure they arrived safely.

"Welcome home, *mi amor*. How is beautiful Evita doing? Does she like her home?"

Roberto had called her "*mi amor.*" What a relief! Roberto was no longer mad at her. For that, she thanked her *Virgencita*.

"I think so," she answered, spirited. "Our *nenita* woke up to eat and went right back to sleep."

"Fantastic! But, have your rest now, my beautiful *mothercita*, she probably won't let you sleep tonight."

"Yes, that's what I hear."

"And how did you get home?" he asked nonchalantly.

She wasn't out of the woods, after all. Would she tell to keep his good mood? She struggled over a decision—she didn't want to lie. She kept quiet, feeling dizzy.

"Elena . . . ?"

"Roberto, we have a beautiful, healthy baby. We're so lucky . . ."

"Did you hire a chauffeured car as I suggested?"

"No, Roberto."

"Then you decided on the . . ."

"*No, mi amor* . . . I couldn't avoid Vilma and Benny. They showed up and . . ."

". . . What?"

"I swear I tried . . ."

"What do you mean you *tried*?"

"What I mean is that I'm alone and scared, and my husband is two thousand miles away, even though I begged him to be near me when the time came, and I have to solve my problems here, which I wouldn't have if you were here!" Elena's fear transformed into anger. She hung up the phone, the tears and anguish she thought belonged to the past returned, burning worse than ever. Roberto was a monster like her father was. The phone rang again and again. Finally, Sandra answered and brought it to her.

"Roberto asks for you," said Sandra, on the verge of tears.

Elena wiped her tears and took the phone. "*Sí*, Roberto."

"Don't you dare hang the phone on me again! Do you hear?"

"I hear you," she answered wearily.

Elena held the phone away from her ear while Roberto ranted. From time to time when she heard quiet she coughed aloud so he would think she was listening. *Oh, Dios, how long would he go on?* Yet he continued the chain of contemptuous insults and rudeness. After a while she interrupted his tirade.

"I'm sorry, Roberto, the baby's crying. I have to go."

"Go, then, and take care of your daughter," he said, adding one final parting shot. "I hope you're a better mother than you are a wife."

CHAPTER XVI

Women From Cuba

When Elena found out that her mother and Doña Pilar were arriving in three days, she was surrounded by uncertainty. She didn't feel the happiness she should have felt, to welcome her mother. Truth was, she didn't want to see anybody—least of all dear Doña Pilar. What she wanted was to disappear before her guests could witness her unhappiness. She could mask her misery, but for how long could she fake joy? She already tried with Sandra, without success. Only with her *bebita* she was able to hide her frustration, trying not to instill gloominess in her little daughter's nascent life. She spoke to her only of a future full of love and happiness.

Were it not for Evita, Roberto wouldn't find Elena waiting at home for his abuse and domination. Her mother's arrival made things worse. What to do to maintain the idea of her daughter's happiness? The peace she felt because her *hijita* had found Mr. Right? Elena had to avoid her dear *mama* finding out the truth at any cost.

After hours of deliberation, and as much as she hated it, she decided to call Roberto and try to patch things up.

"*Hola* Roberto, how're you?"

"Okay."

"How come you haven't called? It's been two days?"

"I don't feel like talking to you."

"How quickly your love has worn off."

"My dignity comes before anything."

"Roberto, I told you I'm sorry."

"I can't forgive or forget your offense that easily."

"For heaven's sake, Roberto, I didn't mean to offend you."

"We talked about that bastard before. You knew all along how I felt about him. To hear his name, I image him watching his friend fondling your bare breast. Knowing exactly how this affects me, the first thing you did was to call Vilma from the hospital and have them visit you."

"Roberto, try to understand. I saw other mothers having company, flowers and gifts; and I was so lonesome! No one cared for me! I felt helpless, vulnerable, without you or any of my family supporting me in such a crucial moment of my life. Vilma is the only friend I have in this country. Calling her was an impulse for which I am paying dearly."

"You could have called Marcia."

"Her husband isn't well and the roads were slippery because of the storm."

They were quiet for a while. Elena blew her nose several times. Finally he broke the silence.

"I don't want you doing things behind my back. This time I'm going to forgive you."

Elena wanted to scream. She wanted him as a mate, not as magnanimous father. When, if ever, would this situation change?

He cleared his throat and was quiet for a moment. "I guess I'm also to blame for leaving you alone when you needed me most. I should have stayed; I'm very sorry I didn't."

That's much better. "But, Evita was early. None of us is to blame"

"Meantime, I went through hell feeling as the laughingstock of those two," he said, bitterly.

"I'm sorry to know you felt that way. I'm also suffering. I love you so," she meant every word.

"I love you, too! I'll make up for this . . . I promise!" he said softly.

She proceeded to tell him about the visitors from Cuba.

"I'm glad for you. I'll be there as soon as I can."

Elena felt the heavy burden lifted. She thought she could fly because of the sensation of lightness about her. She realized how important communication was. Elena ran to the kitchen.

"Sandra," she called out, hugging the young woman. "No more sadness in this house. Roberto is coming home soon. Everything is clear now."

"Is the quarrel over?"

"I apologized and he admitted part of the blame. Now I'm up to having my mother and Doña Pilar here and enjoying them completely."

"That's wonderful! I was so worried."

"Later I'll tell you details; now I have to share the good news with Evita."

Elena ran to the nursery and took her *bebita* in her arms, whirling around like a ballerina. "Darling, Daddy's coming home. Daddy's coming home . . ."

Elena's guests arrived a few days before Roberto. They had the opportunity to enjoy some time together sharing family news. The best news came from her mother. Her sister Alma was no longer thinking of entering the Saint Theresa Convent, and was falling for a young man that moved into the neighborhood. Alma had gotten the courage to confront her father about the man in her life.

"Elena, I'm sure she's copying your example, which is good. Don't you think, Magdalena?" asked Doña Pilar.

"Certainly. Alma told me that if her younger sister had defied her father, she had to do it too."

Sandra was glad to have a letter and fresh news from her family. They all gathered around the sleepy newborn, and graciously agreed that Evita was the most beautiful baby in the world.

Later, after Magdalena and Sandra had retired for the evening, Elena spent some time alone with Doña Pilar.

"I didn't want to ask in front of them," said Doña Pilar, "but how are things going with Roberto and his family? Has your relationship with them improved? Have they mellowed now that you have Evita?"

"Well, Aisha couldn't be happier. Ruth is still a little reserved, but also happy. They can't wait to meet Evita."

"Good! I'm glad. You deserve to be finally appreciated."

"I'm not sure. I have my shortcomings."

"What do you mean?" Doña Pilar asked, with wide-open eyes.

"Roberto's so good to me!" Elena sighed. "But . . . I don't make him happy."

"Wait a moment, my friend. Don't put yourself down."

"I'm all so confused. I don't see clear."

Elena told Doña Pilar why Roberto was infuriated at her and how offended and hurt she was by his insults.

"But, I apologized and now he's returned to his usual sweetness. He regretted not been here for me and the baby, and he sounded genuinely contrite."

"Roberto should have been more understanding." The woman paced the room for a few seconds and then went on, "He knew you were alone among strangers and very vulnerable . . . after all, you were recovering from the birth." Doña Pilar walked back to her place on the sofa.

"Elena, the macho type of man is possessive and thinks of a wife as a slave. He would like to control even her thoughts. Because women allow this behavior they get away with it."

"But Roberto isn't like that."

"I'm afraid that now that you're his wife, he assumes he owns you. And with the birth of the child, the tie gets even tighter."

"Roberto is a good, fair person. He loves me."

"Of course he does! I don't doubt it; otherwise he wouldn't have defied his mother, and his religion." Doña Pilar combed Elena's hair with her fingers, tenderly. "You know I love you. I just want you to be prepared. Understand how Roberto feels every time he remembers what Peter did to you. Benny is there to remind him what he so badly wanted to forget. As much as you like Vilma, cut that friendship if you want peace."

"We're like family away from home. She's grateful to me because I made it possible for her to buy my beauty salon."

"You sold your salon?"

"I'm not going to work anymore, so I offered it to Vilma. She's paying for it at her own pace." Elena thought for a moment, and then continued, "You know, I wanted to pay forward all that you and Gina had done for me."

"Did Roberto agree to the sale?"

"I had to put my foot down . . . He didn't have much of a choice . . . But he doesn't want to see Vilma and Benny in his house."

Elena explained to Doña Pilar everything about the sale, and they conversed some more about their lives.

"Doña Pilar," Elena concluded. "I want to pay you, at least, part of the money you lent me," said Elena eagerly.

"It wasn't a loan, dear. You can keep it."

"I'm very grateful to you for helping me out when I needed it! But I sold my business and now I am able to repay my debt . . . That was what we agreed upon"

"Elena, it was my pleasure and I . . ."

"With that money I want you to help someone else in need," insisted Elena, but to no avail.

Several days later, Roberto arrived from Spain. He used his key to open the front door, flung his hat and jacket on a chair and ran to the nursery. Speechless, he stood by the crib, staring down at his baby, and then exclaimed, grinning, "She's so tiny and—and so ugly . . ."

Suddenly, Elena saw the baby in a new light.

"Roberto, don't say that," she said, heartbroken.

Roberto embraced his wife and kissed her. "You told me she looks like me. Do you really think so?"

"To me, you both are the most beautiful people in the whole world."

"It doesn't matter." He took her face in his hands. "I love you and my little one more than anything . . ."

"She might not be pretty now right after birth, but she's going to grow up to be a beauty. She will be as beautiful as you are handsome. Wait and see—mark my words."

He laughed. "No doubt, love is blind." Taking Elena by the waist, he lifted her into the air. "She's going to look gorgeous in the little dresses I brought for her. In fact, I bought something for every one." He looked around eagerly. "Where are your mother and Doña Pilar?"

"I'm sure they're freshening up to welcome you." She hugged him, and then looked into his eyes. "I missed you; it's so good to have you back."

Later, while the baby slept, the family, including Sandra, clustered around Roberto in the living room. His suitcase lay open on the floor, filled with presents for everyone. For Elena there was an exquisite bottle of Joy perfume by Jean Partout, an elaborated black, hand-embroidered kimono, and a leather handbag, among other things. There were a few Lladro figurines for the house. For each of the women a hand-made lace mantilla with ornamental hair combs. There were two sizes of *Nenuco,* Spanish cologne, for the newborn, along with several dainty dresses, tiny shoes and knitted bonnets.

"*Mi amor, gracias.* I'm dying to see Evita in those beautiful clothes."

"I appreciate this early Christmas, Roberto," said Doña Pilar. "I had been longing for a mantilla like this for ages."

"I never expected to own one," said Magdalena, holding her mantilla close to her face.

"Roberto, do you mind if I send mine to my mother? She'd love a mantilla from Spain," Sandra said.

"Do as you like. It's yours," Roberto answered, smiling. In good humor, he reached for a box from the suitcase and pulled out a surgical mask. "Here's a mask for each one of us. We must wear it each time we approach the baby." Then he added, "We also must wash our hands and rinse them with alcohol before touching Evita."

There was a moment of stunned silence. Elena broke it.

"Are you serious?" she asked.

"Absolutely! We bring home germs. Babies are vulnerable."

"But, Roberto, washing hands is enough. Don't exaggerate."

"A little effort from anyone visiting our *nenita* could result in better health for the baby. Also, whoever is in charge of making the formula must wear a mask and cover their head."

A tense, embarrassing silence followed.

"Is there a problem with that?" Roberto asked, locking eyes with everyone in the room.

From beneath lowered eyelids, Elena watched the changes of expression on her guest's faces. How could Roberto do this to her mother, to Doña Pilar? But his stern face discouraged her from challenging his wishes. Now she should avoid a scene, but later . . .

"It is okay with me," Sandra said, vexed. "*Con su permiso*," she added, and left the room.

"You are in your right, Roberto," said Doña Pilar, smiling. Then she reached for a mask and tried it on. "Do I look funny?"

Magdalena did the same. Her eyes crinkled into a smile. "Do I look like a nurse? I always wanted to be one."

They all smiled, but the atmosphere remained strained.

Later, when Elena and Roberto were alone, she said, "Roberto, they didn't complain, but they weren't happy with your idea."

"My darling, I really don't care what they think. My child and her health are above everything. Taking precautions shouldn't be a sacrifice for anyone. Make sure they follow my orders."

"You cannot order people around like that!"

"It is my house and those are my rules."

"It is my house also and I don't agree."

"Well, you should put your child's welfare first." He rested his hands on her shoulders. "And that's not up for discussion. Okay?"

Elena understood arguing was a lost cause. *Just for the time being, let him think we'll follow his ridiculous orders.*

In bed that night, despite her longing to be in her husband's arms, his inflexible expression earlier kept Elena from surrendering completely during lovemaking. He kissed her with the same passion as always—she was able to respond to the ardent caresses—but she felt a wall between them restraining her.

Through the night, Roberto nudged Elena several times. "Dear, the baby's crying."

"No, she's not. She's just stirring," she would answer.

Finally the baby woke up for her feeding.

"This time she's crying," said Roberto urgently.

"Yes, now she's hungry," said Elena, pushing herself out of bed and shuffling to the nursery, followed by Roberto's trailing words: "Don't forget to wash your hands."

For the first time in their marriage, Elena felt good when Roberto was not around. The women in the house didn't wear masks around Evita and an atmosphere of freedom reigned. They all enjoyed his absence.

CHAPTER XVII

Obsession

One evening, as customary since his arrival from Spain the prior week, Roberto got ready to kiss Evita goodnight. He rinsed his hands with alcohol, put his mask on and lifted his baby from the crib.

"Elena, come here immediately!"

Elena ran to his side. "What's wrong?"

"Look at the baby's eyes . . . she has an infection!"

"What makes you think that?"

"There's pus in her eyes!"

"Let me see," Elena said, looking at her baby closely. She wanted to laugh, but thought better of it, instead she said, "My love—it is only *lagañas.*"

"Are you blind? That's an infection."

"Let my mother and Doña Pilar look at her. After all, my mother raised seven children."

"You are kidding! My child needs her pediatrician." Gesturing with one hand, he added, "Shoo—don't just stay there . . . go . . . call . . ."

"I want my mother and Doña Pilar look at her first," Elena repeated.

"Don't you understand that she needs a doctor? My baby might go blind if we waste time. Go! Call!"

"You are the one who wants the doctor. You call."

Annoyed, he gave the baby to his wife and went to the phone.

"Doctor Williams is on his way," he said when he came back.

Half an hour passed and nerves were eating Roberto. He paced the nursery, then went to the living room and paced some more. "Why is he taking so long?" he mumbled. He walked to the dining room where Elena was folding diapers. "I can't figure out how you can be so unperturbed when your child is sick."

Elena didn't like his tone. "You are the sick one! Evita is fine."

"She's not fine! Woman! Tell me what is it that runs through your veins—Ice?"

The bell rang and Roberto dashed to open the door.

"This way Doctor Williams," he said eagerly, guiding the doctor to the nursery. "Please, doctor, rinse your hands," and Roberto handed the alcohol to the doctor along with a guest towel.

"What's wrong with the baby?" the doctor asked, while drying his hands.

"She has an eye infection."

Doctor Williams examined Evita.

"You mean to tell me that you got me out of my house for this? Ask your wife to clean the baby's eyes."

"I beg of you, please, you do it doctor. This is our first baby. We don't know how to do it."

"I have children who are truly sick and need me. I can't waste my time cleansing sleep from your baby's eyes. You do it!"

"I'll pay you . . ."

"Keep your money." Doctor Williams didn't wait to be escorted out. He left the house, slamming the door behind him.

"Where did you find such a rude doctor? I don't want that jerk seeing my daughter ever again!"

Elena wanted to laugh, but thought better of it. Finally, she had her mother take a look to Evita. After washing her hands with alcohol and slipping on her mask, Magdalena checked Evita. "There's nothing to worry about," she said.

Then, under the pressure of Roberto's close watch, she boiled water and added an iota of boric acid to it. Once the solution was lukewarm, she wiped the baby's eyes with a piece of cotton. Evita burst out crying.

"Be careful! Don't make her cry!" Roberto cried.

"Maybe she won't cry if you do it. Go ahead, do it."

"*Perdón, Señora* Magdalena, pardon me," a contrite apology came from Roberto. "I over-reacted." He placed his hand on her shoulder and said, "I don't know what I'd do if anything happened to my princess.*"*

Doña Pilar approached Elena and whispered over the baby's screams. "Why that face? Be patient with your husband. This obsession is temporary; it will pass soon."

"It better be soon—it's getting on my nerves," Elena answered, rolling her eyes. "I wouldn't want an indifferent father . . . but Roberto's overdoing it. I don't sleep at night; he wakes me for every tiny sound. Then when I come back to bed he's conveniently sound asleep."

"Believe me, child, it's better to be overprotective, rather than not caring," Doña Pilar said, smiling.

That night, at the first nudge from Roberto, Elena responded crabbily: "Will you please stop nudging me every time you hear your princess? I know exactly when she needs my attention."

"What if you don't wake up on time?"

"Then you can get up yourself. You're the father, no? You're driving me crazy," Elena tried not to explode. "If I get sick, who's going to take care of her? Think about it."

"Humm . . . you're right, dear wife," he said in a condescending voice.

She was going to respond, but changed her mind.

Magdalena and Doña Pilar departed on the same day Evita turned five weeks. Elena wanted to ride with them to the airport, but Roberto had other plans.

"I'll take them," he said. "You stay with Evita."

Sandra cut in, "Roberto, I can stay with Evita."

"The *bebita* is too young. She needs her mother."

"But Roberto, I want to go!"

"Elenita, my darling, stay with her, please," he said, sweetly.

They left. Once alone, Sandra said, "Roberto doesn't trust me with Evita. I'm here to help, but he doesn't want me near his baby."

Elena hugged Sandra and said, "You help me enough with other things. Besides, just by being here, you make me feel better. I need moral support in order to deal with this dictator of mine."

"But I don't feel comfortable anymore."

"Don't even think about leaving, okay?"

"I need the job, but Roberto has changed so much . . ."

"*Doña Pilar* told me that this is temporary, and I believe so. I'm sure he'll be back to his old self soon. Let's be patient, Sandra. Support me."

Although Elena missed her guests, she was glad they'd left. Now that she was free to be herself, she didn't have to swallow her indignation every time her husband changed moods or ordered her around. For the sake of peace, she had overlooked Roberto's humiliating behavior because she wanted her mother to leave with the image of a happy daughter. But the next time Roberto put her down; she vowed to give him a piece of her mind.

Roberto returned from the airport and hurried through the ritual of rinsing hands with alcohol and placing his mask. And then ran straight to the nursery. He lifted Evita by the waist and held her in the air, her tiny face almost touching his.

"Careful with her head, it's not strong enough yet," said Elena.

"Please put your mask on, and then talk."

"I'm not staying," Elena said, turning her back to leave. "Supper is ready."

During dinner, Roberto chatted about the trip to the airport, the traffic he encountered on the way, and about the weather. Elena and Sandra followed along with trivial comments. Then, Evita cried and Sandra jumped from the table but Roberto stopped her.

"Sandra, very kind of you, but Elena is the mother and she will check on Evita."

"I am eating now," Elena said casually. "Please, Sandra, go see to the baby.

"That's a mother's duty!" Roberto said, rudely.

"Then let her cry until I finish my food."

Sandra stood paralyzed in the middle, not knowing which way to turn. Elena wasn't about to give in and kept on eating. Roberto angrily slapped the napkin onto the table and left the room.

"Sandra, check on Evita, please. See if she's wet."

"I'm sorry Elena; I don't dare defy Roberto's orders."

"Okay. Crying is good for her lungs," Elena said as she kept on with her dinner. Once done, she washed her hands with water and soap and went to attend Evita without her mask on.

Roberto stayed in the study until ready to retire for the night, and then followed his routine and kissed his *nenita* goodnight. On his way to the bedroom he met Sandra to whom he bid a cold goodnight.

Roberto and Elena met in bed. He turned off the light and turned his back to his wife. She did the same, saying, "Goodnight, Roberto."

There was no reply.

They were careful not to touch each other during the night. At first Elena was concerned about Roberto's coldness and couldn't sleep, but when she heard him snoring, she got mad. How could he fall asleep so soon when they weren't talking to each other?

Next morning Roberto got out of bed early and left the house without breakfast. He was the first one arriving at the office. Impassive, he sat in front of his desk staring at the walls, unable to get rid of the annoying thoughts of his rebellious wife and his dear baby cries.

Last night, Elena had mistreated Evita by allowing her to cry. He shook his head. How could she defy his wishes? And worse, she had defied him in front of Sandra. If she thought he was going to let this pass, she was mistaken. He wouldn't speak to her again until she apologized. If he allowed her behavior to continue, Elena would think she could do whatever she wanted.

But, what disturbed him most was to discover another side to his wife: that of a heartless woman that placed her own selfish interests before her child's needs. The pain of Evita's screaming was engraved on his heart; it was unbelievable that Elena had done nothing about it . . . just kept on eating. At that moment he had used all his will power not to go back and take the abusive mother by the hair and force her to attend to her defenseless child. She must learn that he, and only he, was the head of the household. He supported the family, and his wife should support him.

As the day evolved, Roberto engaged in his work and found a respite from his anger and disillusionment. As the end of the workday neared, he debated what to do. Were it not for his need to look after Evita, he would have preferred to spend the night at a hotel in order to avoid Elena's presence. But, as a second thought, he needed to be home to control irresponsible Elena.

After a long debate, he decided that the best thing to do was to eat out and then go home.

When he arrived, he marched straight to the crib, and went through his usual routine before seeing his princess. His *niñita* was sleeping peacefully, so he suppressed the impulse to pick her up in his protective arms. She was wrapped in one of the receiving blankets he brought from Spain and looked adorable. The delicate aroma of *Nenuco* floated in the air, and he felt good to be home.

Elena emerged from the bedroom across the hall.

"Good evening, Roberto. Did you have dinner?" she asked in a very low voice.

He turned his head a little and noticed that she was wearing a sensual nightgown. He answered gruffly, without looking at her face. "Yes."

"Then, I'm going to bed. Evita is settled for the night," she said, leaving the room.

He caressed Evita's cheeks tenderly, then bent and kissed her forehead. "Darling, I'll be here for you. I'll protect you always."

He went to the bathroom, and when he came back Elena was either asleep or pretended to be. She ignored him completely. No concern whatsoever why he hadn't called during the day and why he came home so late. If that's the way she wanted things to be that was fine with him.

Meanwhile, Sandra was distraught. Roberto refused to speak to her, as if she were to blame for what had happened. The change in Roberto confused her. He had been so nice and courteous, and now was so cold and indifferent. Elena wasn't speaking to her either, and that made her feel like an intruder.

Maybe her job was over and she should leave. After all, Elena didn't need her anymore; she and the baby were doing fine. In addition, she was neglecting her religion. She wasn't able to go to mass on Sundays because of Roberto's wishes. She was amazed that in a country known for its freedom, she was living in a cage: comfortable and beautiful, but still a cage. She had anticipated taking the baby to the nearby park, but Roberto didn't want his precious Evita to leave the house yet. An hour or two on the outside porch, or on the balcony was enough.

Elena interrupted Sandra's rumination.

"Sandra, let's go to the park."

"What?" Sandra looked at Elena, not believing her ears. Elena had Evita bundled up and ready to leave. "Does Roberto know?" Sandra asked.

"This has nothing to do with him."

"Elena, I'm very sorry. I can't go with you."

"Why not, for heaven's sake?"

"You know, I'm also mad at him, I don't approve of what he's doing, but I don't dare defy him. You shouldn't do it, either."

"I refuse to play along with his eccentricity. I have my own ideas and my own rights. Evita is my daughter!"

"And he is her father."

"A paranoid father, I should say! He's making my life miserable. Why be cooped up in a house when we have a beautiful city and a beautiful park so near by?"

"Elena, I never told you, but my father didn't care about his children or his wife. He came home with lipstick smeared all over his clothes and was drunk most of the time. He wanted us out of his sight." Sandra wiped away a tear. "So you see Elena? Even understanding your situation, I can't be on your side. To me there are much worse things than a father exaggerating his care for his first child." She came closer to Evita. "You're a lucky little girl. Your *papito* adores you. All my life I longed for a kind word from my father. It never came."

"Oh Sandra! I'm so sorry. Why did you never tell me?"

"It hurts too much and brings back terrible memories," Sandra said walking away, hiding her tears.

"Wait, Sandra. Thank you for telling me." Elena reached for Sandra and placing a hand on her friend's shoulder, said, "Would you like to come to our beautiful terrace and listen to music? We'll have our own party and Evita will get her dose of fresh air."

Roberto arrived home late, went straight to the nursery to kiss Evita good night, following his usual ritual. Then he sauntered to his room, where he found Elena reading in bed. He entered the bathroom, took his time and read the newspaper. When he finally came out, expecting to find Elena sleeping, or at least pretending to be, he was astonished to see her in bed clad in a sheer negligee. He was glued to the floor. Was he ready to give in to her and take her in his arms? Could he forgive her behavior? No! He wouldn't follow her game. She needed to apologize and promise never to challenge him again. He wasn't going to be her puppet. She would not bend his will with her allure.

"Roberto, are you going to stand there forever?" she asked coquettishly, then, with a come hither gesture, she patted the bed. "I'm waiting for you."

"I can see that."

"Please, don't make me wait any longer. Come to me."

He sat on the edge of the bed and she reached for his hand, squeezing it tenderly. His heart missed a beat. The contact of her hand and her closeness made him realize that he had missed her touch more than he would like to admit. He could see her naked body under the negligee and his excitement grew, his blood boiling with passion. He called on his will and was barely able to control the urge to possess her. But if he wanted her to be a submissive wife and a good mother, he could not give in. He hated to admit that he adored her and wanted her in his arms forever. But that love made him vulnerable and weak. He couldn't allow that.

They locked eyes. Finally he asked, "Do you have something to tell me?"

"I don't like for us to be apart," she said, seductively. "I'm longing for your love and tenderness."

"I'm also longing for you, but I'm very hurt by your contemptuous behavior."

"It was just a misunderstanding. It's time to forget about that, *mi amor*."

He snapped his fingers. "Just like that, eh? I'm very worried about your skills as a mother. The other night you showed no compassion for your defenseless newborn. You heard her cry her lungs out and asked a stranger to find out what was wrong. It is a mother's call of love to attend to the needs of her child."

Elena's eyes flashed with anger.

"Brute! If you care so much, why didn't you pick her up? You are the father. Are you not?"

He leaped from bed, hands fisted, teeth clenched. The vein in his forehead bulged. She ducked from his tirade, waiting a blow.

"I more than fulfill my obligations as a husband and a father," he raged, out of control. "Now you want me to fill yours, too?" He pointed an accusatory finger at her. "Your only duty is to care for our home and child. I doubt if I want to have more children with such an irresponsible woman that chooses to feed herself rather than attend her new-born daughter."

"For heaven's sake, Roberto, you're blowing this out of proportion . . . You are out of your mind for nothing."

"That's the beginning of your rebellion and I'm not going to allow it!"

Roberto rained his fury onto a confused Elena. He lectured endlessly about what the duties of a good wife and mother were; he was so intent upon his reproaches that he didn't give her a chance to defend her point.

Elena couldn't believe what was happening. Roberto stood there blasting about her presumed failure as a mother. Until now she had been sure she was fit to be the best of mothers, but now Roberto had her doubting herself. Maybe the fact that she loved Evita more than anything in the world wasn't enough. Of course, she could have stopped eating to attend Evita, and she should have, but at that moment she wanted to show Roberto that she was tired of not having a life of her own—like going to the airport with her mother when she wanted so much to go. But the master had said "no" and willingly or not, she obeyed.

Amid his insults, Roberto asked:

"Do you regret what you did? Are you willing to learn from this?"

Elena felt she couldn't take it anymore. Her head was about to burst, and she wished she had the power to banish him from her sight. If she complied, he'd stop his soliloquy, so she answered, "*Por supuesto,* I want to be the best of mothers."

As unpredictable as ever, his features softened as if under magic. It was like changing channels on a TV. A new scene appeared and a different story took over. Roberto flew into a fiery passion without warning. He kissed her face, her eyes, blanketed her body with kisses. She was startled by the sudden change. She tried to reciprocate but to no avail—something inside her had died. She couldn't understand Roberto's sudden outburst of anger one second and passionate love the next. He didn't even notice she was not responding . . . he was too involved in his lust.

Once he had satiated his need, she felt used with his overflow of passion. Her body ached and her heart cried for what was missing in their reconciliation. Soon he was snoring heavily and an ocean of confusion swamped her thoughts.

Next day, two-dozen gorgeous long-stemmed red roses arrived at her door. The card read: *Thank you for making me so happy. Yours forever, Roberto.*

She embraced the flowers. "Elena, nothing is perfect, be happy with what you have. Don't long for what cannot be," she lamented, whisking tears away. "You're still young, there's a lot for you to see, and there's hope. Hope never dies."

CHAPTER XVIII

Kosher

Weeks passed by. Things ran peacefully with Sandra and Elena trying to adapt to Roberto's rule of no outings. At first Roberto decreed a year go by before taking Evita out, as a way to avoid his *bebita* catching germs. Finally, only because of his wife's insistence, he agreed to nine months. So, their outings continued to be exclusively to the pediatrician's once a month.

One evening, Roberto was in a very good mood so Elena broached the subject.

"*Mi amor*, I'm concerned about Sandra. She's young and needs to go out and meet people her own age, go to restaurants, and see new places." She caressed his face.

He kissed the palm of her hand and was pensive for a moment, then asked, "Well . . . What do you want me to do?"

"I don't know, but I thought that as clever as you are, you could think of something, so she won't be so bored."

He chuckled. "Leave it to me love. I'll take care of it."

Good! Elena thought. *Maybe he'll come around and take us to dine out. Or maybe he'll arrange a blind date for Sandra. Perhaps he'll realize that a twenty-three-year old young lady can't live like a nun, worse than a nun because nuns go to mass and they see people.*

Elena told Sandra about her conversation with Roberto. They both waited hopefully for a change.

Three days went by. Elena wanted to bring the topic up again; anxious to find out what Roberto was up to. Maybe he'll bring some young man from the office to take Sandra to a restaurant and a show. Sandra was longing to see the show in Radio City Hall. But no, Elena kept quiet and decided to wait, while her curiosity mounted.

At last it happened. Roberto called and asked for both of them to dress up like queens, because that evening he had a big surprise for them.

"Am I included?" asked Elena, nervously.

"Yes."

"What about Evita?"

"I have everything figured out."

"What time should we be ready?"

"Eight."

Well, no doubt he found a reliable nurse to stay with Evita. I knew he would come around. Oh yes, I love you, my Roberto!

Elena hurried to look for Sandra. She found her in the laundry room and, giggling, they spoke about the good news. The two friends danced and sang in unison, full of childish expectations. Sandra borrowed an evening dress from Elena and both dressed up for the coming event. Elena had given Evita her bath and feeding, hoping the baby would behave for the nurse.

Shortly before eight the front door bell rang.

Sandra approached Elena. "It can't be Roberto, so it might be his friend. Should I open the door?"

"I will; it might be your date."

Elena walked to the door and before opening it she glanced at the mirror hanging on the wall. She pushed back a strand of hair from her forehead, approved of what she saw and opened the door. There was Roberto holding a bouquet of red and yellow roses, flanked by two bearded, middle-aged men. They wore small round skullcaps on the back of their heads.

"Darling, hold the door open, please," he said, then handed the flowers to her and showed the men inside.

One of the men pushed a cart covered with a starched white tablecloth. The other carried a bottle of wine inside a sterling silver holder.

"What's going on, Roberto?" Elena asked.

"Since we can't go to a restaurant, I brought the restaurant here." He kissed her. "It's a kosher dinner from Delanceys. And brace yourself because you girls are having a show, right here in our own living room!"

Elena didn't know whether to laugh or cry. Full of resentment, she kissed her much-awaited outing good-bye. *Calm down, Elena, act like you're pleasantly surprised. Appreciate your husband's effort to make you and Sandra happy, even if it is in his own weird, disappointing way . . .*

"Roberto, how nice of you to go to all this trouble," Elena said, without looking at him.

"Just wait and see. We're going to have a banquet and *I am* going to sing for you girls. You see? We won't neglect Evita and neither of you have to lift a finger. Samuel and Jacob will take care of everything." He turned around. "I'm going to see my princess. I'll be back."

Roberto left and the men got busy setting the table. They brought their own dishes, silverware and glasses, starched napkins and even fresh flowers as a centerpiece. Elena and Sandra watched in awe.

"Amazing what Americans can do," said Sandra aloud.

"What money can do, I would say," Jacob said.

They all laughed.

When Roberto returned, a smile in his eyes, he pulled a chair for Sandra, helped her to sit and placed a napkin on her lap. "Gracias," she said. Then he helped Elena the same, kissing her head.

Samuel uncorked the fruity wine bottle serving Roberto a little bit. Roberto swirled the rich burgundy wine, brought it close to his lips, savored its aroma before sampling, and nodded his approval. Samuel then, filled everyone's goblets. Following it, Jacob uncovered the pots and the smell of food wafted gently through the room.

"Mmmmmm! The fish smells so good, it's making me hungry," Elena said, but it was only to compliment the two men. *How could Roberto disappoint Sandra this way? The whole purpose was for Sandra to get out of the house and meet people!* Her eyes flashed fire when she glanced at him.

"This is so good of you, Roberto," said Sandra, listlessly, without conviction. "Thank you!"

"It's my pleasure."

Jacob and Samuel served the meal and remained standing. Roberto addressed them.

"Please, have a seat."

"Thank you, Mr. Carvajal. But we're here to serve you."

"We'd like for you to eat with us. I hope you trust your own food. Is it kosher?" And Roberto laughed loud at his own joke.

The men accepted, gratefully.

Dinner went quietly. The ladies were not in a talkative mood. Roberto did most of the chatting. Before dessert he replenished the goblets with more wine; then he stood and announced that the show was about to begin. He asked what songs they wanted to hear. No requests followed.

"While you think about your choices, I'm going to sing *Granada* and *Madrid*, my favorite songs, which were written by my favorite song-writer: Agustin Lara—who, by the way, has never been to *España*, but several of his songs were inspired by cities in Spain. He has written hundreds of beautiful songs."

Roberto sang without musical accompaniment. Elena couldn't help but marvel at his potent tenor voice. She held her breath; afraid he wouldn't reach the highest notes. But it seemed his voice knew no limits. Gradually, Elena's gray mood lifted, and her resentment vanished. She thought she had never heard *Granada* sung with such passion. She admired his perfect, even teeth and his deep brown eyes, which sparkled, full of life. Then he sang Madrid. Marvelous!

Elena felt, again, the pull of physical attraction to him, to his broad shoulders and strong chest, visible through the fine material of his *guayabera*. Annoyed by her tender feelings towards her husband when she should be mad at him for letting Sandra down, she repressed the urge to throw herself into his arms. She wasn't sure if she were punishing him or herself by not following her impulses.

Once done, Roberto asked Elena what she would like to hear next. Placing aside her concern for Sandra, Elena allowed herself to enjoy the moment, and asked Roberto for songs they both liked, at times even joining in the singing.

The end of the evening arrived. Elena said goodnight to Sandra, and added, "Sorry, dear friend, I'll find a way to convince Roberto for a real outing for you."

"Don't worry. I enjoyed myself tonight," Sandra said with a sad smile.

That night their lovemaking was about love and feelings. Elena surrendered to Roberto's tenderness and felt good that she belonged to this unpredictable man.

Afterwards, Elena brought up Sandra's issue.

"*Mi amor*, let's talk about Sandra."

"What about Sandra?"

"Your gesture tonight was wonderful, but . . ."

"No buts. Dinner tonight was for her. I went out of my way to please her."

"Roberto, *mi vida*, we're a couple and for us it was super. You should have brought a date for her."

"*Elenita del alma mia, Elenita of my soul, por favor.*"

"Since her arrival here we have shut her away from people her own age." Elena traced a finger along his jaw, ran her fingers tenderly through his hair, along his neck and strong shoulders, and then went on. "With all the wonders in the United States, she should spend a day in Manhattan; see some of the great things New York City has to offer. Just like I did when I first arrived here."

"Take it easy, *mi Chiquita linda*. Evita will grow fast and then everything will be different."

"But, *amor*, she needs to meet a young man. Why don't you introduce her to someone from your office? To a friend, or a friend of a friend."

"Darling, let's live our lives, and let Sandra live hers. Don't turn me into cupid, please, *queridisima esposa*."

"She's our responsibility."

"Our responsibility was to pay her way here and a good salary to help her family. I have done that and more."

"More?" asked Elena, disconcerted.

"We treat her like family and we supply her every need."

"Roberto, you either can't, or won't see my point. It would be better if we forget the whole thing for now."

"Right! Let's keep good memories of our evening, *mi vida*," he said pulling her into his arms and humming the tune of *Some Enchanted Evening* into her ear.

CHAPTER XIX

Meddling

Why is life like this? Elena meditated. She had a passionate, generous husband, though difficult. No one is perfect. She had a healthy, adorable daughter and a beautiful home. Why, then, was she not satisfied? Why did she feel something was missing? Why did it bother her that Roberto wasn't fair with Sandra? For him, worldly things like a good salary and a good home were enough to appease his conscience; but for Elena spiritual things were equally important. She was a strong advocate for freedom and independence, thus she felt guilty for going along with her husband in this kind of slavery. She knew that openly opposing his wishes could put and end to their marriage. But, even knowing she could lose her husband, and Evita her father, nevertheless she would find a way to put an end to Sandra's imposed incarceration. To Elena's mind flashed years of confinement in Cuba, her desperate feeling crying for freedom, and how she clang to hope in order to survive. It made Elena want to help Sandra at any cost.

Another dreadful weekend, another boring Saturday with the same pattern. On Sabbath Roberto worshipped God, resting in pajamas from sunrise to sunset, fasting and praying to be forgiven for marrying a Christian who refused to convert. On Sabbath it was forbidden to use electricity, so Roberto wouldn't turn on electric appliances or lights. He just prayed, often standing by the window and gazing at the sky, talking with his God, while Elena's resentment built.

Elena wanted to practice her own religion, but Roberto was opposed to it. Worse, poor Sandra had to pay for it by staying secluded at home. Elena was determined to do something about it, so she spoke with Roberto, explaining that she felt obligated to see that Sandra complied with her religion. After a heavy argument, he slapped the end table and shouted: "No! And that's final." With that, he walked to his office and locked himself.

Elena looked for Sandra and told her to get dressed. "A cab will pick you up and take you to church. This will happen every Sunday."

An hour later, Roberto came out and approached Elena. "I'm sorry I shouted at you," he said sweetly, "but *mi amor*, let's not fight over strangers. I love you."

"I love you too."

He kissed her neck, and as always when she felt his mustache rubbing her skin, she burst into giggles.

"I'll eat you up, Chiquita!" He bit her shoulder, tenderly. "I'm hungry! Why don't you ask Sandra to prepare lunch?"

"I'll set up the table and serve you whatever you want," she said, caressing his face.

"Where's Sandra?"

"I sent her to church in a taxi."

"What? You must be crazy to do a thing like that." He raised a fist in the air and screamed, "You're going against my wishes again."

"As a wife I comply with your commands, but you cannot impose your will on Sandra. She's not your wife, or your daughter."

"She lives under my roof."

"That doesn't mean you own her."

"I don't want to hear this nonsense," he roared.

Evita began to cry. Elena ran to the nursery. Roberto locked himself in his study again. That night he slept on the couch and left early next morning. Sandra had offered him dinner, which he refused. He didn't talk to Elena. Only before going to bed, he visited the nursery to kiss Evita goodnight.

This situation went on for days. One night their bodies brushed accidentally and they ended up making love. The next morning he got up from bed singing their song. He went to the bathroom still singing, as a result, while shaving he cut his skin and bled a little bit. He called Elena. "Look, my love, I bleed for you!"

They kissed, tenderly at first, but soon it turned passionate and they ended up in bed.

In spite of their reconciliation, Roberto never fully digested the idea of his wife sending Sandra to mass on Sundays. He acted differently, like a person whose ego has been hurt, who feels betrayed. Their relationship changed. He cut out his flattering speech and attentions, and made love to her only when he needed to relief himself. Elena missed his tenderness.

With time he will get over this. I'll be patient and wait, Elena convinced herself.

CHAPTER XX

The Big Apple

Finally, Roberto mellowed and went back to his old self; but on the other hand, Elena couldn't stop worrying about Sandra. Spiritually she was better now that she could go to mass every Sunday, but she had no social life. She continued to try to find a way for Sandra to visit New York City. How? She thought her friend Vilma could take Sandra around, maybe after mass-—but on second thought; she didn't dare defy Roberto by contacting Vilma. That would be too much.

Well, I'll grab the bull by the horns and confront Roberto. She'd suggest he arrange a tour around the Big Apple; this way Sandra could see New York without bothering anyone. They discussed it for a long time. At first in a civilized way, but soon it took on high notes. Finally it ended as expected: an emphatic "no." He remained adamant about not letting shy Sandra go alone into a dangerous big city.

"I don't understand your eagerness," Roberto said. "Come December we can take Evita out, and then we'll take Sandra along to see Christmas lights."

Under other circumstances she would have laughed, but Elena was too angry. "Are you serious?" she cried out, but then changed her tone and said calmly, "Christmas is five months away. Sandra's visa will expire before that."

"We'll apply for an extension."

"We're not sure immigration will give an extension this time."

"Why not?"

"Remember? They told us that after a year she needed to leave the country and apply again. In two months it will be a year."

"Why are you so worried?"

"For heaven's sake, Roberto, she hasn't even seen Manhattan. She will have spent one year in New York City and she hasn't left these 4 walls! She hasn't gone to a movie, a park a museum, nothing!"

"She'll return safe and with money. I'm sure she'll tell her family about the automatic washing machines, dishwashers, vacuum cleaners and dozens of other new inventions they don't have in her country"

"You are so selfish and materialistic—you don't know anything about feelings or spiritual needs."

"Hurray! If you know so much, share your knowledge and teach me. Eh?" he said sarcastically.

Elena stood up and left. In her mind fluttered thoughts of how to help Sandra tour the Statue of Liberty, Radio City Hall and some of the places Roberto had taken her.

After deep thoughts, Elena went to see Armand and Marcia, the elderly neighbors whose son Phil had taken her to the hospital when Evita was born. After greetings and some small talk, she opened up and asked for a favor. She would like them to book a tour for Sandra and pay with a check, for which she would reimburse them with cash. She didn't want Roberto to see her cashed check made out to the tour company. If he were to find out the truth, he would be furious and the outcome would be disastrous.

She explained why she was doing things this way and asked them not to reveal her plan to a soul.

"I understand," responded Armand. "We always found your husband a bit strange."

"Well, you know, he comes from a different culture," said Elena, embarrassed. "Sandra is leaving soon and I want her to see the Big Apple for the first time."

And that was how Elena got Sandra to go on a tour. Since Radio City opened its doors at ten in the morning, Sandra was able to slip away after Roberto left for work and had plenty of time to be back before his return.

After the tour, an ebullient Sandra regaled Elena with details. She spoke endlessly about the things she had seen. The young lady couldn't believe the grandiosity of Radio City Hall, which took her breath away. She believed it alone to be worth the price of the tour. She admired even the classy restrooms—exquisite and luxurious with its chandeliers and drapes. Sandra explained that walking on the thick carpets was like sliding on feathers; and that nothing in the world compared with the terrific show. Then, on top of everything, she was able, at last, to eat a ham sandwich.

"Elena, I brought one for you."

"Thanks, Sandra, but you shouldn't have done that."

"Why?"

"You know that Roberto . . ."

"I know! But he isn't here."

"But he'll be here soon. That is a risk I don't want to take." Elena held Sandra's arms tenderly. "I defied him for you because I want you to see things that you might not have the opportunity to see again. I don't feel guilty doing that, but I will feel very guilty if I bring ham to our home knowing that his religion forbids it."

"I'm sorry, Elena. I thought you missed ham as much as I do."

"I miss it all right, but I can live without it."

"Lo siento mucho." Sandra's expression saddened. "Forgive me."

"Don't worry." Elena pulled back a strand of hair covering her eyes. "Do you know what? I'll throw it away right now, because we can't keep pork in a kosher fridge."

"You could hide it. Roberto will never find out."

"Aisha explained all about this and why, so I feel compelled to respect their ways."

Sandra laughed, nervously. "I don't understand you. You're doing worse things behind his back than eating ham."

"It's a matter of ethics. Helping you doesn't bother my conscience. I do it because I can't bear watching him enslaving you. I can't participate . . ."

"I appreciate it a lot." Sandra tapped Elena's shoulder and looked her in the eye. "But, I'm very worried. I don't know what I'd do if Roberto catches us."

"Don't be negative. Everything's going to be just fine. Next week you're going to the Roxy Theater. That's another marvel in the city."

"I'm frightened and excited at the same time. You really have courage doing this."

"My dear Sandra, you're afraid, but you're facing your fear. That's what courage is all about. You are part of what's going on."

By the time Roberto arrived that evening, Sandra had changed clothes and was ready to serve diner. Though Elena knew how nervous Sandra was, she felt relieved that she didn't let it show.

The following Wednesday, Sandra's went to the Roxy. Their neighbor Armand drove her to the Port Authority bus station and wrote down instructions on where and how to catch the bus back home. On her way back, she took the New Jersey bus, and got off two blocks from home. Then, under a sizzling July sun, she arrived damp with perspiration. She forgot to borrow the key from Elena so she rang the bell. Elena greeted her at the door.

"Oh dear, thank you," said Sandra, embracing her friend.

"It was wonderful! *Dios mio*, now I know how much I've been missing . . ."

"Tell me, which show did you like best?" asked Elena, as they walked to the kitchen. "Last week's or today's?"

"It's hard to tell," said Sandra, gulping down a glass of cold water. "But, I think I like Radio City's best." She paused for a moment. "They're different, though. The first one was more spectacular because of the out-of-this-world stage show, and the Rockettes. Today's was more of a presentation of well-known stars, and more talking, which I missed most of it—too fast and too many jokes. *Pero si,* I loved both, really. The Roxy building is old, very elegant and sophisticated. Radio City is more contemporary, ultra modern, I should say."

"Did you eat a meal this time?"

"Yes! And guess what—forbidden shellfish! Shrimp, crab . . ."

"Gosh, I miss *mariscos* more than *jamon*," said Elena, rolling her eyes.

"Should I bring some for you next time?"

"Of course not! But thank you."

"Okay. Could you manage the baby and the house alone? How was Evita?"

"*Un angelito.*"

"Meaning we can keep doing this?"

"Yes, as long as I can slip you away."

"Where are you sending me next?"

"How would you like to go to the Statue of Liberty?"

"I can't wait!"

So it was arranged, and it went well. On returning, Sandra repeated once and again about what she had seen and how it had affected her.

"When crossing the river aboard the ferry," she said, her eyes shinning with a new light, "the wind blew my hair around and I felt so good. I saw the grandiose Lady of Liberty approaching us as if offering freedom and independence to me and to the millions of slaves around the world. Elena, I cannot describe my feelings—I only know it took my breath away. I wanted that moment to never end."

"You are really inspired . . ."

"Yes!" Her face turned crimson with emotion. "I felt strong, as if I were another person. What a nice sensation to see so many different kinds of people, speaking different languages and dressed with clothes from their own country." She smoothed her skirt. "Elena, even the hot weather, so much like Cuba's, helped create my perfect day."

"I'm glad you enjoyed it that much. It was worth the risk of sneaking you out." Elena paused for a moment, then, as to assure herself, exclaimed, "Oh yes, I'm glad I did!"

"But Elena, I don't know how I'm going to live without this kind of life now that I've experienced it. I'm afraid I will never adapt to my old boring world."

"I didn't know you were so passionate . . ." Elena laughed, nervously.

"If I can't stay in this country, I prefer not to have discovered this kind of life. Elena, do you think Roberto will help me come back?"

"I know he'll try." A sudden pang hit Elena's stomach and a dark feeling settled in. *Oh God, what have I done to Sandra? I might have spoiled her life forever. Now I realize that it's true that you don't miss what you never had. Why on earth did I meddle with the life of this good, naïve girl? Although with good intentions, I might have destroyed this girl's happiness.*

Days passed and Elena didn't mention the next tour. She wasn't sure that she wanted to keep sending Sandra into a world she wasn't ready for.

The following Sunday, after coming back from church, Sandra showed up at the terrace carrying Evita. "Elena, *la nenita* just said my name, listen to her." With her finger, Sandra played with Evita's lips while asking the baby to repeat *Sandra*. "Say it again. Come on, *chiquitita*, say *Sandra*."

After a few tries, the baby repeated 'ma ma ma ma.'

"Did you hear it? She's saying 'Sandra.'"

Elena burst into laughter. "Yes, I believe she did!"

Later that evening, while setting the table, Sandra asked, "Elena, where are you sending me next?"

There it was, the question Elena dreaded so much. She thought hard before answering. She tried to sound casual when finally she spoke. "Let's wait two or three weeks. Do you mind?"

"What ever you say," said Sandra, with a tinge of disappointment. "Do you know where I'm going next?"

"Well, I have happy memories of a restaurant built amid a vast area of lush greenery in the heart of Central Park. It's called Tavern on the Green—and it's unique, gorgeous—it surpassed any dream."

"Can you tell me a little about it? Sort of be able to put a face to my dream."

"Sure, the place is like a fairy tale. When Roberto took me we didn't have Evita yet, so his attention was only for me. We had a scrumptious dinner; two waiters served us. Each brought a silver tray with a small whole hen decorated with feathers and green vegetables. I didn't know how to eat it or what silverware use. Roberto laughed about it and later we danced under the stars. We left the place on a horse-drawn carriage under a full moon. My happiness was beyond words."

"What a pity that Roberto has changed so much!" Sandra said.

"I know! I noticed his change after our honeymoon . . . Then, our lives changed when I was so ill during my pregnancy. But what really confuses me is his sickly obsession with Evita." "It's good to know he adores his child."

"I don't think it is the right way of showing it," said Elena, sadly.

"It is a passing thing. Don't worry too much about it."

"You're right."

Sandra told Elena how eagerly she was waiting for another tour. She also insisted on sharing the expenses. After some resistance, Elena finally agreed on splitting the cost and arranged an outing for the following week.

"I can't wait, I'm so excited," said Sandra wringing her hands. "What should I wear?"

Elena felt uneasy sending a young lady alone, and wished for something to happen, so Sandra couldn't go. The day arrived and Sandra showed such childish joy that Elena's worries worsened.

"Elena, can I borrow your house key? That way I won't bother you when I came back."

"Good idea." Elena handed the key and embraced her friend. "Sandra, be very careful. Will you please?"

"Of course, I will. Don't worry!"

Once alone, Elena spent some time with Evita. Later, she wrote a letter to her mother and another to *Doña* Pilar, sending both of them pictures of the baby.

Around two in the afternoon, she heard the front door. *That can't be Sandra! It's too early for her to be back.*

Elena went to investigate, and froze at the sight of her husband standing in the living room. He rushed toward her and held her tightly in his arms. "My darling, I yearned for my family and came home to have lunch with my gorgeous wife. But, what's wrong, you're shaking." He looked into her eyes. "What on earth is wrong? Is Evita sick?"

Elena shook her head.

"Say something!"

She managed to say, "She's fine."

"Are you sure?"

What to do . . . what to say to cover for Sandra's absence, she wondered with dismay.

"Are you sure?"

"What makes you think Evita's sick?" She tried to sound casual, but her voice broke.

He hurried to the nursery and found the baby sound asleep. He kissed his finger and placed it on Evita's forehead. He went back to Elena. "Elena, you scared the living daylights out of me!" Then, he shouted, "Sandra, I'm here for lunch." There was silence. He shouted again, "Sandra!"

"*Mi amor*, if you're in a hurry I'll fix something really quickly. Come with me to the kitchen." She pulled him by the hand tenderly, but she was still shaking.

Roberto held the back of the chair. "Okay, Elena, where is Sandra?"

Elena prayed: *Virgencita, I need help. I don't dare to lie and say she's sick in her room. Oh, maybe yes. That would be a lie on top of another lie. So, should I tell the truth? Oh, no!*

"Why are you finding this so hard? Go find Sandra."

"I'll fix your lunch."

"If you weren't so nervous, I wouldn't insist. But I want to see Sandra right now."

"Well . . . Okay . . . Here goes. She was very sad with a letter from her mother. I sent her to the park to clear her head."

"With what authority did you send Sandra alone to the park? Why didn't you call me first? You're not a single woman living alone and doing as she wishes."

"I'm sorry, Roberto. She was so distressed and crying. I wanted to help."

"We have a nice garden where she can relax safely. Why send her all the way to the park?"

"Because she's tired of being shut in, that's why."

"You should have called me and we could have thought of something. But that's typical of you—you want to do things your own way, forgetting that you are not a single woman."

"I have said I'm sorry." Elena walked to the fridge. "I'll hurry and fix your lunch."

"I'm not leaving; I'll wait for Sandra."

"I thought you were in a hurry."

"I was, before you spoiled my day. Now that I think about it-—I'm going to look for her in the park."

"Don't worry. Sandra will be back as soon as she feels better. Please! Let's respect her privacy."

"She can have privacy and safety in our own backyard."

He left, slamming the door. Elena's fear rose. There was no way she would get out of this mess. If it was wrong that she allowed Sandra to go to the park, imagine when he found out she wasn't in the park? What then? Once more Elena prayed hard for a miracle. She went to the nursery where Evita was napping. She wanted to take the baby in her arms for comfort, but, if she cut short the baby's nap, Evita would be cranky. She heard the door and went back to the living room.

"She wasn't in the park. Where in the hell did you send her? Say something! Where's that woman?"

Elena was stumped for an answer.

"Where?" he shouted.

"I . . . I . . . don't know."

"So, you don't know, eh? Don't worry, I'll be waiting right here for her. We'll see if you really don't know."

With that Robert sat and waited. At times he paced the room, only to go back to the couch. Elena stared at the grandfather clock, wishing desperately that its hands would break off and time ceased.

Evita woke up and began babbling to herself. *Evita, please cry,* Elena begged. *Cry as hard as you can so I can seek refuge within the sanctuary of your innocence.*

But no, Evita chose to sing little musical notes in her throat and make glorious, happy noises, ignoring the bitter scene being staged in her home with her own parents playing main roles.

Time passed. Roberto's face darkened with anger. Meanwhile, not knowing what to do, Elena visited the bathroom a few times, on another occasion she went to the kitchen, unable to utter a word. A series of familiar mechanical sounds announced that the clock was about to chime the hour. And then, unaware and indifferent of the importance to freeze life right at this moment, the pendulum swung three times. The resonant echo of each gong penetrated into Elena's chest as if it were a sword wounding her heart.

Some time later the front door flung open and Sandra let herself in, shouting her return, her radiant face flushed with happiness.

The girl almost fainted when she saw Roberto. Her face turned ashen, her knees began to shake. Elena feared Sandra would collapse, but shaking in fear she wasn't able to do anything. The thick, icy silence enveloped them; it could be cut with a knife. Then, the stillness broke when the bomb exploded. Roberto stared daggers at Sandra.

"Pack your things and leave my house right now."

Elena threw herself at Roberto's feet, "No, please. You're a fair person, listen to me, please."

He jumped to his feet and pushed her hard. Raising a menacing hand, he almost slapped her, but stopped, just an inch from her face. "Shut up! Don't make me break your lying face!" He gestured for Elena to leave the room. "Get out of my sight! Go!"

She whirled away, a sobbing Sandra following close behind.

It would be so nice to go to her room, cover her head with a pillow and forget the whole world, but her tiny daughter needed her. While Sandra left for her bedroom to pack, Elena entered the nursery and stood before the crib where Evita, her hands in front of her face, played with her fingers. On seeing her mother the child raised her arms and arched upward, as if asking to be picked up. Elena took the baby in her arms, kissing her face tenderly, and then changed her diaper.

When she was sure Roberto had locked himself in his office, she carried Evita in her arms and marched on to see Sandra. She found her packing her bags, tears running down her cheeks.

"What's going to happen to you, Elena?" Sandra asked between sobs.

"I'll survive, but I'm worried about you, my friend. Nothing I say or do is going to persuade Roberto to change his mind—he's furious beyond words."

"I know! He must feel betrayed, as you felt when he lied to you, remember?"

"But I forgave him . . ."

"With time, he will forgive you, too."

Elena released a deep sigh. "I don't know about that. His big ego has been terribly wounded." She placed Evita on the bed. "Oh, God, what I'm going to do now?" lamented Sandra, sitting on the suitcase to force it closed. "I should wait at the airport tonight. It's safe there."

"Out of the question."

"But, Elena, I have to get out of this house, and I don't have enough money for a hotel after my trip today." Sandra dried her tears, but in vain.

"Yes, I know! Here is what you will do. Go to see Marcia and Armand, tell them what happened, and spend the night there. Armand can make your flight reservation. They will take care of you."

"What about my return ticket?"

"Once you're ready to leave, and with your suit case in hand, ask Roberto for it. He is sending you away; he will have no other choice but to give it to you."

"I'm so sad, and so sorry things have to end this way!" Hugging Elena, Sandra said with a broken voice, "Please, let's keep in touch, *si*?"

Elena hid her grief. She swallowed hard to hold back the tears screaming to get out. "But of course!" she said, returning the embrace. And listen, once in *Habana* go to see Doña Pilar. I'm sure she'll find another job for you, so you can come back soon."

"I'll do that as soon as I arrive," said Sandra with a little spark in her eyes.

Then Sandra lifted Evita, took the child in her arms and hugged her tightly to her chest for a while, then kissed her cheeks, wetting the baby's face with her tears. "I'll miss you, *mi niña adorada*."

Some time later, Elena heard Sandra knocking at the door to Roberto's office. She slipped down the hallway in order to hear well. Finally, he opened the door.

"Señor Roberto, I'm sorry for . . ."

"Spare me!" he said rudely, and handled Sandra two envelopes. "Here's your return ticket and some money to arrange your journey back home any way you like. Since now you are an independent woman . . . you'll know what to do." He shut the door in her face.

Things were done the way Elena planned. Marcia informed Elena that Armand took Sandra to the airport and saw her leave without incident.

The day after the fight Roberto left the house with a piece of luggage and his brief case. Elena let two days pass and then called the office. She was told that Señor Carvajal had called from Greece to advise them that he was taking some time off. He left a message for Elena: if she needed anything, call the office.

CHAPTER XXI

Decisions

A week went by, lonely days filled with uncertainty. Elena shared her feelings with Evita to break the silence, and tried to keep her sanity. She didn't want to speculate about Roberto's reasons for leaving them behind without saying where he was going, without so much as a goodbye. She wanted to see things objectively, and struggled to be fair.

Tired of being cooped up in the house, one day she took Evita for a stroll in the park, defying Roberto's order. But, why not? He wasn't there to stop them. After pushing the carriage for a while along the park, she sat on a bench and directed her thoughts to her little girl.

Dear child, I'm sorry that your Dad is away from us. Now I know I shouldn't have gone against his wishes. But, gosh, I would have felt terrible if Sandra went back to Cuba without visiting some of the wonderful things New York is known for. I felt strongly about that.

On the other hand, now I feel very sad without Sandra and without your daddy. But you know, honey, I never expected such a strong reaction from your Dad. I never expected to lose Sandra and your father at the same time. But he has been cruel, punishing us this way. Yes my darling, he's punishing you too, when you have nothing to do with this quarrel. It's cowardly and selfish of him to act like this.

If he loves you as much as he says he does, why did he leave you behind? He accused me of being irresponsible. If he is the responsible one in our family, then he should stay close to protect you from what he called my irresponsibility. Right now he doesn't know how you are doing, or what could be happening to you. Not even a call to find out if we are still alive. If I were to follow my instincts, I would go somewhere, so he would find an empty house whenever he decides to come back. But I cannot do that to you, my precious baby. I will never lift a finger to hurt you, no matter what. Not even if my emotions are trampled. Not until you grow up and can understand.

With both Roberto and Sandra gone, Evita had been acting nervously, waking up during the night and wetting her diapers more often. Was it possible that the child sensed something was wrong? It wasn't fair that so early in life she was paying for the sins of her parents.

After their trip to the park, Evita slept throughout the night, which allowed Elena to sleep also. From that day on, Elena took the baby out everyday with the same results.

One morning, when ready to leave for their stroll in the park, a messenger delivered a telegram from Greece. Elena was flabbergasted; Roberto would arrive in two days. She felt happy he was alive and well, but the thought that he was capable of leaving his family behind in a strange country only to escape a crisis, made her mad.

He'd blown everything out of proportion. She'd only kept from him what Evita's nanny was doing. It was not as if his wife were cheating on him with a lover, or anything like that.

She took Evita from the carriage and held her up in the air, their faces touching. The child displayed a cute toothless smile. "My darling Evita," she blurted out with relief, "your father is coming back. I'm so happy! He didn't abandon us after all!"

Later on, when pushing the carriage around the park, her euphoria dimmed. What if Roberto is coming back to take his things out of the house? Maybe he decided on a separation, still worse, a divorce? But, no, surely he wouldn't do that to Evita.

Elena strolled through the park; her mind full of ambivalent feelings and clashing thoughts. Once back home, she counted anxiously the hours that separated her from her difficult husband.

Finally Roberto arrived. The couple locked eyes for a moment; he hugged his wife without emotion, gave her a perfunctory kiss on the cheek, and went straight to the nursery to rinse his hands with alcohol. Though Evita was napping, he picked her up avidly.

"My beloved baby," he said, "I can't tell you how much I missed you!" He kissed her face, her head, and her hands.

He ambled carefully to the living room where he placed Evita in her carriage and then he opened his luggage. "Look, *preciosa*, do you think this will fit you?" He showed her a navy blue dress followed by a display of little outfits and a brightly colored embroidered dress. Then he pulled out a bathrobe. "Maybe this is too big now, but soon it will fit you. But look, this coat is size two . . . not too long to wait." Then he took out a doll and a few more toys.

Elena approached them. "Roberto, Evita will enjoy everything, thanks." She paused for a moment. "Please, will you tell me just why you took off the way you did?"

He looked into her eyes. "So I wouldn't loose control and hurt you!"

"It wasn't like I was unfaithful."

"I would have killed you for that!"

"I hope you think of your daughter before . . ."

"This isn't the time to talk."

"Then, when?"

"Tonight."

For a moment she had thought that after seeing Evita, Roberto was going to leave. She asked, just to make sure, "Are you staying for dinner?"

"Of course."

By the evening Evita had her bath and soon after fell asleep. Elena and Roberto ate dinner in silence. Afterwards Elena cleaned up the kitchen while Roberto unpacked. Deliberately, she postponed the moment to face Roberto by lingering in the kitchen longer than was necessary. He had showed indifference towards her, but displayed the best of dispositions with Evita. The baby seemed happy with all the attention her father poured on her, and when tickled, she laughed loudly.

Though Elena loved the happy scene between Evita and her Dad, it was bittersweet, as she foresaw no future as a family. To be alone with her husband gave her the shivers . . . She always had hated arguments, but tonight she would not take his bullying, nor his criticism.

Finally, Roberto entered his office. Not long after, Elena followed him. He was at the desk sorting papers.

"Come in. Sit down, please." She sat and he did the same across from her. "Sorry, Elena, I didn't bring you any souvenir this time."

He didn't sound apologetic.

"I wasn't expecting any."

"Good! Let's talk." He scowled and coughed a little. "I left after what you did to me to meditate and clear my mind. I was very angry and capable to do something I'm

215

sure I would have regretted. I talked to God and prayed a lot. Now I can be objective and we can talk." He cleared his throat. "What do you have to say?"

I'm not going to apologize, if that's what you expect, she thought, then asked, "Do you want to hear my side of the story?"

"I know what happened, but go ahead . . ."

"Promise you won't stop me, even if my version doesn't match yours."

"Oh, we have two versions?" he asked, with a half smile.

"All stories do."

"Okay, I promise not to interrupt."

"Then I'll get to the point." She sighed deeply. "Remember how I nagged you about Sandra? I felt terrible that day in and day out she remained locked in this house when there was so much for her to discover and see. This might have been the only time in her life that she could visit New York. Yet she couldn't even go out to the park? She was treated like a slave?"

"Sandra came to work. She wasn't here on vacation and I paid her very well."

"You are right . . . But Sandra is a childless single woman. She worked for us, and by law she was entitled to a weekly day off."

"We treated her like a member of our family," he interjected.

"Then, it would have been better to treat her as an employee and let her have a day off to do as she pleased."

"It is impossible to reason with you," he said losing patience.

"You promised to hear me without interruption."

He scratched his head. "Sorry! Go on."

"You forced me to lie . . ."

"What? What?" he shouted.

"Please, Roberto, control yourself. Use your objectivity. It has cost you a lot of money, a cruise, and two weeks without your family."

"For me it was a sacrifice to leave everything behind in order to cool off and, all alone, thinking about the future of our family."

Pobrecito, all the way to Greece to be alone! Why didn't you choose any city around the US?

"Explain yourself. How is it that I forced you to lie?"

"Since we weren't able to show Sandra a little of New York before she left for Cuba, I asked you to send her on a tour. You wouldn't hear of it—I was compelled to act on my own and keep it from you. Respecting your wishes of not seeing Vilma and Benny ever again, I didn't ask them to take Sandra, which would have been the thing to do. I didn't take her myself either, that would have been an affront to you. But because I am a resourceful person who can think for herself, I found a way for Sandra to see New York without hurting anybody."

"So, you risked our future?"

"I didn't think our future was at risk. I never imagined it would provoke such uncontrollable rage in you."

"You know I hate lies," he interrupted angrily.

"Yes, but you have lied to me! Let me remind you. You kept your religion from me for a very long time, and that's a lie. In the end I forgave you."

The veins on his forehead swelled. He became crimson. He slapped the arm of the chair and said in a low voice, "You're right! Thanks for reminding me. I remember how much I had to beg your forgiveness." Grinding his teeth, he added, "Now it's your turn to apologize."

She fixed her eyes on his. "Will you please, Roberto, forgive me for lying to you?" Then, she averted her gaze. "I should have fought for Sandra openly no matter the consequences. Instead, I wanted to keep peace in the household at any cost."

"You can see that it was a temporary peace."

"I know that now."

"Very well. I accept your apology. I would like to negotiate some points . . . Please, will you open your mind, listen to me and bring out your best disposition . . ." He slowly ran his fingers through his hair, and then said with a spark of kindness in his eyes, "I love you more than I'd like to admit, and I would like more than anything else for us to be a happy family."

He stood up and went for a glass of water, sipped from it and sat in the chair again.

Elena didn't know what to make of the change of heart in Roberto. His conciliatory tone confused her. Would it be possible that he wanted to change? Maybe he was changing already. Oh, she'd recite the rosary twenty times if he did!

"We all grow up with a dream," he went on. "At least I did! But, given my Latin background and growing up surrounded by the Arab culture, unfortunately, those ways crept up. My concept of women is that they are there to please their man, and follow orders graciously, with love."

Elena cringed. How silly to think he wanted to change! "You also grew up in the US. Did any of this culture creep up on you?"

"Of course, that's why I make concessions."

"To me you sound apologetic. Is that, by any chance, one of your concessions?"

He smiled mischievously. "No interruptions . . . Remember?"

"Sorry."

"During my youth I was like a blacksmith, forging in my mind the image of the woman I wanted." He seemed to be faraway, absorbed by memories. "I searched for an ideal wife to form a family. That's why I never took Gina seriously, or any of the gorgeous women before her. They were just too independent . . . impossible to mold. Then you came along, fitting every one of my expectations and I fell at your feet. You were beautiful, sweet, naïve but clever, moldable, a romantic dreamer, warm, respectful of family ties, a caring daughter . . ."

Elena burst into spontaneous laughter. "Stop! With all those qualities I surpassed your expectations. Right?"

Roberto was silent for a while, staring at her with eyes full of love, but a sad expression covered his face. Then he said dreamily, "It's a shame, *mi Elenita*, that your passion for independence is in the way of what could be a happy marriage and memorable love."

"What is a "happy marriage" to you?"

"To have a loving and trusting wife who complies with her husband's wishes."

"Then what you want is a servant not a wife." She sighed. "Contrary to what you want, I want a husband to support my hunger for knowledge and self-reliance. While you want to be obeyed, I'm longing for equality."

"Men and women can't be equals," he said with authority.

"We are equals," she retorted.

Roberto rolled his eyes and let it pass.

"I don't object to you learning all you want," he went on. "I praise that you have confidence in yourself. You'll instill that in our children. My darling Elena, you're very young and there is a lot of time ahead of you to achieve what you want. But, for now, your future should be dedicated to our child, and later to all that will follow.

He paced the room a little and came back to the chair.

"Each group, each institution, is led by one person. In a home the leader is the husband; only one ruler. If two captains steered a boat, the boat would sink. I am the captain in our family. Two heads and one goal is what makes a sound, strong, and healthy family."

Elena understood Roberto's goal, but his dreams didn't match hers. If he would agree to steer the boat together, she might, maybe, consider it. But to have a lot of children and become one of them was out of the question. Not negotiable.

Roberto's monologue went on and on. The fact that some arguments sounded reasonable and others farfetched made Elena's doubts worse. She wanted to scream, ask him to be quiet for a moment; anxiety was draining her. She needed to put an end to his charade.

Finally, she got to her feet. "Roberto, I'm very tired. Could we continue with this tomorrow, please?"

He stood in front of her, staring at her roguishly.

"Darling Elenita," he said softly. "For me it is a torment to see you so close, and feel as if you were miles away." He held her arms with concern, and pleaded, "May I stay in your room?"

"Of course. I'll stay in the guest room."

"Don't play games with me, *mi querida*. I'm crazy about you."

"Roberto, now that I don't have any help with Evita, I'm exhausted. I prefer to rest alone."

"I promise I won't touch you."

"That's a tale that not even you believe. Good night."

"I swear I only want to feel you are near me."

"See you tomorrow." She smiled, and left the room.

CHAPTER XXII

Your Adoring Husband

Next morning, Elena woke up early. Roberto had already left the guest room, and Evita was still asleep, the house was quite. Around midmorning three-dozen red roses arrived. The card read: *Your adoring husband.*

"Roberto, why are you doing this to me?" Elena's words resounded around the house. She sat in the anteroom and stayed there for long time, thinking about what to do, aware of how much depended on her decision. To sleep with Roberto tonight would be like giving up any possibility of change, and continue submissively the way women in her generation always had.

Elena knew this was, perhaps, her only opportunity to pressure Roberto to a change. She also knew that she had to play clever and be subtle in order to get him to be more flexible and less chauvinistic. The fact that Evita had not been baptized preoccupied her, the fact that she was not allowed to go to mass bothered her and the silly idea to wait a year before taking Evita out annoyed her beyond words. Could she play games with him before having sex and coax him into complying with her needs? She would try tonight.

She went to the kitchen and placed the flowers in a vase with water, and took the chicken out from the fridge. Then she heard Evita. The baby was used to getting attention right away, so after cooing and talking to herself for a while, she burst out crying to let mommy know she was hungry.

Elena, as well as Evita, missed Sandra immensely. Everything was easier when the nanny was here. She hoped the baby wouldn't spoil tonight's plan. "*Bebita, por favor,* behave and don't disturb us tonight," she said, wishing Evita could understand.

In the evening, Elena was setting the table, the roses as centerpiece, when Roberto arrived with a bottle of champagne. He placed the bottle on the table, and embraced her.

"This is to celebrate our love and another beginning on our life."

What on earth is he talking about? We haven't made up yet. Oh, God! Why he has to look so appealing and handsome, making it harder for me to remain indifferent.

"But we still have a lot of things to discuss before we kiss and make up." She tried to sound stern.

"Darling wife, don't you know that love conquers all? The hardest thing to find is real love. Let's be grateful to God and don't take it for granted."

"But, I want you to understand my . . ."

"*Mi mujercita preciosa,*" he said, lifting her up in the air. "I don't think anyone could love more than I'm loving you right now." He took her face in his hands and looked into her eyes—then kissed her neck. It tickled, and she burst into giggles.

Right away she was disgusted with herself for falling, once more, into Roberto's manipulations.

He opened the champagne and they toasted. Then, teasing and giggling, he carried her in his arms to the bedroom. They made fulfilling love, unloading the accumulated passion held for so long.

Evita woke up and they left the bed to attend their baby. After the evening bath, Elena placed her *bebita* in the playpen while they dined. They had an enjoyable evening, amused by the gurgling and chattering of their offspring. Much to her chagrin, Elena felt her heart bursting with love and happiness. Blinded by love, she had melted under the heat of Roberto's charm and surrendered to his passion. That very night, again and again, they entwined their hungry bodies transcending to one soul.

Friday evening Roberto showed up accompanied by a middle-aged nurse-aid.

"This is Alice. Alice, this is Elena, my wife."

They shook hands and sat in the living room, Roberto next to his wife.

"Darling," he said. "Alice is staying with us for the week-end."

"How come?"

"Because I'm taking you to dinner on Sunday: I would like Alice to stay with Evita."

Elena eyed Alice and then the overnight case sitting by the woman. "But, we don't need her until Sunday?"

"I want Evita to get used to her. And you would have time to make sure they get along." He squeezed her hands tenderly, and gazed at her. "Do you think it might work?"

"It might . . . if I ever recuperate from the shock."

During the weekend Roberto watched Alice like a hawk. Elena felt embarrassed.

Finally, she called his attention. "*Mi amor*, Alice knows what she's doing. Leave her alone."

"It's fine, Mrs. Carvajal. I'm good with babies, no matter who's watching."

When Sunday arrived, Elena inquired, "How should I dress for this dinner party?"

"Casual. We're going to the airport."

"What for?"

"To pick up a client."

"Do you need me for that?"

"I think so. He's traveling with his wife. We'll take them to dinner."

"How old are they?"

"You ask too many questions, dear," he laughed playfully. "Wait and find out yourself. Agreed, Mrs. Carvajal?"

They left for the airport. To her amazement, as soon as they left the house Elena found herself painfully missing her little one. Now she was the one full of apprehensions for leaving Evita with a perfect stranger, even though Roberto had the best of recommendations from the hospital where Alice worked. Life was funny. She was sure that if Roberto had not imposed his rules so forcefully, she herself would have followed them naturally; with the exception, of course, of wearing the silly masks, the rinsing hands with alcohol, and going to the park.

Driving through the tunnel connecting New Jersey with the Port Authority, Elena heard herself saying, "*Por favor* dear, take me back home."

"What?"

"I can't bear to leave our baby."

Roberto almost stopped the car right there; his eyes wide. As soon as the traffic allowed, he made the turn and drove back. Once at the house, he leaped from the car, helped her out and embraced her tightly.

"I thought I couldn't love you more, my darling Elenita. I adore you! I'll be back as soon as I can." He left her at the front door and took off.

She ran straight to the nursery. "My baby," she said, picking up Evita. "Here I am."

"Anything wrong, Mrs. Carvajal?"

"I'm sorry, Alice. Suddenly I felt I couldn't go anywhere without my daughter. I hope you don't mind. I swear it's nothing personal."

"It is okay with me. But it's strange . . . after spending the week-end training me, you decided . . ."

"Sorry! It's my first time leaving her. Well, I don't understand why. One thing is for sure, when I get over this, you will be the only person I trust with my baby."

"I appreciate you saying that! Call me whenever you need me."

Shortly before midnight, Roberto returned home and went directly to the bedroom.

"Roberto, you are back. I didn't expect you so early."

He kissed her. "Is that why you are all bundled up already?" He paused for a moment, staring at her. "Sweetheart, please, come downstairs with me. We have a guest."

"What?"

"I have a surprise for you."

"I love surprises. I'll get dressed," she said getting up.

"A robe is enough."

What's going on here? A surprise? Maybe his mother? Mine?

The couple hurried to the living room where Elena met a smiling Sandra, who sprang up from a chair and hugged Elena. They embraced for a long time.

"Roberto, you were right. This is indeed a surprise! How on earth did all of this happen?"

"I realized how valuable Sandra was to our family, so I placed a call to Cuba and apologized." Softly, he patted Sandra's back. "She agreed to come back, and here she is."

"Sandra, I'm so happy to see you."

"So am I. How's Evita?"

"She's fine . . . except for missing you a lot!"

Uneventful weeks went by. With Sandra's help, Elena wasn't tired, but animated and in good humor. Roberto gave Sandra Sundays off to go to church and use the day as she liked. The ambience was agreeable and he found the peace of mind he longed for.

One evening he arrived home excited by some news he wanted to share with his wife. After he played with Evita a bit, he turned to Elena.

"I want to tell you what happened in the office today." He held her chin with his fingers. "In a way it concerns you."

"I like that!"

They sat on the back porch, sipping tomato juice.

"I am all ears," Elena said, unable to hold her curiosity.

"Well, this afternoon I had a visit from a young Cuban couple, friends of *Doña* Pilar."

"I wonder why she didn't tell me anything."

"Well, this wasn't a social visit."

"Business?"

"It might be. It seems that a revolutionary group in the mountains of *Oriente* is working to overthrow *Batista* from power. Apparently they know, from good sources, that a revolution is breeding, so he is withdrawing his money little by little and sending it to Switzerland. In the meantime they need some kind of business arrangement in order to stay in the US. Doña Pilar wants me to advise them."

"What can you do?"

"He is a known accountant in *Habana*, but his English isn't very good. It would be hard for him to find a job in the States. He can help me here or in Spain," he said, thoughtfully. "Or we can become partners . . . we'll see."

"I'm happy you can do something for Doña Pilar."

"I'll benefit too." He paused. "They're lonely; they miss Cuba and their family. I invited them for dinner tomorrow. Is this okay with you?"

"Anything for Doña Pilar's friends."

CHAPTER XXIII

Maritza And Daniel

The next evening, the guests arrived at seven with two bottles of wine and a box of chocolates. After the greetings they were introduced to Evita. Roberto asked, with the best of his charm, that please rinse their hands with alcohol, which the guests complied, grinning.

A Caribbean dinner was served to please the couple, who missed the cuisine of their country. The guests were appreciative of the menu: the spice *picadillo* with a hint of sweet; *arroz blanco y platanos fritos,* and a salad of beautiful, fresh tomatoes tossed with small pieces of purple onion and cilantro. They had *natilla* for dessert, an old favorite of Elena's. To top it off, dessert and after-dinner drinks were served in the living room along with espresso.

Maritza was twenty-six and Esteban thirty-three. She had large; almond shaped black eyes and was high-spirited. She laughed a lot and when she turned her head lush dark hair bounced. Tall and fit, Esteban Martinez had short, curly, chestnut hair and light brown eyes. Good looking, well educated and talkative, he held the floor longer than he should.

They got along well and felt as if they had known each other forever. At first the conversation revolved around prominent names of Cuban aristocracy, friends of the

Martinez's, who like them, were taking their money out of the country, anticipating an imminent revolution. Elena was a little embarrassed because she only knew these names from Cuba's social pages in the newspapers, so she couldn't share any mutual experiences.

To her relief, they changed topic. Maritza spoke about Doña Pilar and her family, Elena fully involved herself in the conversation, giving free reign to her memories, reliving her friendship with Doña Pilar. Elena told many stories about the woman's well-kept secret acts of philanthropy, some of which she had witnessed.

All in all, Elena had the best of times with her newly acquired friends. She enjoyed seeing her charismatic husband toasting, chatting and telling jokes, making everyone laugh. *This was the Roberto she loved and admired.*

At one point Esteban asked to see Elena's four karat, blue diamond ring. She took it off and handed it to him. After admiring it from all angles, Esteban returned it saying, "It matches your beauty."

Elena thanked him and extended her hand in a clear sign for him to place the ring upon her finger, which he did.

Roberto's change of attitude was immediate. He stood up and gripped the back of the armchair. His eyes full of fire, he said, curtly, "All of a sudden I don't feel well. Good night!"

He left the room with a stern face. Elena froze. Angry, she didn't know what to say or do. How could he act like that? What kind of moron was he?

Esteban followed Roberto's act of rudeness by asking to use the phone. He pulled out a card from his pocket and dialed a number from the taxi company that had brought them to the house earlier. He procured their jackets, kissed

Elena's cheeks lightly and walked towards the front door, refusing politely Elena's invitation to wait for the cab inside. Maritza hugged Elena, thanked her for the dinner and followed her husband out of the door.

Elena bolted into Roberto's studio without knocking. She found him sitting in front of his desk with his head resting in his hands. He didn't move. She waited a moment, and then shouted, "What got into you to make you behave like a lunatic?"

He leaped from the desk chair and shook her shoulders. "Don't play dumb with me!"

"Let go of me! What the devil's wrong with you?"

"As if you don't know!"

"No. I don't know!"

"So, flirting is your natural state, then?"

"What are you talking about?"

"You were flirting with that conceited bastard! You gave in into his flattery and asked him to put the ring on your finger . . . as if asking him to take you to bed!"

"Stop! You must be mad! Crazy!"

"If you call me crazy again, I swear we will both be sorry!"

"What the hell did I do?"

"You didn't respect me, or Maritza. You and that son-of-a-bitch carried on right in front of my nose."

"My God! You're blinded by jealousy. When you cool off, we'll talk."

Elena scampered off toward the door. Roberto grabbed her hair and flung her onto a chair. "Ouch . . . ! Beast!" she complained.

"We'll talk right now!" he ordered.

"Okay! Explain! What's eating you?"

He sat on the edge of the desk, close to her. "Be grateful that I was able to restrain the impulse to throw that jerk out of my house!"

Exasperated, Elena asked, "For Christ's sake, what on earth made you think we were flirting?"

"When he said that the diamond matched your beauty, you melted. Your eyes sparkled and the coquette in you surfaced."

"Unless you explain yourself, I don't know what you're talking about."

"Don't tell me you're that naïve!"

"Naïve, stupid, whatever you want to call it; what the devil is on your mind?"

He stood in front of her and pressed a finger at her forehead, his eyes spitting hate.

"Hell, Elena, when you are married, the ring on your finger is a symbol of union—the woman surrenders to her man." Roberto slammed the desk. "You understand now what you did, damn you?"

Elena was stunned. She has never heard of this. Could it be possible? It made sense, though. All of the sudden she was ashamed of herself and thought of Maritza. What kind of impression had she given the woman? *Oh, God, have I misled Esteban?*

She heard Roberto ask, "You have nothing to say?"

"Oh, yes! If what you say is true . . ." She thought for a moment. "I should apologize to these people."

"You really didn't know?"

"Of course not! Still, your lack of trust in me infuriates me." She paced the room and Roberto sat behind the desk, obviously relieved that Elena hadn't acted on bad faith.

"Damn you, Roberto!" she went on. "You should have told me instead of chastising me like a child."

"I never knew you were that ignorant."

"I'd rather be thought of as ignorant than a cheat."

"You have a lot to learn yet." He began sorting papers, dismissing her.

"Good night," Elena said harshly, and walked away.

"I'll follow you in a bit," he answered.

Elena stepped into her bedroom, lost in a sea of contradictory feelings. How could she have been so careless? If she had thought about it before acting, she'd have remembered that a lady does not behave that way. It was definitely inappropriate, at least childish. She covered her face with her hands as if shutting from her mind the image of herself extending a hand for Esteban to do what he did. Why didn't she show the damn ring to him without taking it off? Well, *nobleza obliga*. She was wrong, and she could apologize to Roberto, even if he had blown things out of proportion, again.

When he emerged from the office some time later, Elena was already in bed. She sat up.

"I have given a lot of thought to this embarrassing incident," she prompted with great effort. "I don't understand how I can be . . . well . . . so careless?"

"As long as you acknowledge it . . . I'm sure you won't do it again," he said, but he didn't show much conviction.

"If you know me you know that I never would do anything to shame you." She was silent for a few moments. "People don't cheat in front of their spouses," she said, almost to herself.

He undressed and went to bed quietly, keeping his thoughts to himself.

In the days to come, they ignored their wrangle and soon it became history.

Several weeks passed.

One day the phone rang and Sandra answered. She summoned Elena and announced that Maritza was on the line.

"What does she want?"

"She didn't say."

Elena answered, and after the preliminary pleasantries, Maritza invited the couple for dinner at their new house, which they had rented furnished two weeks earlier.

"Thank you Maritza, I'll talk to Roberto and let you know."

"They're talking in Roberto's office right now."

"How come?" asked Elena surprised.

"Roberto invited Esteban to his office. After two hours, Esteban called me. They both had agreed to dine at our home any day and time you choose. Now you and I are to set the date. Is tomorrow good for you?"

"We can't leave Evita."

"Roberto said Evita and Sandra would come along."

Was Roberto breaking his own rule of not taking their daughter out until she was one year old?

"Is that so . . ."

Maritza and Elena chatted for a while. Still Elena couldn't make up her mind, so she promised to call back once her decision was made.

On his arrival home that evening, Roberto explained to his wife the events of the day. It so happened that Señor Orlando Morales, Doña Pilar's husband, called from Cuba with a great idea for a business. He wanted Roberto and Esteban together, so they could discuss the details.

"Do you see, that's why I asked Esteban to come to the office. '*Borrón y cuenta nueva*' Esteban said, so we started on a clean slate."

"Very interesting . . ."

"Mr. Morales, Esteban and I agreed that this was the perfect time to take all their money out of Cuba."

Obviously Roberto was teeming with new ideas. His optimism overwhelmed him. He wanted to keep growing, and the faster, the better. He put aside his principles in lieu of the possibility for greater gain. Elena was disappointed to note that once again, her husband was not true to his ethics. Some days ago he considered Esteban despicable for flirting with her. Although he thought Elena partially to blame, he excused her naïveté. What excuse did he have for Esteban? Now her husband easily overlooked what he had taken as an insult. Elena began to doubt her husband's integrity.

Roberto interrupted her ponderings. "Since you need a little help to decide, we will go to dinner tomorrow."

"What about Evita?"

"The whole family is going. We'll all enjoy that."

"I'm not sure. Don't you mind breaking your own rules?"

He smiled mischievously and held her chin with two fingers.

"Rules are made to be broken, dear wife."

"You're disappointing me, dear husband."

"As I've told you . . ." He reached for her head and then caressed her hair, tenderly. "Darling, you still have a lot to learn. I want to create an empire for my family," he said, emphatically.

"I don't like what I'm learning here. I'd rather learn integrity from you."

"That's fine, Elenita. But when you see the results, I will be your champion . . . mark my words."

"I'm so confused! Do you remember the saying 'do as I say, not as I do'?"

He stared at her intently for seconds. "I'm only doing this for you . . ."

"Please, spare me! I don't buy that."

"Because Doña Pilar is your dear friend, I accepted this business with her husband and Esteban."

To avoid a quarrel, Elena bit her lip and said sarcastically, "Whatever—you're always sooo generous. Thank you, in Doña Pilar's name and mine."

"I don't appreciate your sarcasm . . . What's wrong with you?"

"Nothing, Roberto. Forget it."

CHAPTER XXIV

Dinner

The dinner party went well. Esteban hired a chef, who ran things smoothly. The food was superb and the ambience friendly. While they ate, Sandra took Evita to the solarium, where they played with the tons of toys they brought from home.

They had dessert in the solarium and they chatted and played with Evita. To Elena's awe, Roberto dispensed with his ritual of hand sterilization and acted almost like a normal father, though he still fussed over his child.

The men excused themselves and went to discuss business in the privacy of the *biblioteca*. Maritza and Elena remained in the solarium with Sandra and the baby. They listened to music, and Maritza showed albums of the family's pictures. The time passed quickly, and Elena began to worry. It was getting late. Close to midnight, she went to look for her husband.

She knocked on the door and Esteban called out, "Come in, please."

She opened the door a little and saw a huge desk, the top covered with all kind of papers, scattered around.

"Excuse me," she said, stepping in. "Roberto, it's long pass Evita's bedtime."

"Oh, *mi querida*, I'm so sorry." Roberto slapped the side of his head lightly. "We lost our sense of time." He stood by her, and held her chin. "We're leaving at once. Go on, get ready."

"We're ready."

"Did Evita eat?"

"Of course, we came prepared."

They gathered their things and Elena kissed the hostess' cheek. Roberto carried sleepy Evita to the car and effusively thanked the couple before hitting the road. Once on the way, Roberto explained to Elena the bright future that lay before them. For business purpose they had lined up a trip to Spain and another one to Mexico.

"Who's going, you or Esteban?"

"The first trip I'm going alone, sort of preparing the way."

"Thank God Sandra's here."

"Honey, while I'm away, no outing. I don't want the baby leaving the house. You either. Do you hear?"

Again with that! Aloud, she said, "We need to discuss that."

"It's not negotiable. While I'm away, you will respect my rules."

"You're the one breaking the rules! You even forgot your baby's bedtime."

"Please, Elena, don't rain on my parade. I'm very happy with the great business' deal I've landed. I need absolute peace of mind to multiply my money, as well as Esteban's and *Señor* Morales's. I need your help."

Discouraged, Elena didn't know what to say. She didn't know if she should insist, or humor him. Evita gave signs of waking up. Elena turned her head to watch, and smiled at the way Sandra talked and hummed to the baby. She really appreciated Sandra.

"When are you planning on traveling?" she asked.

"Very soon. Why do you ask?"

She was pensive. Maybe it would be better to speak her mind now, while he was in a good mood. So, she spoke.

"The thing is that I don't want to be cooped up in the house waiting for your return."

"Elena, please! I'm not going to be gone forever." He slapped the wheel and said impatiently, "Now, will you please let me drive in peace?"

"Then we'll talk at home."

"No. It's too late and I need a clear head to think about this big business. Our future is more important than worrying because you don't want stay at home."

I'll let it pass for now, Mr. Dictator, but we'll talk before you leave.

During the following days, before his departure, Roberto was so busy that Elena saw very little of him. Then, the night before his trip, after passionate lovemaking, she spoke out about what has been on her mind for many days.

"Roberto, *mi amor*, let's talk about our situation."

He smiled. "What do you mean *our situation*?"

She laid on top of him, smiling provocatively, a gratifying gaze in her eyes. Their faces were very close.

"Yes, now that you're leaving we need to agree on something," she said brushing his nose against hers.

"Agree on what?"

"While you're away, I'd like to take Evita to the park once in a while, weather permitting, of course."

His expression changed radically, and he pushed her off to the side. "Elena, for heaven's sake, I thought it was clear I need my piece of mind . . ."

"What about mine, eh?"

"I carry the full responsibility of our family so you can go through life without worries. Doesn't that give you peace?"

"It's not enough; I need to feel free . . ."

"Free to do what, woman?"

"To go out of the house. To go grocery shopping, to the park, to breathe fresh air . . ."

"Go outside your house for fresh air, swim, get a suntan, order the groceries by phone and leave me alone to do my job!"

He got out of bed, clearly angered by her rebellion.

"Don't do that to us, Roberto," she pleaded.

"Do what? How dare you! You're the one ruining our lives with your obsession for freedom. Why can't you wait in the house until my return?"

"At least tell me why?"

"I panic to think my family may be in danger, outside in public."

"What can happen to us?"

"A kidnapping. An accident. Germs!"

"A deadly accident could happen in our pool; and Evita could be kidnapped from her own room. It happened to Lindbergh's child, kidnapped from his room . . ."

"You're irresponsible beyond words. I'm leaving tomorrow and you are putting ill-fated ideas in my head. Are you senseless? Can you not learn?"

"I want you to be aware that accidents happen anywhere: sitting in the living room, sleeping in your own bed. I believe in destiny."

"The only thing you should believe in is giving support to your husband, who's risking everything in life for his family."

Furious, he stomped out to the bathroom.

I'm so frustrated; I want to shout at him: "Go to Hell, bastard!" But, I can't do that when he's about to fly so faraway. What if the plane doesn't make it? I won't be able to forgive myself. She counted to ten before following him to the bathroom. She knocked on the door.

"Roberto, let's talk."

"Talk! I'm listening."

"I want to apologize. I don't want you to go away like this." She tried to sound cordial. She hid her wishes to slap his face.

He opened the door and confronted her. "Like what?"

"Mad at me. I want you to concentrate only on your business. We'll be all right here."

"If my mother knew about your behavior, for sure she wouldn't like you as much as she does."

"Your mother's fair, she would understand my point. She would be on my side, if you told things as they really are."

"I'll never understand you. A second ago you sounded apologetic and now you're ready to fight again."

"Sorry. My only wish is to send you off knowing that Evita and I will stay right at home waiting for you."

He let go a deep loud sigh of relief, approached her and took her face in his hands. Gazing into her eyes, he said, "I don't know what I'm going to do with you, neither what would I do without you, darling." Then he placed her head against his chest and ran his fingers through her hair, twining a curl around his finger. "But I'd rather die to lose you."

Why can't I be happy with what I have, instead of dreaming of what I can't have? Why is independence so important to me?

She felt good resting her head on his burly chest, with his strong hands stroking her hair. She placed her arms around his neck and reached for his lips. The towel around his waist fell to the floor, and his manhood brushed her body. Both of them surrendered to the call of love and their bodies and souls transcended the earth, wrapped in sublime desire.

CHAPTER XXV

Change Of Conscience

The next day Roberto left for Spain. He called daily at different times, obviously checking on Elena. He was always in the best of moods because business went better than expected. For the moment, Elena placed her dreams of independence on hold and followed Roberto's wishes.

Meanwhile, Roberto was in Barcelona searching for a port of entry and an officer to take care of customs when the cargo arrived. The goods he took to Barcelona were illicit, so he needed an accomplice when the ship anchored. The purchase was made in the United States with money from Esteban and Señor Morales, his new associates. He exercised the utmost caution, knowing the price to pay for not following Spanish Dictator Francisco Franco's strict laws against smugglers.

But he was used to risk. During the Second World War, he defied death in daily air missions. He was luckier than most of his friend's who didn't return, a nightmare that never left him. After the war ended, he made most of his money by selling several diamond rocks from Amsterdam and smuggling pharmaceutical goods to Spain—never drugs. At that time he didn't value life, but now that he was in love and had a family, he was extremely careful. He'll stop at nothing to keep his family safe and happy.

The day after his arrival in Barcelona, Roberto had a lavish lunch with a customs officer. All went well and the man agreed to help. It would cost a small fortune but the arrangement covered several shipments. When they were done with lunch, each went their own way, rather than go home for a siesta. Roberto wanted to walk off the calories of rich food. He opted to walk along *Las Ramblas de las Flores*, his mind filled with grand thoughts. He was about to make a fortune and fulfill his dreams of helping the needy.

From three to six, Barcelona slept. The radio and the only television channel in the province played the national anthem at twelve and retired from the air for the whole afternoon. Stores closed and the streets were deserted—a dead city.

The picturesque sights, on a side street, attracted him. On the cobbled footpaths you could stretch out your arms and almost touch the buildings between. He had visited *Las Ramblas* often and never noticed this lovely hidden place.

He noticed a poster outside a small stone building announcing an old American movie, *Blossoms in the Dust*, starring Greer Carson and Walter Pigeon. Since it was a benefit to help orphan children the salon was open earlier. The matinee began at 5 pm and he was in time for the first show. It would have been nice to have Elena with him. She loved movies, and this one had great reviews. If the long distance calling booth hadn't been closed at the time, he would've called her. With his adorable Elena on his mind, he entered the *salon de fiesta*.

Roberto Carvajal never thought that a simple movie could influence his future the way that one did. It was the biography of Etna Gladney who fought all her life for abandoned orphans. She believed that there weren't illegitimate children but illegitimate fathers. She struggled against the court of Texas until finally the word "illegitimate" was banned from the birth certificate of newborn babies. There was a knot in his throat, and he fought tears all through the film.

Though Roberto didn't want to admit it, the hat of illegitimate father fit him perfectly. When the film was over, a nagging thought tormented him. Memories of the past overshadowed his happy present. He could no longer deny that in this part of the world he had an illegitimate daughter. As much as he hated the truth, he had to accept that he had fathered a bastard child. The thought of his fling with Anita had come back to haunt him. Was he ever going to do anything about it?

Once he took care of the most pressing part of business in Barcelona, he left his hotel and went to spend time with his mother Aisha and his Sister Ruth in Valencia, approximately one hundred sixty miles away.

They were thrilled to see him and it felt good to be at home. He enjoyed being the object of so much pampering. His mother's warmth and the cozy ambience brought to mind, again, his abandoned child. He kept thinking of the little girl he fathered, his own flesh and blood, and whom he had never met. Now he was in the same country as his little girl, and he didn't even know her name.

Selfishly, he had banned the fruit of his sin from his life, afraid to lose Elena. At the time, he thought it was enough to make arrangements with a bank in Madrid to provide money regularly for her support. Emilio, his mother's chauffeur, and his wife Marina, provided her a home. They'd tried to communicate with him when the baby was born, but Roberto had been adamant about not receiving any kind of news from what was his well-guarded secret nightmare.

On Saturday morning he turned down his mother's invitation to go to the synagogue. Instead, he decided to go to Emilio's house, determined to do something about his out-of-wedlock daughter. At ten o'clock in the morning he summoned a taxi.

Upon arriving at the house, he saw Anita sitting off in the courtyard scanning a magazine, while a small girl played under a leafy tree. His heart skipped a bit, as he realized that this could be his child. For a second he couldn't move. He felt terrible for not giving this innocent *niña* what all children deserve: their father's name.

Controlling the impulse to jump over the fence and run to meet his daughter, he nervously walked around to the front of the house and knocked on the front door. Marina opened it, and almost fainted at the sight of him.

"Señor Roberto, *que gusto verlo!*" she cried, extending her hand. "Come in."

Ignoring her hand, he instead hugged the hearty woman. "How are you*, mi querida* Marina?"

"Full of aches, as always." She signaled a chair and they sat across from each other."

"I'm sorry to hear that. We must do something about that."

"Don't worry. Mine is a lost case." She shrugged. "Anything to drink, *Señor* Roberto?" she asked, while taking off her brown apron.

"*Nada, gracias.*" He went straight to the point. "How's Anita doing with the baby?"

"*Por favor, Señor*, I prefer not to talk about that."

His eyes widened. "Isn't she a good mother?"

"She's lazy. She only looks after herself."

"Does she mistreat the baby?" he asked anxiously.

"Oh Jesus, no! I baptized that girl; I'm her second mother and take care that no harm comes to my godchild."

"Then what's the problem?"

"She's slovenly." Marina secured her chignon with a pin and went on. "As long as she lives here, I force her to look after my little Azucena."

"Azucena? It shows your love for her."

"Oh, si, yo la quiero mucho." The woman's eyes filled with tears. "Azucenita is pure, white and soft, just like the flower bearing her name. She's beautiful, and a good girl too."

Roberto leaped to his feet and reached for Marina's tough, calloused hand. "Take me to meet Azucena, *por favor.*"

Walking behind Marina, Roberto couldn't help but wonder about his sudden change of heart for the *muchachita* he abandoned before birth and the powerful message he got from the story of Edna Gladney. Now, an unknown three-year-old girl had him all stirred up. Was it really caring for his daughter, or was it a sense of guilt? He was on the way to find out.

Anita turned to look at them when they entered the courtyard. When she saw Roberto, she leaped from the chair and rushed toward him.

"Oh, Roberto, you came back to us," she exclaimed, reaching to caress his face.

Immediately he raised his hand to stop her. "Don't confuse things, woman. I'm here for my daughter," he said, dryly.

"Azucena, look who's here!" announced Marina, calling the little girl's attention. "*Tu papa!*"

Roberto stared in awe at Azucena. The little girl was a vision, the most beautiful child he had ever seen. Curly red hair framed the translucent skin of her angelic face. A turned-up nose made her look very cute, adorable. But Roberto was angered to see she was unkempt, dirty, and her nose running.

Next to him was Marina carrying the child in her arms. Roberto said *"Hola,"* and touched her uncombed hair softly. Azucena grabbed his wrist and clutched his forefinger in her little hand. He felt the tiny pressure right in his heart.

"Chatita, ese es tu papa," said Anita. "Give him a kiss."

The child pressed her face against his, leaving a sticky smear on his cheek.

"Take your daughter and wash her face and hands," he snapped.

Anita jumped in quickly, "If you had told me you were coming, I'd have prepared her." She took the little girl from Marina's arms. "After all, she's been playing with dirt." Then, as she walked away, her last words trailed. "It's normal for a child to be *sucia.*"

Mother and daughter disappeared from sight.

"Marina, let's go inside now; if you don't mind," said Roberto.

"Si. Vamos."

They walked back to the living room and renewed the conversation.

"I understand you now, Marina."

"What do you mean?"

"About Anita being careless with Azucena."

"I'm sorry! You let me know next time you want to see her. Azucenita will be spotless." She smoothed her skirt. "Sit down, please."

Roberto laid a hand on her shoulder. "Thanks. I'm leaving now."

"Please, wait to see *mi niña.*"

"I can't now, but I'll be back tomorrow. I want to talk with Emilio."

"At what time are you coming tomorrow?"

"Around six."

It was time to leave and Roberto left with more doubts than the ones he brought in with him. His main worry now was to face the fact that his daughter was a Christian. She had been baptized and Marina was the godmother. This, alone, was a problem; he shouldn't see Azucena again. He could fall hard for that adorable doll. It was, for sure, an easy task to fall for Azucena; he must avoid that.

Roberto replayed the scene on meeting his daughter. Azucena had gazed at him and smiled, showing cute dimples. And then, when he felt her tiny fingers wrapping around his, he could have fainted at that moment . . . he sensed a bond between them that he suspected would last forever. The thought of taking his daughter with him crossed his mind . . . but he couldn't hurt Anita by taking away Azucena from her. It would be so very nice if he could bring that cutie with him to the States. His heart ached—he was so confused!

That evening when Roberto arrived home, his mother intuited right away that something out of the ordinary had happened. As much as Aisha asked, he was loath to share his worries with her. To Aisha's and Ruth's chagrin, he had a glass of milk and went to bed without dinner. He didn't like the Spanish custom dinner at ten or eleven and bed long after midnight.

He called Elena first thing in the morning and was pleased to learn everything was fine at home. Elena was very sweet on the phone and told him how much she missed him. Evita was well, learning new things daily. The first tooth was breaking through the gum, making her sore and a bit cranky. As he hung up, he smiled and said to himself, "My baby's going through her first encounter with pain. I hope that's the only pain she'll ever experience."

Next day Roberto spoke with Emilio, as he wanted to know more about Anita and her role as a mother. For what Emilio told him, Roberto affirmed that the couple was crazy about Azucena. They wanted the little girl to grow up as a Catholic and took her to church every Sunday. They knew that Anita took advantage of the couple adoration for the girl, and threatened to move herself and Azucena out of their home at the most insignificant provocation.

"If she moves from your house I won't support her," Roberto said, firmly.

"She's under the impression that once she's out of my house she alone would manage the money we receive from you."

"Let her know right away that she's mistaken. Put an end to her extortion once and for all."

They spoke extensively and Roberto emphasized to Emilio that one of the reasons he had for not keeping a close relationship with his daughter was his religion.

"The child is lovable but she is a Christian, and you know I'm Jewish. Besides, I suspect that if I keep seeing her, I would love her to pieces. I don't want to do that; I respect my family in the States."

"I understand," Emilio said, dabbing his tired eyes with a handkerchief.

"I want a monthly report on how mother and daughter are doing . . . and pictures of the little girl as she grows up." Roberto reached into his pocket and removed his money clip, full of bulky Spanish bills. He extended a wad of money to Emilio. "Here's some extra money to buy a dress and a big, talking doll for Azucena."

There was a short pause, and then Emilio asked.

"Can I tell her it comes from you?"

"Yes. She should know that even though I don't see her, I do care and think of her."

CHAPTER XXVI

Ocean Liner

Elena welcomed Roberto, who joyfully arrived home laden with gifts. It was late evening and Evita was sleeping. He restrained his urge to take her in his arms; instead he kissed his finger and placed it gingerly on her forehead. Then he sent his thoughts to his little girl: *I'll play with you tomorrow and will make up for the time I was away.*

Exhausted from the long trip, Roberto went straight to bed. Followed by Elena. He ardently desired his wife, but thought of leaving lovemaking for the morning, when rested. Elena gave him a passionate, lingering kiss, then, with her fingers played around his hairy chest. He tried to stop her, but soon succumbed to her appeal and made love to her with all the passion accumulated during his absence. He felt whole and very happy to be back home in the amorous arms of an adorable wife. He totally concentrated on his present state of well-being. He tried to brush away from his mind any trace of the memory of his little daughter in Spain.

Many happy weeks reigned in the Carvajal household. Roberto was busy making money, very involved with his new partner Esteban, and both couples saw each other often. Stronger ties seemed to wrap tighter around the

Carvajal marriage. The past dark clouds hanging over their happiness seemed to be gone.

One evening Roberto arrived home dangling a brown envelope in the air. "Surprise, surprise," he chanted, then kissed his wife and placed the envelope in her hand. "Here are the tickets! We're going on vacation, my darling."

"What! When? Where?"

"On a Mediterranean cruise."

"How come?"

"It's a bridge tournament with important business men."

"Will the wives go also?"

"I don't know and I don't care as long as my family is with me."

The following days were a myriad of dreams for Elena. It was just one of her wishes to be aboard a luxurious ship. She took great care packing, not only her own luggage, but Evita's and Sandra's.

The cruise day arrived. Elena had the family looking their best in order to make her husband proud. Even though it was late September, the warm weather and the blue skies allowed her to wear her wide brimmed hat and her chic, simple summer lace dress. She wore inconspicuous jewelry and felt good about herself, fit to be among elegant ladies. Evita looked gorgeous in her pink, embroidered set of cotton dress and light coat. Sandra fitted the group as well and complemented the family.

When Roberto saw them exclaimed: "Whoa . . . You all look fabulous! I'll be the envy of everyone on the whole ship!"

On the way to the port in New York, sitting in the back of the taxi, Elena's thoughts took leave and she remembered how many times she had dreamt of being surrounded by nothing but the ocean. Thank God and Roberto another of her dreams was on its way to becoming a reality. She wondered how Sandra felt about experiencing an adventure like this. Evita, interested by her new surroundings, was content and quiet. Elena planned to take lots of pictures for Evita to remember about her first cruise around the Mediterranean.

They arrived at the port and Elena tried to restrain her thoughts so she could concentrate on what she was doing and where they were going. She followed Roberto, who knew what to do and had covered all the steps before boarding the ship. He'd completed all the paperwork needed and carried with him their passports, tickets and boarding cards.

Finally they were inside the luxury cruise ship. Elena drank in the grandiosity of the enormous boat and decided it was bigger than the whole city of Santiago de Cuba. All the bulletins on the various halls enthralled her. There were going to be shows, afternoon piano concerts, tea, contests . . .

"Look, Elena," Roberto called her attention. "This is our group." He signaled to an announcement of the Bridge Tournament. "They're meeting at five on the deck to see the boat off."

"How nice! Are we going to be there?"

"Yes. First let's settle Sandra and Evita in the cabin."

They took the elevator up to the second deck and then walked through the hallways until they arrived at their staterooms. Although Elena had seen luxurious cabins in pictures and movies, this one exceeded her expectations. It was just like a penthouse apartment, or like a presidential suite in the Waldorf Astoria. She thanked God for the fairy tale she was living.

Roberto took off his jacket and grabbed Evita from Sandra's arms. "My princess, we're here. Your first of many trips abroad," he said, raising her into the air.

Elena took off her hat and walked through the cabin, drawing open the drapes to allow the harbor view to fill the room. She pushed open the door to the bathroom and found it was large and inviting, with gold fixtures and marble walls. She never expected the bathroom to be as luxurious and comfortable as the ones in her house.

Lightheaded, Elena returned to the bedroom where Roberto played with Evita on the bed. He got up and told his wife to take care of the baby while he freshened up. Elena took Evita in her arms and asked Sandra how she liked the ship.

"I've been thanking my lucky star. This is just unbelievable!"

"I'm so happy you have this opportunity. It's good you're with us," Elena said.

When ready, Roberto and Elena left the cabin for the deck where their party gathered for lunch. Roberto nudged Elena every time she stopped, or craned her head to see her surroundings.

"My love, we'll be here long enough. You have plenty of time to see all of this at your own pace."

"Of course, *mi amor*. I'll control myself."

With effort Elena paid attention to her path. The couple arrived in a crowded large room filled with people, voices and laughter. Joyful passengers bustle about excitedly. Men and women held drinks in animated conversations.

Roberto laid his hand on her arm. "Darling," he spoke close to her ear, "let's circulate among the people to find the other players."

They mingled about the crowd, Roberto's hand like a vise on her arm, as if afraid of losing her. He craned about, searching for familiar faces.

"There! It's Francisco," he exclaimed, and directed his steps towards a tall, handsome man.

"Roberto, finally! I'd been looking for you!" They hugged. "I saw your name in the list of passengers."

"Good!" And then Roberto placed his arm on Elena's waist. "Francisco, this is Elena, my wife," he said, smiling.

Emanating charm, Francisco bowed before Elena. With a seductive smile, took her hand softly and touched it to his lips. "At your feet, *encantadora Dama.*"

The smile on Roberto's face twisted into a frown. "What do you think you're doing?" he sneered, grabbing Francisco by the lapel.

"Putting myself at your wife's feet," the man said, shoving away Roberto's hand. "The gesture of a gentleman," he continued, locking eyes with Roberto.

"'A gentleman's gesture.' Where on earth is the gentleman?"

"You insult me."

"As I meant."

Crimson faced, his jaw clenched, Francisco murmured, "I demand an explanation. But we will not argue before the lady. I'll look for you later." He left, his head high, his back ramrod straight.

Elena held tight Roberto's arm. "Why did you do that? Tell me!"

"Yes, I will."

But he did not say a word. Elena remembered the issue with Esteban and Maritza.

"Why, Roberto?" she asked again. "Are you crazy?"

"Don't you call me crazy. I'm not crazy! I've good reasons."

"I hope so! But I'd like to know what they are."

"Let's sit somewhere," he said, searching for a table.

He spotted a couple of empty bar stools and they sat. Elena allowed some time to pass, and then asked again.

"Please, Roberto, will you tell me now?"

He spoke over the voices and laughter from the people. "For now, suffice it to say that he's a scoundrel."

"What do you mean?"

"He's a womanizer."

"Why did you befriend him, then?"

"Because of business," he was silent for seconds. "And education."

Elena raised her voice. "But why did you act as if you were such good friends when you met him?"

Roberto jumped to his feet and grabbed Elena's arm, "Our place is with our daughter, not wasting time with this useless conversation."

Pulling Elena along with him, he inched through the crowd.

Silently, Elena stayed by his side, once more confused by his abrupt reaction. When she met Roberto, he'd always bowed and kissed her hand. In fact, her mother's and Doña Pilar's as well. Such gallantry swept her off her feet. And today she felt good when such a handsome, distinguished man had bowed to her, taken her hand in his, and gently kissed it. No doubt this had infuriated Roberto. But why? She was eager to hear what he had to say about his absurd burst of jealousy.

She recalled the incident with Esteban. Elena admitted that had been because of her naiveté. However, what happened today was beyond her understanding. She hadn't done anything wrong. Francisco had simply acted like any other debonair, European gentleman. Roberto claimed that

Francisco was a scoundrel, if that were the case, why did he befriend him? Why was he glad to see him? She needed an answer.

Back at the stateroom, Roberto made himself comfortable and began to read pamphlets with information about the ship and circulars about social events taking place. He occasionally chatted and played with Evita, totally ignoring his wife, as if she were to blame for the demons tormenting him.

Elena occupied herself listening to the soothing music coming from speakers. Suddenly, a whistle blast from the vessel pierced her ears, and more noisy laughter and cheers filled the air. The ship began to move—motors in full gear marked the beginning of the voyage.

Dinners were classified in three sittings. Musical bells announced when the restaurant opened for each group. As the crowd heard the bells, they dispersed in order to freshen up and march on to the dining room. Little by little, the clamor outside dwindled.

Roberto had signed Sandra up for the first sitting. That way, she would be back in time to care for Evita, while Roberto and Elena went to the third turn.

"Sandra, they're calling for dinner," said Elena, taking Evita from her.

"It isn't necessary," Roberto interrupted.

The women looked at him in surprise.

"How come?" Elena asked.

"We're eating in the cabin tonight."

"Why? Let's eat at the restaurant," Elena said.

"I don't feel like going anywhere," he replayed, coldly.

Another disappointment. Elena yearned to say, "I want to see the dining room. I want to show off my pretty dress. But, she held her tongue. She didn't want to fight on the first night of the cruise and spoil what could be a second honeymoon. She wanted to enjoy the amazing surroundings—and she wanted Roberto to enjoy it too. She could kill him if he spoiled her wonderful voyage. Oh, whom was she kidding? They'd argue later when she insisted on an explanation for his prior fit of anger.

That night in bed, Roberto said goodnight and turned his back to Elena.

"*Un momento*, Roberto. We need to talk."

"Can you wait until tomorrow? I'm tired."

Grabbing his arm, Elena stared at him steadily. "It's only going to take few minutes. Tell me about Francisco."

"I don't trust him. He's trying to take advantage of your naïveté."

"Why you don't trust him?"

"Don't ask! A good wife trusts her husband's judgment."

"Then why don't you trust my judgment?"

Roberto sat up, angry. "Because you are a flirt!"

"Damn you Roberto! What do you mean I'm a flirt?"

"The way you looked at Francisco. Your eyes lit up. You smiled at him provocatively."

She took her head in her hands. "You are insane!"

"And you are a coquette!"

"I'm not taking more of your insults!"

"Then stop giving me reasons to insult you!"

"You're just suspicious because you do the things you accused me of . . . you and your filthy mind."

"Enough! I'm fed up with your insubordination."

"Keep torturing yourself. I'm going to sleep," she said with finality and lay down, hoping she could sleep.

He pointed a finger at her. "You should have stayed at home."

"You bastard!" she said, holding back tears.

Who gave this man the power to upset me this much? I did! Yes, God—but, until when?

Maybe if Roberto had beaten her, it wouldn't have hurt as much as his hurtful words. When was she going to understand that her expectations for a change in the macho man she had married were only a wishful thinking? Was she rationalizing her life with Roberto as a defense against his emotional abuse?

Sleep eluded her. She lay in bed, her eyes wide open, and her attention fixed on the soothing movement of the ship on top of the ocean. How nice it would be to lie down on one of the chaise lounges lying on the deck—how nice to look at the starry sky and talk to God. But she needed the approval of her maniacal husband. She was only an object that belonged to a man. A man? An animal! But she would keep dreaming about freedom and independence, because some day her dreams would come true. After all, she was imprisoned by hope.

What could have been a wonderful and delightful cruise for Elena it turned to be a very sad one. Because the Carvajal family stayed cooped up in the cabin for the rest of the trip. Elena's pretty dresses and jewelries remained packed. The only outing for the family was to informal lunches at the deck. The weight of the disappointment was so heavy that it impaired Elena's wish to appear happy for Evita and Sandra's sake. The suppressed anger infected her spirit. If she were able to send Roberto to Hell, to scream at his face that he was behaving like a son-of-a-bitch, her resentment might decrease. But she had to wait until she felt calm enough. The way she felt at the moment could make her lose control. She'd try to parch things up for the voyage to have a better ending.

CHAPTER XXVII

The Truth Is Out

Elena hoped for a joyful cruising, but it never happened. The rest of the trip followed the same odious pattern.

The afternoon before arriving in New York, after lunch on the deck, Roberto took the family back to the cabin. While Roberto went to the bathroom, Elena said to Sandra, "Hey, let's walk around."

"Where?"

Elena answered full of enthusiasm, "I'd love to visit the boutiques. They have amazing things from different parts of the world."

"No, Elena. Not without telling Roberto."

"We know what his answer would be."

"After what happened last time, I don't dare do it again."

"I take responsibility . . ."

"Oh, sorry, Elena. No."

Roberto reappeared. He played a little bit with Evita. Then he gave Elena a perfunctory kiss.

"I'll see you all after the game," he said and left.

As soon as Roberto left, Elena said to Sandra, "I'll take Evita to the swimming pool. Shops would bore her. See you later."

With this, Elena pushed Evita's stroller down to the exclusive First Class swimming pool. She took the elevator three stories to the Dolphin deck, from where she saw Francisco by the pool. Confused and nervous, she met his gaze. How to act? She didn't want more problems with Roberto. She tried to leave, but it was too late. Francisco smiled at her, grabbed a towel and wrapped it around his hips, leaving exposed his muscular, hairy torso. To her shame, she noticed he was wearing a very brief swimming suit.

Francisco approached her.

"*Encantadora Señora,*" he said. "It is a pleasure to see you again. Where do you hide?"

He towered over her. She felt uncomfortable under his appraising stare. She gave him a tight-lipped smile, and said nothing. He smiled at the sight of the stroller.

He pulled up the cover of the carriage.

"Hi, gorgeous baby," he said to Evita. "What's your name?"

"Her name is Evita," Elena said.

"Beautiful name for a beautiful *bebita.*" He looked intensely at the child, and then smiled maliciously. "Oh, but she's very different from her red haired sister in Spain."

Stunned, Elena locked eyes with Francisco. "What are you talking about? She doesn't have a sister."

"I'm terribly sorry, Señora," he said with a sly smile. "I thought you knew."

Elena frowned and asked, "Knew what?"

"After all, Roberto did tell me that he'd told you."

"Told me what?"

"About Azucena, his daughter in Spain, of course."

Elena didn't know what to say, what to think.

"You know, I think I don't believe you . . ."

"Good. I'm glad you don't. It's much better and easier that way."

Then it dawned on her. Maybe Roberto had had a daughter way before she met him, and didn't say anything to avoid misunderstandings. Of course! That was it.

"How old is the girl you're talking about?"

"Look, I'm sorry I started this." Francisco coughed nervously. "Forget the whole thing, please."

"No, now you must tell me . . ."

"My dear lady, please forgive me. You better ask your husband instead." With this Francisco bent and kissed her hand. Deeply disturbed Elena jerked it away and headed for the cabin.

She found Sandra looking through the glass window, clearly mesmerized by the white foam dancing on the waves.

Distraught, Elena handed Evita to Sandra. "Will you please, take care of Evita? I'm going to take a bath."

"Are you okay?" Sandra asked, concerned. "What happened?"

"Later."

Elena stumbled into the bathroom and prepared a stemming bubble bath. Once the tub was full and soapsuds covered the surface, she submerged herself completely, and then raised her face to the surface, feeling hot drops of water dripping down her cheeks. *I'm not going to cry,* she told herself as a moan escaped her throat. Disobeying tears slid down her cheeks.

Would Aisha remain silent if Roberto had a daughter? Her mother-in-law was a fair person. Wouldn't she have said something to Elena if she knew?

Is this why Roberto had kept them confined to the cabin during the whole miserable trip? So Francisco wouldn't inadvertently, or otherwise, reveal the truth to Elena? Could it be true that Roberto conceived a daughter while married to her? Otherwise, why would he hide it from her? He certainly would have told her something if this daughter were the product of a past relationship. Wouldn't he?

As Elena's muddled mind tried to figure out when this could have happened, she stopped fighting her tears and sobbed freely. *You rotten bastard! You sanctimonious, controlling pig! You betrayed me in the worst way of all. Why can't I just kill you?*

Had it happened during the year he spent in Barcelona trying to disentangle from Gina? How old was this girl? If she found out and it proved Roberto had been unfaithful, what would she do then? Could she forgive him? Could she leave him? How about Evita? She needed her father, and he adored her. A painful sob caught in her chest as she felt her heart breaking.

Elena didn't know how long she sat in the tub lost in misery. A shiver awoke her from her trance. The water was cold and the soapsuds were gone; the only warmth in her body came from the stubborn tears still rolling down her cheeks. She wiped them slowly, feeling a strange sense of hollow calm. She stepped out of the tub and wrapped her goose pump riddled body with a luxurious towel. She dried off, powdered with perfumed talcum and stepped out of the bathroom, peeking around the cabin. She heard Sandra and Evita playing in their next-door room. She closed the door to their room and went to the closet. She picked the most striking and stylish evening gown and held it against her body.

Tonight was Captain's night, the last and most elegant night of the trip. Elena unpacked her jewelry and set it on the bed. She began to dress, taking great care with each detail.

The tightly fitted black sequin dress molded her figure, enhancing her curves. She arranged her hair into a chignon, topping it with a black and silver laced *mantilla*, which she held together with an ornamental *peineta*. Discrete with the jewelry, she wore only a set of small diamond earrings and a diamond ring, along with sequin sandals with very high thin heels. Elena brought her makeup kit from the bathroom and sat in front of the mirror, and mechanically made up her face. Foundation. Powder. Rouge. Mascara. Red lipstick. She moistened her fingers with the Joy perfume Roberto had brought from Spain and dabbed it behind her ears and neck.

"Where the hell do you think you're going?"

Elena's heart skipped a beat when she saw Roberto's reflection behind her in the mirror.

"I asked you a question, Elena."

"I heard it the first time."

Roberto stared at her, confused, and for the first time since Elena had met him, he was at a loss for words.

"I am going to the captain's party," she responded deliberately.

"Who gave you permission?"

"I don't need permission. I am an adult."

Again, Roberto was speechless. Elena stood and turned to face him. A vein pulsed in his temple and his face grew flushed.

"The question is whether I'm going alone . . . or whether you are coming with me."

Roberto pierced her with his stare, clenching and unclenching his fists. She added, "If your reluctance to get out of this room is fear of encountering, oh, say Francisco, because he might have unpleasant things to say, then it's too late. There's no need for hiding anymore."

Roberto's face went white. He stepped aside as Elena walked past him out of the room.

"Sandra, please get yourself and Evita ready for tonight's party. We should leave soon," Elena told an astonished Sandra, who was standing wide-eyed behind Roberto.

Then she addressed Roberto.

"We are going. Decide whether or not you're coming with us."

CHAPTER XXVIII

Captain's Night

They sat comfortably in the lobby while Elena made the necessary calls. There was a private office, meant to help the passengers. Elena quickly worked out the details for the event. Roberto would not be joining them. Sandra would take his place at the table in the dinning room. Elena called for a baby sitter for Evita.

Once everything was taken care of, they went to meet the captain. There was a line from the hallway to the cocktail lounge where Captain White stood greeting his guests. Elena and Sandra took their places, waiting in silence. Many in the line spoke to Evita, who loved the attention and smiled, wrinkling her nose. Finally, they met the handsome captain, who graciously shook Elena's hand and spoke some gallantries.

Then, slowly, they made their way to the cabin where the baby sitter was waiting. The middle-aged woman introduced herself as Ashima Dylan and explained that an employee brought her to the cabin and asked to wait for Mrs. Carvajal. Sandra and Ashima changed Evita into her pajamas and left her to sleep. After giving the woman the necessary instructions regarding Evita, Elena and Sandra left for the dining room.

Once there, they were ushered to an imposing table for twelve. She noticed an empty chair at their table. One guest was still to arrive. In spite of Elena's low spirits, she admired the grandiosity of the dining room and the exquisite setting of the table. Her eyes traveled around mesmerized by the glittering, fashionable dresses the other women wore.

With the best of her smiles, Elena introduced Sandra and herself. The gentlemen stood until the two women sat while the ladies reciprocated her smile, saying their names, of which she retained none. They were delighted to meet Mrs. Carvajal and asked about her husband. Elena gave the same explanation to those who asked: "My husband isn't feeling well. If he feels better, he'll join us for dessert."

Elena caught herself craning her neck and stealing glances at the door hoping and dreading the sight of Roberto's imposing figure walking towards them.

Did she want to see him? No. She did not! *Liar.* She found herself apologizing for making people repeat what they said, but her mind was not with these elegant people or the captain, who sat at an even more opulent table in the center of the room. She couldn't stop thinking of Roberto's betrayal. What a bastard he ended up to be.

"Is that right, Mrs. Carvajal?"

Elena was brought back to the moment by . . . what's-his-name? The Swiss banker or something like that.

"I'm sorry," Elena apologized for the tenth time. With that she stood up and added, "Pardon me . . . I'll be right back."

The four gentlemen at the table stood when Elena got up and the ladies watched her with concern. Sandra stood up at almost the same time Elena did.

"May I go with you?" Sandra asked.

"Thank you, dear. I'm going *al baño.*"

"Are you OK?"

"I'm fine. I'll be back soon."

Smugly, Elena walked away under the approving gaze of men. She looked around first, disoriented; the place was sumptuous and she fell swallowed by it. She couldn't stop thinking of her bastard husband's betrayal. "How different from her red haired sister from Spain." The cruel words danced in her head. Her proper husband was nothing but a lying, self-serving, son-of-a-bitch. With his air of superiority and holier-than-thou attitude he had made her feel unworthy and stupid, when all along it was he who was the lesser human.

On the mist of her displacement, she saw Francisco. *Oh, Jesus, I don't need this now.* She couldn't help but notice his distinguished figure . . . such an attractive man. On the pool she found him seductively handsome and well built . . . and now, in a tuxedo he was the cynic Red Butler in *Gone with the Wind.* He walked towards her.

"Señora Carvajal!" Francisco said, as he bent over slightly and raised her hand to his lips. With her hand inches from him, he looked deeply into her eyes. "I'm impressed! What a regal way to wear a mantilla. You look like a queen. No . . . . You are a queen!" Suavely he brushed his lips on her hand, his unblinking eyes fixed on hers.

Against her will, she found herself trembling with excitement. She looked around afraid that Roberto was watching.

"Your husband is at the front deck," he said. "Big mistake . . ." he added insolently. "If you were my wife, I'd be attached to you for life."

Elena turned around; stern faced, and began walking away. "Goodnight, *Señor*," she said.

"*Un momento, bella dama*, you're going the wrong way."

"Excuse me?"

"The lavatories are this way." With a mischievous smile, Francisco pointed in the opposite direction.

She felt the blood rushing to her face. She wanted to run away. So much for her dignified retreat. She had to change direction as gracefully as possible—her exuberant high heels didn't help any and she envisioned herself tripping and falling, her tight dress rising exposing her legs and more. As in *Phantom of the Opera*, she saw the huge chandelier falling down on her; her head was spinning. She lost her balance for a moment . . . and found herself in Francisco's strong arms.

"Careful, my fair lady," said Francisco trying gallantly to suppress a smile.

Elena immediately tried to get out of his embrace.

"Sorry," she murmured.

"Please allow me to walk you to the Ladies' room."

"Thank you, but I'm perfectly capable of walking myself . . . Your presence compromises me."

"It was a pleasure helping a gorgeous lady in distress." He bowed with a smirk on his lips. "At your feet, Madam."

When Elena went back to the table, she was aghast to see Francisco occupying the empty chair. He seemed to have nothing better to do but to embarrass her. His mischievous eyes searched for hers relentlessly. Elena nervously, fiddled with the silver wear and Waterford crystal settled in front of her.

This delightful anguish momentarily replaced the pain caused by Roberto's treason.

"Señora Carvajal, are you joining us for the grand show tonight?" asked Francisco from across the table.

"I'm sorry, my husband and baby are waiting for me."

"It is a pity that you and your lovely friend miss tonight's farewell spectacle. It was brought directly from Vegas, especially for tonight."

"Sandra, I want you to go," said Elena.

"Me? Alone? No Elena . . ." said Sandra.

"If you allow me the pleasure of your company, I would be delighted to accompany you," said Francisco with a seductive smile.

Sandra smiled and her eyes became beacons. "Yes, I'd like to go," she prompted; a light of her own illuminating her face. Obviously, she chose to forget Roberto's orders and welcomed the tempting situation enticing her.

Elena felt a surge of happiness mixed with a bit of anxiety for her friend.

"I'm glad, Sandra, it's settled." Elena gazed at Francisco. "Señor Francisco, please, I expect Sandra back before dawn. I hold you accountable for her safety."

Elena returned to the cabin alone. Roberto wasn't there. She dismissed the sitter and went to check on Evita.

"Such a sleepy angel!" said Elena, as she caught a tear running down her own cheek.

Sandra arrived before dawn.

"What a night!" she exclaimed, as she hugged Elena.

"Did you have good time?"

"Good time sounds so inadequate. I had the most marvelous time!"

"What made it so marvelous?"

"Francisco! He held me tight as we danced after the show, and he told me the sweetest things you can imagine."

"Sandra, stop there. He's a womanizer."

"I know! His passionate goodnight kiss said it all." She walked away, and then stopped. "I've no regrets. Now I'll keep dreaming . . . wrapped in his kiss."

It was good that Sandra understood. Let her dream while I pack.

After packing, Elena sat and waited for Roberto with the lights on. She dozed off as the sun was rising, only to be awakened a few minutes later by the sound of the unlocking door. Roberto's silhouette filled the doorframe. Their eyes locked, and Elena was shocked at his haggard face. Beard stubble darkened his handsome features, his eyes red-rimmed, his suit and tie rumpled. She didn't know whether to caress and comfort him, or hit him over the head with the night lamp, so she did nothing but stare.

"We need to talk," shouted Elena breaking the interminable silence.

"I'm sick."

"I don't care! This can't wait."

Roberto moved slowly, with slumped shoulders, towards the bed.

"I understand why you are the way you are." Elena said dryly. "You don't trust anyone. You are insecure and miserable because you are always afraid to be lied to and betrayed. You are jealous and controlling because you don't want to be made a fool of; you are afraid I'm going to treat you like you treated me."

"Elena, let me speak."

"No! You speak later. Like the saying goes, *El leon cree que todos son de su condicion.* This is obvious to me now. You are a liar and a cheat. I have to suffer your betrayal while you make my life a living hell in case I was to do the same to you. Well, on this, we are very different, Roberto."

"Elena, please, listens . . . I never meant to hurt you. You are my life, the only woman for me."

"Love and trust go hand-in-hand. Without trust there can't be love. After all the anger and hurt you've caused me, the prevalent feeling in my heart now is anger. I can't imagine living with someone day in and day out, always waiting for the stab in the back. I would go mad."

"So, you've never lied to me?"

Elena saw in Roberto's face the fight for control as he clenched his jaw.

"Everybody lies every now and then; inconsequential, white lies. I'm not talking about that, I have to lie to you so I can go out to the park, go for a walk, have a life! You oppress me, crush my spirit, and treat me as if you own me! I'm not your property; I'm your wife!

"Our life had been dominated by your threatening lies: your religion and now your unfaithfulness." Elena stood and paced the floor. Then, she stopped in front of him. "What in the name of God do you want me to do now? Tell me!" She raised her voice, her menacing hands inches from his face. He seized them.

"Anything you want, but don't leave me," he said vehemently. She fought to get her hands free, but he tightened his grip.

"Let go of me," she cried out.

"I am going to speak now!"

"More lies?"

"I swear to tell you how things really happened."

"I don't want to see you again. I'm leaving you and there's nothing you can do to stop me!"

He let go of her. "Please, sit here," he pleaded.

"I have more important things to do than listening to your lies."

"I solemnly swear by our daughter Evita that I won't lie."

She sat next to him. "Fine! Talk!"

Roberto told Elena how he met Anita.

"Then, Francisco was the owner of the bordello?"

"Yes. He also brags about enticing the wives of his business associates."

"Why didn't you tell me all these before? Tonight I trusted Sandra with him."

"What did you do?"

"I sent her with him to watch the farewell show."

"Is she back?"

"Oh, yes!"

He made a gesture that she read as wanting to blame her, but seemingly thought better of it.

"Elena, whatever you decide . . . I beg of you, do not leave me."

"It's too soon to decide one way or the other."

"Please, Elena, don't torture me. I need to know in order to continue living."

"I can't. For now, let's get some rest."

"I can't rest not knowing . . ." he said with a catch in his voice.

"I don't care, but *I* need my rest!"

"But, do I have any hope?" He begged.

"I don't think so. Besides everything else, now I have to consider you as an awful father. How could you leave a daughter behind and put her out of your concern for so long?

"I didn't want to loose you!"

"Enough! You make me sick. I don't want you in my bed . . . Not now . . . or ever. Did you hear?"

With this she got to her feet, leaving a humiliated Roberto wanting for words.

Chapter XXIX

It Is Over

In the early hours of a bright afternoon, the Carvajal family arrived home. No one spoke during the long drive to New Jersey. The thick silence could be beaten up and not budge an inch. Along the way Evita sensed the tension and went through crying spells. Sandra would try to soothe the child, but Evita's sobs lessened only in Elena's arms.

At home, Roberto tried to console her and sang songs to no avail. Finally he kissed the child and returned her to his wife.

"Elena, if you need me, I'll be in my office," said Roberto softly, disappearing from sight.

Elena bathed and fed Evita, and did everything she could to make the child comfortable. When the girl finally fell asleep, Elena went to see Roberto. She entered without knocking. He looked up in surprise.

"We need to talk," Elena said curtly.

He pulled out a chair for her, and answered hopefully. "Of course!"

"I want to raise Evita in a peaceful, loving home."

"No question about that."

"Then you have to leave the house right now!"

Roberto froze, mouth open. Nervously, he ran his fingers through his hair. "You can't be that cruel . . . you know you and Evita are my reason for living. You are my most cherished possessions."

Elena noticed his efforts to suppress his desperation; but remained unmoved. She went on. "I know," she said. "But we belong to no one. I am free; I am independent and have a right to my opinions and actions. You refused to acknowledge that and now you've lost me. You've seen us as your belongings. You took me for granted, but no more! I have no respect for you!"

He stood in front of her, nostrils flared, a look of shock in his sad expression. Finally, he cleared his throat and said, "I'll move to the guest room. I won't bother you . . ."

"Right now I can't stand your presence. Respect my wishes and leave."

He thought for a while. His pronounced veins popping on his sweaty forehead, his eyes filled with tears. "Have it your way. I'll leave at once."

"Thank you."

"If, or when you need anything, don't hesitate and let me know. Please, ask Sandra to call me at the office everyday to let me know about Evita." He approached her and brushed her cheeks with his lips tenderly. "Take care of my baby." He wiped off his tears and walked away toward the bedroom. A moment later, he returned carrying his luggage, the same bag he had used on the cruise and hadn't yet unpacked. With a pang, she watched him leave.

Sandra spoke softly behind her. "Elena, I heard the door. Was that Roberto?"

"Yes. He's gone. You are to call him daily to report on Evita."

"Oh, Elena, I hope you don't regret this."

"Don't you worry."

After a long bath to soak away her travel weariness, Elena went to check on Evita. She seemed to be resting peacefully, but underneath closed lids her eyes moved restlessly. Elena placed the palm of her hand on the girl's forehead. It was cool to the touch. Elena blessed her child and went to her bedroom, and checked the intercom to be sure it was on. Satisfied, she climbed into bed.

She performed all the tricks she knew in order to force herself to sleep. She meditated, she prayed, and she counted sheep. And then, she gave up. She confronted the big problem hanging over her head. Was she making the right decision? When older, would Evita forgive her mother for growing up without her father? It was such a move . . .

Around midnight she heard a disturbing sound from the nursery. She dashed to her daughter's bed and found her gasping for air, her breath wheezing in her lungs. "Oh, God! My baby!"

Sandra heard and came running.

"Hurry! Ask Doctor Williams to come at once!" Elena urged.

Sandra ran from the room and returned almost immediately.

"He's on his way."

"Call Roberto!"

"Where is he staying?"

"I don't know . . ."

"What happened to Evita?"

"I found her wheezing, gasping for air . . . She can't breathe."

"*Pobrecita mi niña* . . . Let's pray for her . . ."

"You pray! I have to do something . . ." said Elena, anxiously. She kept Evita leaning on her shoulder upright and lifting her up occasionally, while pacing the floor agitatedly.

Doctor Williams arrived. He took one look and declared: "This child is having an asthma attack." Then he took out of his briefcase an infant atomizer and sprayed Evita's nose. Soon, the girl closed her mouth and began to breathe.

"Doctor Williams, this is the worst scare I've had in my life. Tell me what happened? Why?"

"Asthma is a chronic, common disease that affects the lung's airways." The doctor wrapped Evita in her blanket and placed two pillows under her head. "Its mainly an inflammation of the airways, which leads to the symptoms she's having now."

"Is she going to be all right?"

"For now, yes."

"Don't scare me, what do you mean "for now"?"

"Unfortunately, asthma never goes away completely, but with treatment, it can be controlled."

Elena felt as if an icy hand scraped deeply inside her chest, searing her heart. She coughed in order to gain stability. She held her head between her hands and let out, "Oh no . . . !" She paused. "What are we fighting against? What am I going to do?"

"Airway constriction, inflammation and mucus, that's what makes breathing difficult and causes the wheezing."

"How often can that happen? What can I do to avoid it?"

"Nothing! We cannot predict an attack of asthma. But, you can be alert, and at the first symptom, call me."

And Doctor Williams plainly addressed all the concerns that the young mother voiced.

"Please, I'd like you to tell all this to Roberto, will you?"

"Of course, I'll be happy." He laughed. "I remember when he made me come at midnight in a snow storm, because his new-born had sleep in her eyes."

"He thought it was an infection," answered Elena, promptly.

"Imagine now that his baby has a real condition . . ." said the Doctor, putting away his glasses and shutting closed his briefcase.

CHAPTER XXX

Keep Hope Alive

When Roberto found out about Evita, he rushed to the house and to her side.

"*Mi princesa, mi vida*," he told his little daughter, then asked Elena, "Is it okay to hold her?"

"Of course," she quickly answered, and somehow felt that Evita was safe now that her father was at her side.

He rinsed his hands with alcohol and covered his face with the surgical mask. This time Elena didn't think it was an exaggeration at all. He might have failed as a husband, but as a father there was no better.

She hated the man but admired the father.

He sat there for hours, jumping to his feet every time Evita coughed. "How long will it take for the wheezing and dry cough to go away?" he asked, anxiously.

"Until the dryness in her chest loosen up and the inflammation goes away."

"I have to stay here until then."

"You don't have to . . ."

"I know, but I'm staying. Ask Sandra to prepare the guest room, please."

Elena's first impulse was to ask Roberto to leave; but Evita needed her father, and Elena was convinced of this.

Roberto spent Monday and Tuesday night by his daughter's side. Wednesday morning Elena told Sandra she was going to run errands. She'd been feeling peculiar for the last several days, but because of Evita's illness, she hadn't done anything about it.

After Doctor Osvaldo Moreno checked Elena and ran some tests, he rubbed his hands together and announced: "My dear Elena, congratulations! You are expecting your second baby."

She thought of her plan to divorce Roberto, and worried. How was she going to do it now? She stared at the doctor in disbelief. She wanted to feel good with the words that had made her so happy the last time she had heard them. Unfortunately, right now she didn't welcome the news.

"Anything wrong?"

She heard the words amidst her concerns. Then she spoke hesitantly, "I'm in the middle of a separation."

Doctor Moreno raised an eyebrow. "I thought you and Roberto were happily married!"

"We are not," said Elena, eyes filling with tears.

"Do you want to tell me about it? I might be able to help."

"Thank you, doctor, But I don't want to talk about it right now."

"Whatever you do, *hijita,* balance out the good and the bad," he said, making seesaw motions with his hands.

"Thank you! I'll do just that."

When Elena arrived home, Roberto was still there. He didn't ask where she had been, but she could tell it was a struggle not to do so. During dinner, he announced sternly that since Evita was better, he was leaving early the next day.

Elena appreciated his not talking about their situation and not asking for her decision. Before he left he told Elena how much he missed his family and how sorry he was for not having valued what he had. That he had learned his lesson and hoped she found it in her heart to forgive him.

"I'll keep hoping until the end. I trust you'll make the right decision," he said in a sad tone.

The day after Roberto left, he called Sandra and wanted a detailed account of Evita's day. He didn't ask to talk to his wife.

I'll not talk to him either, and I will not tell him, yet, that I'm expecting. First I need to study my options and decide what I'm going to do.

On Friday, Roberto visited his daughter. He greeted Elena and went straight to the nursery. He lifted his little girl and kissed her head. "*Mi princesita, te quiero mucho,*" he murmured in her ear.

Three weeks passed by. Elena went out every day. She visited churches, malls and grocery stores, enjoying the sweet taste of freedom. She couldn't go back to living imprisoned, even if the cage was made of gold.

One day she took the bus to the Port Authority Station and from there she hailed a yellow cab to Fifth Avenue. She enjoyed window-shopping in New York, and even more now doing her heart's desire. But, she also realized the importance of children growing up with both parents. How would she support herself and two kids if she divorced Roberto? She knew poverty, so she wouldn't like her children to go through it. The way things were now, she didn't even own half of their home, or anything else for that matter. She could try to earn a living with one child, but not with another on the way.

As much as Elena enjoyed her freedom, she pondered how much free time she would have to be with her children, if she had to work to support them. What kind of rearing could she provide? She turned her head and saw a family walking at leisure along the street. The father carried his little girl on his shoulders. The image of Evita popped up in her mind, and she thought of her little girl growing up without a Dad.

Maybe Roberto had learned his lesson. She really hoped so. What to do?

With a throbbing heart, finally Elena reached a decision.

A haggard Roberto showed up at the front door. Elena followed him to the nursery.

He replied to Sandra's offer, politely, "I'd like herbal tea, please."

"Roberto, I want to talk with you before you leave," said Elena.

"Why not right now?"

"Okay." Then Elena addressed Sandra. "Will you please bring the tea to the office?"

Roberto followed Elena to his office. She sat at the desk and he sat across from her. "Have you reached a decision?" he asked.

"Yes, Roberto. I have."

They kept silent for a while. He broke it.

"Well . . . ?"

Sandra brought the tea and sat it on the desk.

"Well . . . ?" asked Roberto again when Sandra left.

"If we want to save our marriage, there are many things to mend."

"Elena, of course I want our marriage to work. What do I need to do?"

"First of all, you aren't entirely to blame for the failure of our relationship. I allowed you to walk all over me and was a parrot at your side. No more!"

"What does all of this have to do with me having a daughter in Spain?"

"That was the straw that broke the camel's back. By then I was already fed up with your unfairness. I took so much from you because I thought you were perfect, but you are nothing but a phony." Elena pushed back the hair on her forehead. "I want us to begin a new life the way it should have been."

"I'm listening," he said, solemnly.

"You have a strange idea about equality in a marriage." She paused for a few seconds, and then continued. "You don't own me. Your children will ask permission from you. I will not. I will, however, be a homemaker and a mother." She sustained his steely gaze. "I am not your shadow any longer. I won't let you make me feel bad about myself anymore."

"So far, I don't have any problem with that. In fact, I'll help you!"

"One moment! I haven't finished yet. I don't have any idea of how much money you have or how much you make. Why isn't my name in the ownership papers of this house? How do you stand financially? I want to be your co-owner in everything. I want to be your equal."

Roberto sat there, looking at her as if for the first time. He moved his head slowly in disbelief.

"As an equal," she went on, "I want us, together, to manage the monthly spending of our house and review every bill. I want also to help your child in Spain. I want you to be a supportive father. I believe the saying: 'what you do to others will come back to haunt you'."

With a hint of a smile, Roberto asked, "Who brain-washed you?"

"I don't trust you, so I realized that if I stayed with you, I have to use your own tactics."

He jumped to his feet.

"You offend me!" he said, incensed. And then changed tone. "Oh, Elena, how much you have changed. If there's a truth in my life, that's my undying love for you. I swear I never wanted to hurt you. I kept things from you afraid to lose you. It worked against me, though." His eyes shone with the tears he fought not to let out. "You don't respect me anymore, and that's my worst punishment. It's my fault, I know, but, I just can't stand it . . . !" he spoke, obviously, with a knot in his throat.

"I can't help it, Roberto, it's your own doing." She sighed deeply.

They locked eyes. Then he cleared his throat. "The last few weeks I suffered enough without my family. Still, I can endure that much better than living with a wife who doesn't respect her husband."

"It's hard to respect someone that doesn't have respect for you."

"Okay. Again, have it your way, Elenita."

"Does that mean . . ."

"I'm leaving. I'll be here always for you and Evita. Don't ever hesitate to call me if you need anything. My heart and thoughts will be with you unconditionally. I'll be waiting, Elenita. Hope never dies"

He walked past her and stroked her head tenderly, then said, in a whisper, "Until we meet again, my love."

It was difficult for Elena not to call him back, but she wanted him to pay for his sins. He must! And then, some day, she'll tell him about the new baby she was expecting, the child he had been wishing for.

"*Después*, yes, later!" Elena told herself aloud. "*Cuando el se gane mi respeto;* then I will tell him!"

Keep hoping, Elena! Hope is the last to go!

FIN